AN ITALIAN WIFE

An
Italian Wife

Ann Hood

W. W. NORTON & COMPANY

NEW YORK • LONDON

These stories have appeared in: "The Summer of Ice," *Five Chapters*; "Coney Island Dreams," *The Atlantic*; "Dear Mussolini," *The Hartford Courant*, "Best New Fiction in the Northeast"; "Waiting for Churchill," *Five Points*; "La Vigilia," *Blue Christmas: Holiday Stories for the Rest of Us*, edited by John Dufresne (Books & Books, 2011); "Crooning With Dino," *Post Road*.

For information about permission to reproduce selections from this book, write to Permissions, W. W. Norton & Company, Inc., 500 Fifth Avenue, New York, NY 10110

For information about special discounts for bulk purchases, please contact W. W. Norton Special Sales at specialsales@wwnorton.com or 800-233-4830

Manufacturing by Courier Westford
Book design by Barbara Bachman
Production manager: Louise Parasmo

Library of Congress Cataloging-in-Publication Data

Hood, Ann, 1956–
An Italian wife / Ann Hood. — First edition.
pages cm
ISBN 978-0-393-24166-2 (hardcover)
1. Italian Americans—Fiction. 2. Italian American families—Fiction.
3. Family life—Fiction. 4. Immigrants—Fiction. I. Title.
PS3558.O537I83 2014
813'.54—dc23

2014013801

W. W. Norton & Company, Inc.
500 Fifth Avenue, New York, N.Y. 10110
www.wwnorton.com

W. W. Norton & Company Ltd.
Castle House, 75/76 Wells Street, London W1T 3QT

1 2 3 4 5 6 7 8 9 0

For Gogo

Contents

The

RIMALDI FAMILY

JOSEPHINE AND VINCENZO

...

Their Children:

Carmine Concetta Giulia Elisabetta Chiara Isabella Valentina/Martha

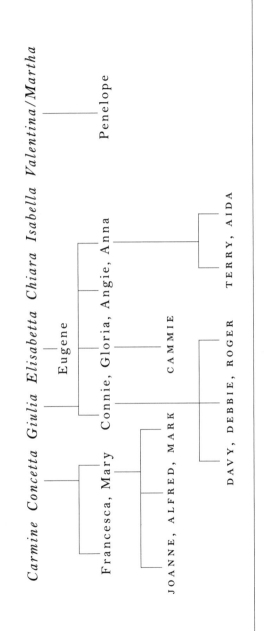

Francesca, Mary   Connie, Gloria, Angie, Anna

Eugene

Penelope

JOANNE, ALFRED, MARK   CAMMIE

DAVY, DEBBIE, ROGER   TERRY, AIDA

Part One

1889–1925

Salute

IN AMERICA, ANYTHING WAS POSSIBLE. THIS WAS WHAT Josephine's husband told her before he left their village to catch the ship in Naples. She didn't know him, this husband of hers. Their marriage had been arranged by their parents long ago, before Josephine had breasts or menstruated for the first time. He was considered a step up for her family: his parents owned land in the next village, and pigs, and even a cow. He had been to Rome, where for two years he worked as a guard at the king's palace. "Vincenzo Rimaldi," Josephine's mother had told her from the very day the betrothal was set, when Josephine was only eight years old. "He will give you a good life. You will have fresh milk every day. And pork all year long. And most important, you will have land. Land is better than gold, Josephine."

Josephine had nodded, but really she would rather have gold than land or pigs. She liked pretty things, shiny things, things that glittered. She collected rocks with veins of fool's gold, or pieces of flint that sparkled in the sun. Once she found something bright-blue and unidentifiable and she kept it in her apron pocket, believing it must be valuable.

Because her husband-to-be was eleven years older than Josephine, she didn't meet him until the day of her wedding. He was away in Rome; he was taking care of all that land.

A week before her fifteenth birthday, her mother woke her and explained that her wedding would be today. The husband-to-be had managed to book a spot in steerage on a ship to America and he would not be back for some time. The families had decided it was better for the wedding to happen right away, before he left. If God was smiling on them so much as to get him a ticket on that boat, then perhaps he would send them a child right away too.

"I knew this match was a fortunate one," Josephine's mother said, making a quick sign of the cross and kissing the silver crucifix that dangled from the black rosary beads she wore around her neck. "You are so lucky, Josephine," her mother told her, pinching Josephine's cheeks. "America! Imagine it!"

"I can't, Mama. I don't even know for certain where it is." Josephine was trying not to cry. What she did know about America was that it was far away, across a vast, turbulent ocean. She would be happy to marry any boy in her own village, someone without a cow, someone staying put.

"Who cares where it is?" her mother said dismissively. "Everyone there is rich. Money spills out of their pockets. They live in big houses and have many cows and pigs. You're blessed, Josephine," she said, making another sign of the cross. "Now, get up so I can get you ready."

Josephine had gone to sleep the night before, happily watching the moon rise outside her window. It was her fav-

orite moon, a crescent, with a star shining bright beside it.
Now her life was about to change completely. Nothing would
be the same after today.

Her mother unfolded a white lace dress and held it up for
Josephine to see. "This is the dress my mother made for me
when I got married. Now you will wear it."

Josephine fingered the fine lace.

"You know how the dogs are when they're in heat?" her
mother asked, busying herself by laying out undergarments
and stockings, taking a cameo from its satin box.

She didn't look at Josephine, who was frowning at her
mother. Why would they talk about something like dogs on
the morning before she got married? Josephine's stomach
churned uncomfortably.

"You know how the boy dog climbs up on the female dog
and moves on her?"

"Yes," Josephine said hesitantly.

"All of God's things do that, Josephine. That's how we
reproduce."

"Reproduce?" Josephine repeated.

Her mother sighed. She glanced at Josephine ever so briefly.
"That's what you will have to do tonight with Vincenzo."

"What?" Josephine said.

This was too much. In a few minutes her whole life had been
turned upside down. She went to sleep distantly betrothed,
and woke to learn she would get married today, that her husband would leave her in three days' time and go to America,
where he would eventually send for her. And now this thing
with the dogs. She could picture it, their own long-dead dog

Jacko, mounting any female dog that passed—bigger ones, smaller ones, it didn't mater; Jacko was indiscriminate—and jerking around inside them, sputtering and drooling.

"You will do it tonight and you will do it anytime Vincenzo wants you to. This is what a wife does for a husband."

"But Mama—"

"There's no more to say about it. Now, get dressed. His family is already on their way."

...

UNTIL TODAY, JOSEPHINE'S days had been her own to do whatever she wished. There were always chores: water to haul from the well in the center of the village, clothes to wash and hang along string hung from tree branches to dry, bread to bake, pasta to roll out and shape, vegetables and fruits to cook or can or bottle or set in the sun to dry; there was always something to sweep, or candle wax to scrape off the shrines in the church, or helping the nuns with their flock of sheep. But even with all of these things to get done every day, Josephine still had time to wander the hills outside the village, to pick wildflowers there, or wade barefoot in the stream. "She's too dreamy," people told her mother. "She has her head in the clouds." But her parents indulged her, buying her paper and colored pencils so she could make pictures and even letting the nuns teach her to read.

But standing here in the too-tight lace dress—"Hold your breath!" her mother had ordered, so that she could button all the tiny pearl buttons that ran up the back—with the silk

stockings held up by garters that dug into her thighs and
the shoes a size too small, Josephine realized that if she let
it, this marriage would ruin her life. She would no longer be
able to draw with her colored pencils if her husband decided
he wanted to have his way with her. She would no longer be
able to walk in the cool stream, letting the hems of her skirts
get wet and muddy. She would live far away in America.

This last thought made her throat tighten. Below her, she
heard voices, loud and celebratory, shouts of *"Salute!"* and the
clinking of glasses. She smelled pork roasting, onions frying,
sweet things baking.

Josephine sat stiffly on her bed and unbuttoned the shoes.
In her tight dress, it was hard to move, so it took her a long
time, grunting and sweating to finally get the shoes off. Then
she unfastened the garters and slid the silk stockings down
her legs. She had climbed out her bedroom window many
times, but it was difficult in her wedding dress. As she wig-
gled outside, she heard a seam split, and smiled. When she
lowered herself to the ground, she glimpsed all the people
who had gathered for the wedding. They were inside and outside; they were familiar and they were strangers.

Josephine took off at a gallop, splitting another seam as
she ran out through the fence that marked the land they
farmed and into the field behind the houses. The grass felt
cool and damp on her feet. She ran until she no longer heard
the sounds of the wedding party. She ran until she reached
the stream, where the nuns' sheep drank and chewed. Josephine opened her arms wide and ran as fast as she could into
the water. She didn't bother to lift her hem. She slipped on
some wet stones and splattered mud on the white lace and her

face. She stayed in the water until her mind calmed. Then, barefoot and muddy and wet, she went to meet her husband.

HIS FAMILY FROWNED at her and the people from the village whispered when the bride showed up late and dirty and dripping. But Josephine didn't care. She took the veil resting on a table and placed it over her face, clutched the wildflowers she had stopped to pick on her way back, and walked through the crowd.

Her eyes moved past the priest to the short man waiting beside him. The man was grinning at her. Josephine wished her mother had not told her about dogs, because she had thought of Jacko, and this man who was about to become her husband resembled Jacko. He was short and barrel-chested, with a slightly pushed-in face and unruly brown hair. She made the sign of the cross because she needed all the help she could get, then took her place on the other side of the priest.

It was over so quickly that Josephine hardly had time to think. The priest said words, everyone said prayers, he made Vincenzo repeat something after him, and they were done. Married, just like that. Vincenzo lifted her veil and with his fat thumb wiped a smear of mud from her cheek before he kissed her right on the mouth with his cold, rubbery lips. Everyone cheered wildly as they watched him claim her. Josephine tried not to gag or to cry. When Vincenzo took her hand and held it triumphantly in the air, the crowd cheered again. This time, she couldn't hold back the tears, and as they turned to face everyone, she saw the women nodding at her sympathetically.

For the rest of the day, they ate and drank and danced. When the sun set, they lit candles and ate more and drank more. The music grew louder, the dancing more frenetic. She danced with her girlfriends, and sneaked ladlefuls of wine. Although she didn't like the taste very much, she liked how it made her lightheaded. She was someone who was prone to drinking too much of it. Josephine, full and sleepy, had almost forgotten they were all celebrating her wedding when she felt a hand on her elbow.

"Josephine," her husband said to her, and her girlfriends moved away shyly.

She watched them slip back into the crowd.

"It's time for us to go upstairs now," he said.

Josephine chewed her bottom lip and said finally, "But the party."

He laughed at this, and led her into the house, still holding on to her elbow. To her surprise, a group of men followed them inside and up the stairs. Even though Vincenzo closed the bedroom door firmly behind them, the men stayed in the hall, shouting instructions and making jokes.

"Would you like me to light a candle?" Vincenzo asked her politely. "Or would you prefer the dark?"

Josephine shrugged, but he couldn't see her of course. Out the window, she saw the same moon that just last night had made her smile so dreamily. Now it shed the only light in the room, making Vincenzo shadowy and sinister. Sometimes, when Josephine sipped too much wine, the room spun when she lay down. She liked that giddy feeling, and wished for it tonight. But everything stayed firmly rooted.

As quick as the wedding itself, Vincenzo had unbuttoned

his pants, pulled down her bloomers, climbed on top of her, and stuck his thing inside her. For a brief moment it hurt, but then it just felt strange. Before Josephine could decide how she felt, Vincenzo moved quickly, three or four times, quivered, and collapsed on her.

"Maybe when I send for you to come to America," he said, "you will bring me a son."

He rolled off her and shouted to the men waiting outside the door, "Go home now, you pigs. It's done."

The men shouted back, "Good luck! Congratulations!" and then noisily ran down the stairs and back to the party.

Vincenzo started to snore immediately while Josephine tried to find a spot away from him in the narrow bed. Finally, she got up and took off the wedding dress, slipping on her white nightgown. She combed her hair, thinking that if that was all there was to it, she didn't mind so much. She hadn't liked his hot breath on her neck, but otherwise it was fast, boring.

Climbing onto the edge of the bed, Josephine gazed out the window. That star next to the moon, she thought, was the symbol of love. It broke her heart to look at it, so she closed her eyes tight, and waited for sleep.

THE NEXT MORNING, Josephine was woken up by the sight of her mother-in-law, Concetta Rimaldi, bursting into her bedroom.

Vincenzo was gone and Josephine was alone in the bed, still clinging to the very edge.

"Up!" Concetta ordered. She had the same pushed-in

face as her son, and the same unruly hair, except hers was already silver.

"Up!" she said again, this time slapping Josephine on the thigh.

Josephine jumped off the bed, wondering what strange thing was going to happen now. Had it really been only twenty-four hours ago that she'd been happy?

Concetta yanked the sheet off the bed and held it up to the sunlight. Embarrassed, Josephine saw a rust stain of blood right where she had lain while Vincenzo poked at her. Concetta lowered the sheet and smiled. "Good girl," she said, patting Josephine's arm. "Good girl."

Then Josephine watched as Concetta took that sheet and hung it out the window for everyone to see.

"Signora," Josephine said, "this makes me ashamed." She pointed to the window.

"Foolish girl," Concetta said. "You have nothing to be ashamed of."

Josephine began to follow her mother-in-law out the door. But Concetta stopped her.

"No, no, no," she said. "You stay here and wait for your husband. Now that I've checked your virginity, the marriage is good." She kissed Josephine once on each cheek, her breath citrusy, like she'd just eaten oranges. "Put a fresh sheet on the bed, and then wait for him there."

She didn't have to wait long. Vincenzo came bounding up the stairs with two bowls of coffee and a plate of warm bread.

"Good girl," he told her.

Was this what everyone was going to be saying to her as long as that bloody sheet hung out the window? Josephine watched him slurp his coffee and tear the bread with his teeth. She thought again of Jacko, and turned away from the sight of her husband eating.

"Eat up," Vincenzo told her. "I don't leave for three more days. You'll need your energy."

That was when she understood what was in store for her. The two of them would be locked in this room for three whole days. But then, Josephine reasoned, he would leave for America and she would be free again. Slowly, she chewed a small piece of bread. Anything could happen in the meantime. His boat could sink in the ocean. He could fall in love with a rich American and never send for her. He could be trampled by a horse, fall sick with consumption, or simply disappear.

"Finally," Vincenzo said, "you're smiling."

"Yes," Josephine said.

"You're beautiful when you smile," he said gently.

He wasn't awful, Josephine decided. And it was only three days. He asked her to lie down, and she did. Then he unzipped his pants, lifted her nightgown, moved about jerkily three or four times, quivered, and collapsed on her. It was so ridiculous that Josephine had to work on not laughing out loud.

Over the next three days, he did this every six or seven hours. In between, he brought Josephine food, and let her sit and draw. It was so silly, that her mood improved greatly, and by the time he left, he was certain he had married the most good-natured, lighthearted girl in all of Italy.

Josephine walked him to the edge of her village, where the cobblestones ended and a winding dirt path began. That path, she had been told, went all the way down the mountain to a bigger road that eventually worked its way to the city of Naples.

"Good-bye then," Vincenzo said.

Josephine nodded at him and smiled.

He touched her cheek lightly. "You are a treasure," he told her. "I only hope I've given you a son. That when I send for you, there will be two coming to America."

Josephine waved to him, and practically ran back home. The entire thing felt like a dream already. In her house, she hummed as she punched down the dough that had just finished its first rising, and brought a platter of small perfect tomatoes outside to sit in the sun.

NINE YEARS LATER, her mother came running into the house, out of breath, and grinning broadly.

"Finally," she said, "Vincenzo has sent for you."

Josephine frowned, trying to remember this man who was her husband. But in the years that had passed between them, his face had faded into a smudge, and she could not remember what his voice sounded like. From time to time, she had received a letter from him, telling her how hard he was working and all of the things he was doing to prepare for her arrival. He rented a house, and then he bought that house. He planted the fields around it and he began to save money. She read his letters as if they were chapters in a serial novel. They seemed to have nothing at all to do with her life, which was moving along pleasantly at home. There was no baby produced from those long-forgotten three days after the wedding, and Josephine continued on just as she had before the interruption of marriage.

But now, it seemed, she really would have to go.

A week later, she, too, had traveled the cobblestones to the dirt path down the mountain. She had ridden a cart all the way into Naples, where water sparkled more brilliantly than any rocks she had found. Excitement rose in her as she boarded the big ship. For a long time, she stood at the railing, watching the lights of Naples twinkle at her until they finally disappeared. By then, the ship was in the ocean. There was nothing but endless sky, water, and stars.

Josephine shivered in the cold, damp air. But still she did not move. She stood, waiting for her life to unfold. She stood, ready.

The Summer of Ice

Y EARS LATER, JOSEPHINE WOULD THINK OF THAT SUM-
mer of 1918 as the summer of ice. Already, it had become the
summer of the Great War. People blamed everything on
the fact that the world had gone mad. Dogs howled into the
night. Hail as big as plums fell from the sky, not once, but
twice that summer. Father Leone held special Masses to pray
for the boys going off to war. The village filled the church
for those Masses, crying as Father Leone, with his head of
slick, wavy hair and his large, drooping handlebar mustache,
invoked the names of the town boys who had gone. It was said
that the Virgin Mary cried real tears after these Masses. A
special representative from the Boston Archdiocese was coming to investigate. But for Josephine, even with the howling
dogs and brutal hail, even with the weeping Virgin, and her
own son, Carmine, being old enough to join the Army, that
summer was ordinary, until Alfredo Petrocelli, the ice man,
got the Spanish Influenza.

On Mondays, the rag man came. He walked down the
street calling, "Rags! Rags for sale!" His rags spilled from
pails attached to a wire pole that he carried across his shoul-

ders. He wore rags too, the rag man. Tied around his head, his neck, his waist, his wrists and ankles. The rag man was colorful, a burst of brightness every Monday afternoon. Josephine looked forward to hearing him call out his arrival, and always felt disappointed if he failed to come, which happened from time to time because the rag man was a drunk.

The coal man came on Tuesdays. Covered in soot, with grime in every crease and hole, the coal man drove his dirty red truck up and down the streets, spilling coal as he went. The neighborhood children ran behind the truck, collecting the pieces that fell. Josephine didn't like the coal man. She didn't like the way black grime lay beneath his fingernails, or how he blew his nose, releasing a stream of black snot into a dirty handkerchief. The coal man coughed and sniffed and cleared his thick phlegmy throat. Josephine imagined he cried black tears and urinated black piss. Still, when her daughter Isabella gave her a lump of coal that had fallen from his truck, Josephine buried it in a secret place, believing that, if left alone, it would turn into a diamond. Even now, she liked things that sparkled.

On Wednesdays, Tino the Turnip came with his horse-drawn wagon filled with fruits and vegetables. He was called Turnip because he was long and thin and covered in warts. Still, he always had the freshest fruits and vegetables. And he always brought something exotic: peaches or grapefruit. The prices for these were especially dear, but he was known to give them away for free at the end of the day, along with any bruised or half-rotten fruit he hadn't sold. Josephine would ask him to save her anything that no one else wanted, and late Wednesday afternoons, Tino the Turnip would come and leave her a basket of red peppers gone soft, string beans that were too thin, smashed raspberries. Once, he left her a mango. Another time, a green vegetable with hard, bumpy skin that even Tino didn't know the name for.

Jacques LaSalle came by noisily and early on Thursday mornings. He sharpened knives, bought and sold pans, shod horses, collected cans. Anything metal, Jacques took care of. Josephine avoided him if she could, and never let her children roam the streets until she heard him clink away. Jacques did not button his pants and let his penis swing free. He was simpleminded, everyone said. He meant no harm, he was just an idiot. But Josephine didn't like to see that long, pencil-thin penis hanging out. When he moved, climbing in or out of his cart, bending forward to set the sharpening wheel spinning, his penis swung left and right. Once, Josephine noticed it was partially erect, and she felt queasy around him after that.

Fridays were the best. On Fridays, the ice man came. In a way, he was the complete opposite of the coal man, everything about him sleek and clean and cold. Where the coal man was black, the ice man was blue. He swung enormous blocks of ice from his truck with large metal tongs, smooth and easy. Josephine liked watching him work his way up the street toward her house, liked his smooth, tanned hands, the half-moon of his fingernails. His name was Alfredo Petrocelli, and he came from a village in the Old Country not far from her own. Josephine looked forward to his arrival. When she saw Alfredo, she knew it was Friday, and another week was coming to an end.

But in June of that summer of 1918, right after her son, Carmine, left for Coney Island to make his fortune, Alfredo

Petrocelli did not come with ice. Josephine was already feeling all wrong inside. How else could a person feel after her only son decided to leave home for a strange place like Coney Island?

Carmine had been born exactly nine months after Josephine arrived in America. She had been met at the docks in New York by Vincenzo's cousin from Jersey City. All of the people in Vincenzo's family had that same pushed-in face, and she remembered thinking that if they never had children, it would be better than having ones that looked like that. (As it turned out, the two youngest girls had that unfortunate face. The others were all beautiful, with large, aquiline noses and full, pouty mouths). The cousin—she never learned his name—escorted her to the train station, handed her a ticket, helped her with her trunk, and walked away before the train even left the station. Josephine sat, clutching her ticket, her heart doing strange flips and flops as a swirl of people speaking English surrounded her. The language sounded harsh. Unwelcoming. But soon she relaxed, watching the lights of cities and seaside towns pass before her. America was a shiny place, Josephine learned. It glittered. She believed she could be happy there, even with Vincenzo.

That night, even though she was tired and achy and hungry from so many weeks of travel, Vincenzo climbed on top of her and moved around inside her five or six times, then collapsed beside her. In the nine years since he had married her right before going off to America, she had forgotten what he looked like exactly, until she saw the cousin from Jersey City. She had forgotten this part too. Or rather, she had remembered that he required a minute or two of her time, that it felt like nothing but an itch she wanted to scratch, and then it was over. Since she had last seen her husband, he had grown fat, so although it was as quick as before, his weight on top of her made it hard to breathe. Still, she could hold her breath until he was done. Then Josephine would sit up, take long deep breaths, and go and wash herself. By the time she got back into bed, Vincenzo was snoring.

During her first couple of weeks in America, they didn't talk very much. He went off to work in the mill that sat on the river at the bottom of the hill, and she did the same types of chores she had done back home. She baked bread and made pasta and tended the garden; she darned his clothes and crocheted a blanket for their bed; she stewed and bottled and canned fruits and vegetables; she walked to the church and helped the nuns clean the altar and dress the saints. Life in America, Josephine thought those first weeks, was very much like life in the Old Country. All of her neighbors spoke Italian and they had all come from villages right near her own. Vincenzo didn't have the same desire he'd had when they got married. Every few nights, he forced her legs apart and heaved his fat body on top of hers. Push, push, push, push. Done. Holding her breath, Josephine began to count how many thrusts it took him to finish. It was never more than six.

After her first week in America, Josephine fell asleep smiling. Here, there was always someone to gossip with while picking the ripe tomatoes. There was always someone with news of the war, or someone who knew details of Father Leone's life. It was said he was from Florence, an artist himself, perhaps of noble birth. He was so holy, Josephine was told, that the pope wrote him letters of admiration and respect. In

America, things grew with more abandon. Melons were juicier, tomatoes redder, eggplants larger. She had many rooms to wander, windows to make curtains for, a stove with six burners. For the few thrusts and grunts Vincenzo required, it was worth it to be in America.

But on the fourteenth morning of her arrival, Josephine woke up with the room spinning like it did when she had too much wine. Vincenzo was already moving about the kitchen, and she called for him to come, something was wrong. By the time he came, she was throwing up in the chamber pot.

"I'm sick," she told him. "I think I'm dying."

She thought she would never stop puking. But by the afternoon, weak and exhausted, it stopped. Josephine threw away the eggs she'd collected from her neighbor the day before. Fresh eggs make you talk too much. Old eggs make you sick; she knew that. But when this continued every morning for several days, Vincenzo grinned at her and said, "You're pregnant. Finally." With her head in the chamber pot, and the room upside down, she couldn't tell him what she was thinking: Finally? I hardly know you. For her, this pregnancy had happened too fast.

JOSEPHINE NEVER UNDERSTOOD why she had been so blessed after her wedding that she did not get pregnant. Because once she came to America, all she did was have babies. It was as if this country was so abundant, so full of plenty, that babies grew in her with the same ease that vegetables filled her garden. First she had Carmine, then Concetta, Giulia, Elisabetta. Vincenzo strutted like a rooster, showing off his virility. "All

I have to do is look at my wife," he liked to say, "and poof! She has a baby." But it wasn't poof! to Josephine. Each baby was bigger and harder to deliver, and she became more swollen and lethargic with each pregnancy. Her breasts grew big, and leaked milk even when there wasn't a baby or two latched onto them. Often, she had a baby at each breast and a third one waiting her turn.

Once she delivered a baby, the only relief was that Vincenzo would leave her alone for a few months. But soon, those months would pass, and one night, he would push aside the babies flopped around the bed, shove Josephine's legs open, and heave his ever fatter body onto hers. Even worse, either because he had grown so fat, or because he was getting older, it took him longer. Sometimes Josephine counted all the way to thirteen before he grunted and rolled off her. All the while he was pushing into her, babies cried and tugged at her and her breasts leaked out milk.

When she woke up puking with the fifth baby, Josephine broke into tears. Throwing up into the chamber pot while she nursed Giulia and Elisabetta, who was only three months old, she caught sight of Vincenzo standing in the doorway grinning down at her.

"Remember this," she told him. "You will never touch me again."

But when that fifth baby, another girl, was stillborn, Josephine was so heartbroken and guilty that she went back on her threat and soon had two more babies, Chiara and Isabella, whom they called Bella. In her mind, whenever Josephine looked at that seventh baby, she didn't think *Bella*; she thought *basta*. Enough.

———

UP THE HILL, in a rundown house in the woods, lived a *strega*, a witch. Josephine had heard stories about the things this woman could do. She could make a man fall in love with a woman. She could bring financial ruin to a family. She could cure sciatica and migraine headaches. She could even, it was rumored, see into the future. She had told Magdalena down the hill that her baby would be born with feet like a fish, and it came to pass. She had seen early death for Giorgio the barber, and hadn't he been trampled by his own horse before he reached thirty? And his wife pregnant with twins at the time.

Josephine wondered if the *strega* could keep her from getting pregnant again. Ever since that fifth baby had been born dead, Josephine believed she was to blame. She had told her husband he could not touch her again, but she knew that it was his right to have her anytime he wanted. Hadn't her own mother told her that on her wedding day? It was her duty, even if it meant looking like a cow and smelling of spoiled milk and baby spit-up all the time.

One afternoon, after she lit a candle wax on the altar, she saw Father Leone emerging from the confessional. Josephine rushed to catch up with him.

"Josephine," he said, obviously pleased to see her. He pointed to her flat stomach. "No new babies for the Rimaldis this year?"

Josephine took a step back. It was as if he had read her mind. "Father," she managed. The smell of incense and melting wax was making her dizzy and she actually swayed slightly.

"Whoa," Father Leone said, catching her by the elbows and holding her up.

Josephine looked into his dark eyes. He had very long lashes that curled up, like a girl's.

"I have a question," she said, her throat too dry to continue.

"Sit here," he said. "I'll get you some water." Gently, he led her into the front pew and ran to bring her a glass of water.

When he sat beside her, Josephine foolishly thought his eyes lingered on her breasts, which were filling with milk, which meant it was time for her to go home to feed her babies. What was wrong with her? she wondered as she gulped down the water. Here was a man so holy, the pope wrote him letters of admiration. Having babies made women act crazy; this was a fact. Marianna next door had tried to drown herself in the river after her third baby. Catalina from Sicily ran naked through the streets when she was nine months pregnant. Women knew this. Babies did something to them.

"I'm so tired," Josephine said at last.

"Babies," the priest said, nodding, "they take your strength."

"Yes!" Josephine said. "And Vincenzo . . . " She didn't know how to say what she wanted to say. Father Leone was sitting so close she could smell his cologne, a spicy scent that filled her mouth. Her nipples were starting to tingle. She had to go. Her breasts were growing hard with milk and soon it would leak out, embarrassing her.

"Vincenzo insists on you continuing to be his wife," the priest said, nodding again.

Was he reprimanding her? Josephine wondered.

"This is your job, of course. Didn't Jesus order us to be fruitful and multiply?" His Tuscan accent made it difficult for her to understand him exactly. He pronounced each vowel at the end of his words with a great and confusing flourish.

Josephine dropped her head. "I suppose so," she said. Now her breasts were hot and aching.

Father Leone cupped her chin in his soft hand and lifted her face so that he could look right at her. "How could Vincenzo, or any mortal, keep away from you? You, Josephine, are so beautiful, and so womanly. Look. Look at your breasts even now, flowing with life."

Josephine couldn't really move her head because he held on to her like that, but she glanced down to see a wet stain spreading across the front of her dress. Her cheeks turned red with shame.

"What's this?" Father Leone said. "You should never be ashamed of being fruitful and multiplying. Of nourishing God's children."

"But Father," she said, "look at me. Like a cow."

The same hand that had so gently cupped her chin now reached back and gave her a quick, hard slap. Josephine's hand shot to her face.

"You are a woman," Father Leone said sharply. He frowned at her, his dark eyes flashing. "How can I convince you that your body is a gift to your husband and to all of God's children?"

Even with her breasts leaking milk, the ache in them got worse. "Thank you, Father," she said. "But I have to go now."

"Why?" he asked her.

Trying not to show her embarrassment, Josephine looked

away from him and said, "You're a man of God, you don't need to worry about these mundane things, Father. But when my milk comes in, it's painful to not release it."

"Ah!" Father Leone said. "But you have such a long walk. In pain."

"That's all right, Father."

Once again, Father Leone lifted Josephine's chin. "Do you believe that I am a child of God?" he asked her.

Confused, thinking perhaps his accent had led her to misunderstand, she said, "Are *you* a child of God? Why, of course."

"Then it would be perfectly appropriate for you to nourish me, wouldn't it?"

Josephine searched his eyes but saw nothing there but compassion.

Father Leone nodded at her. "This will be an offering to God, Josephine," he said brusquely. "Offer me your milk."

Glancing around the empty church, Josephine wondered what to do.

"God is waiting, Josephine," he said, impatient.

Quickly, she unbuttoned her dress. The priest, without ceremony or lust, bent his head and gently put her sore nipple into his mouth. The pain made her groan and she worried he would misunderstand. But Father Leone seemed to take no notice of it, or her. He just greedily sucked her milk, first from one breast, then the other. Sucking hard, using his hand to gently pump it.

When he lifted his head, his lips were shiny with her milk. Josephine hurriedly buttoned her dress, and Father Leone raised his hand, making a dramatic sign of the cross in the air between them, his deep voice intoning, "In the name of the Father, and of the Son, and of the Holy Spirit." He pressed his thumb against her forehead. "You have given God a gift, and in turn, he blesses you."

Josephine swallowed hard. She believed she'd had a holy experience. While she had given her milk to God through Father Leone, something deep within her had stirred. She was damp everywhere, under her arms, between her breasts, even between her legs.

"Go home, Josephine," Father Leone said, "and be a wife to your husband. God orders you to do this."

PERHAPS, JOSEPHINE THOUGHT as she made her way to the witch's house, it was possible to do her duty as a wife and to stop having babies. Ever since that day last week in the church, Josephine had felt closer to God. The priest was indeed a holy man. At church on Sunday, she had gazed up at him as he stood delivering God's words, and that same something had stirred in her.

With Bella in a sling swaying in front of her, Josephine walked all the way to the *strega*'s house through the woods so no one would see her. One thing everyone knew that the witch could do was to stop a pregnancy before the baby got too big. This was a sin, but women regularly came to the witch for that. Josephine didn't want anyone to think that was what she was doing.

Barefoot, she walked through the quiet woods. Except for her daughter sleeping against her, Josephine could have been back in the Old Country, walking to the stream. The moss was soft and squishy beneath her feet, and she spotted mushrooms that would be good cooked in red sauce. Josephine couldn't remember when she had last felt so peaceful. At home, there was always a baby needing to be nursed or fed or changed or washed; there was always a meal to cook, clothes to clean; there was Vincenzo, already wanting her, even though Bella was just ten weeks old. She could tell the way his puffy eyes lingered on her breasts as she nursed Bella and Chiara, then Elisabetta.

Her breasts were so sore and swollen, covered in fat blue veins, that Josephine could not understand how they brought desire to him. But they did. He had never once even touched them, or seen them, until Carmine was born and she was nursing him. But Vincenzo ogled them anytime she had them out, which was most of the day. Sometimes Josephine wondered if other women's husbands touched them. Or if every man did what Vincenzo did. She was too embarrassed to ask, but there were times when something in her longed for Vincenzo, fat Vincenzo, to caress her, to kiss her mouth, to touch her thighs.

Once, so long ago now that she could not even remember when, between babies, she was washing herself in the big silver tub they kept outside, and her soapy hands gently scrubbed her thighs, then her inner thighs. Small charges, like electricity, shot through her. Tentatively, she washed where her babies came out. Usually, she did this hurriedly and with great efficiency. But this day, because she was alone in her yard and the touch of her own soapy hands had sent these small jolts through her, she washed herself there more carefully. Slowly, she rubbed herself, keeping her hand soapy and slippery. Yes. It felt good to be touched there. But also silly. And wrong. Josephine got out of the tub quickly and went and confessed this to Father Leone, who made her say a rosary for trying to find pleasure in such a sinful way.

But it wasn't pleasure she had been after, Josephine thought as she made her way to the *strega*'s house, which had come into view. It was tenderness. How tenderly Father Leone had taken her milk. Tenderness like this was a holy experience, wasn't it?

Josephine realized that the witch was standing outside the house, hands on her hips, watching Josephine approach. To Josephine's surprise, the *strega* was beautiful. Her hair was in a thick black braid down her back, and her skin was smooth and clear. She had surprising violet eyes, and she wore pants, like a man. She was smiling at Josephine.

"Don't worry," the witch said, "you will find that tenderness. But not for ten more years."

Josephine stopped in her tracks. The woman was most definitely a *strega*, to know what was in Josephine's heart.

"That's why you came, isn't it?"

"No," Josephine said slowly. But even as she said it, she wondered if perhaps it was why she had come.

The witch looked down at Bella, still sleeping, and something crossed her face, then passed.

"What?" Josephine said.

The witch's violet eyes rested on Josephine's face. "Why did you come then?"

Unsettled by the way she had looked at the baby, Josephine struggled for the words. "This is my seventh baby in ten years," she began.

"Too many, eh?"

"No. But enough."

The witch laughed. She told Josephine to wait and she disappeared into the house. When she returned, she held a brown bag filled with sticks and twigs and dried flowers. "After you and your husband have intercourse, make tea with this. It will get rid of any babies you make."

"Oh, I don't want to get rid of them!" Josephine explained. "I don't want any more at all."

The witch laughed again. "Then tell your husband to leave you alone," she said. "That's the only way to prevent babies for certain."

"But the priest says I have to be with Vincenzo. Jesus ordered it."

The witch laughed, a sharp, rough sound.

Then, unexpectedly, she drew Josephine into her arms, and soothed her, like a mother comforts a child. Her embrace, so strong and tender, brought tears to Josephine's eyes. She thought of her own mother, back home—for Josephine always thought of that tiny village as home. Josephine could picture her rough, red hands, the line of dirt beneath her fingernails, the coffee-colored mark on her cheek. She could picture her mother the day Josephine left. She had stood straight and tall and dry-eyed. *This is what we do for our children*, her mother had whispered. *We let them go, even as our heart breaks in two.*

But as soon as the *strega* released Josephine, she turned and walked away.

Josephine called out to her, but the woman went inside the house without even looking back. Her mother had not waited for her either. Josephine had turned around once on that road that eventually led to Naples, expecting her mother to be standing there, only to find her gone. Now, unsettled, Josephine made her slow way toward home.

ON THE FRIDAY in June that the ice man did not come, Josephine had not been a wife to Vincenzo in a long time. Although there had been a night here and there over those years when he had managed to make her open her legs to him, she always got up and made a cup of that tea from the bag the *strega* had given her. The children were no longer babies, and Josephine's body had remarkably returned to its former slender self. Her breasts still sagged more than she would have liked, but the blue veins had vanished, and she noticed men admiring her when she leaned forward or wore certain dresses that showed off her full bosom.

Vincenzo had grown so fat that he waddled when he walked. His hair had thinned, and he'd bought himself a black toupee that sat on top of his head like a crow. At night, he put the toupee on the lamp by the bed, and more than once Josephine had woken to think a cat had gotten into their room. Every once in a while, Josephine tried to talk to her husband. But he never seemed very interested. After dinner, he burped loud and long, sending giggles through the children, then shoved himself away from the table, heaving his large body up. He straightened his toupee and went to play cards and drink grappa down the street.

No ice for a week in June meant meat went bad, drinks

grew warm, everything had to be eaten right away. There were rumors that Alfredo Petrocelli had the Spanish Influenza and surely would die. But Josephine chose not to believe this. She thought of his cool hands, his muscles straining as he hoisted blocks of ice, his clean clear face. If anyone got the Spanish Influenza, surely it would be the filthy coal man. Or that Jacques LaSalle with his thing hanging out all the time.

The next Friday morning, with all of the children at school or at work in the mill, Josephine was surprised when she heard a racket in the backyard.

She stepped outside, still in her thin housedress, and found a man who was not Alfredo Petrocelli standing there with a block of ice. Aware of the sweat marks staining under her arms, and of her breasts against the flimsy dress, Josephine folded her arms across her chest.

"You there!" she called to the man. "You startled me."

He turned and Josephine's knees wobbled. Tall, with blond hair and green eyes staring back at her from a tanned face, the man in the black pants and white sleeveless T-shirt was the most beautiful thing she had ever seen.

"Sorry," he said in English. "I don't know the drill."

Josephine frowned. "Drill?" she repeated.

"I'm filling in for my cousin Al," the man said, in rapid-fire English with no hint of an Italian accent. An American. "He's pretty sick." He studied her for a minute, then laughed. "You don't know a word I'm saying, do you?"

She shrugged and took a tentative step toward him. That's when she realized she was barefoot, and her legs were bare as well. Bare arms, bare legs, no shoes, a flimsy dress hardly concealing what was beneath it. What was this man going to think of her? He was looking at her, and a blush rose on his cheeks.

"Sorry to stare," he said in terrible Italian. "But you're really beautiful."

Now color rose in her cheeks. "No," she said, waving his compliment away with her hands.

His hand grabbed one of hers, and before she could pull it away, he was shaking it and saying, "Tommy Petrocelli. Your new temporary ice man."

"Your Italian is awful," she told him, the heat from his hand spreading up her arm, making her sweat even more.

"Sorry," he said again. "I was born in the good old U S of A. My father is Al's father's brother. *Tio?*" he said, raising his eyebrows.

"*Tio,*" she said, then. "Uncle."

He laughed. "Your English is terrible," he kidded her. "My mother is French, but she's been here forever."

Josephine nodded, even though she had no idea what French was.

"Ah," she said. "Do you want to come inside for a drink?"

"Sure," he said. "Great."

He still held on to her hand, and when they both realized this, he dropped it quickly.

Sitting in her hot kitchen at the table, beads of sweat on his forehead, he quickly drank the lemonade she gave him. They sat quietly.

"Even the glass is sweating," Josephine said finally, pointing.

He laughed. Then they were silent again.

"Mrs. . . . " he began.

"Josephine," she said.

"Josephine. Have you ever heard the saying that every person has a soul mate?"

She frowned at the word.

He reached across the table and placed his hand on her collarbone. "Soul mate," he repeated. "Some people, like me, believe that everyone has a soul mate, wandering the Earth somewhere. Not everyone finds theirs. But if you do, you recognize her immediately."

"Like fate?" she said, the pressure of his hand on her collarbone making her heart do strange things.

"Stronger, even. Two souls wander the planet, and if you are very, very lucky, you find each other."

He dropped his hand quickly and stood. "I've got to go," he said. "I'm sorry."

She wanted to tell him to stop apologizing. Was it them he was talking about? Soul mates? When he turned and looked at her out there, something had happened to her. Was he saying it had happened to him as well? Was this what people meant by love? Josephine wondered. But by the time she raced outside, he was gone.

THE WHOLE NEXT WEEK, as first the rag man, then the coal man, came, Josephine thought about soul mates. Two people wandering the Earth, searching for each other. Hadn't he said soul mates recognize each other immediately? She fed her children and slaughtered a chicken and sewed new dresses for the older girls and watched her fat husband eating, slurping and chomping. Maybe she had married Vincenzo simply to get her to America on that Friday when Tommy Petrocelli would find her. Soul mates, reaching across time and continents. She wondered what Father Leone thought of this idea. Did souls have mates?

Tino the Turnip left her a half-rotten pineapple. Jacques LaSalle clanked by, his penis swinging. Josephine asked about Alfredo Petrocelli. Had anyone heard anything about him? Was he better? And although she didn't wish Alfredo any harm, she was happy when Rose Palmieri said she'd heard he was still sick with the Spanish Influenza.

On Friday morning, after Vincenzo waddled out of the house, after she'd fed all the children and sent them off, Josephine took a bath in the big silver tub. She put lavender in the water, and rubbed aloe from the plant she kept by the stove to treat burns on her feet and elbows. Then she put on a dress, one of the ones that made men look at her when she wore it. And she swept her hair up with a sparkling pin.

Then, Josephine Rimaldi sat and waited. Just when she decided he wasn't going to come, he appeared. He walked right into the house, and said her name, so soft and tender that tears spilled from her eyes. He reached for her, and she nodded.

Tommy Petrocelli kneeled in front of her. He slowly lifted her dress and ran his large, cool hands up her thighs, as if he knew this was the very place where jolts of electricity shot through her. When his hand touched her down there and found her wet, Josephine was embarrassed. But then Tommy did the most remarkable thing. He kissed her down there. He licked her and sucked her and she heard someone moaning, loud. That feeling she'd had so long ago in the tub was back again. But at the point she had stopped, guilty and ashamed, Tommy kept going. The noise grew louder. Such moaning! Josephine was gripping Tommy's head now, shoving herself into him, and she realized she was making all the noise. But she couldn't stop herself. He was doing something to her, something she had been longing for. And when she found it, she knew. Her scream was like the cats in heat, but longer and more intense.

As soon as it ended, Tommy pulled down his pants and lifted her onto the table, where he entered her. She was still trembling, wondering what had happened to her, when she realized he was not moving. He was inside her, and he was looking at her.

"Do you believe it?" he whispered.

She knew what he meant: soul mates. Her voice seemed to have vanished, but she managed to nod. Tommy Petrocelli was her soul mate. They were—incredibly, wonderfully—in love. So many questions bubbled up in Josephine's throat that a strange, choking sound came from her. Would he take her and all these children with him somewhere?

He took the pin from her hair, and he began to kiss her. Without those fast thrusts, Josephine was able to actually feel Tommy inside her. Soon she was clawing at him, begging him to move inside her. He moved so slowly that she thought she might die from the pleasure of it. And again those jolts were shooting through her, and she heard herself moaning, and she was digging her nails into his hard shoulders. Soon he was moving faster and grunting, and then she actually felt him come inside her.

"Feel my heart," she whispered. It was beating wildly. "I might die," she said.

"*Le petit mort,*" Tommy said.

"Death?"

"It's French. They call it the little death."

FOR TWO MORE FRIDAYS he came to her, his hands cold from delivering ice. She brought him into the bed she shared with Vincenzo. She imagined leaving her husband, following Tommy Petrocelli anywhere he wanted her to. Everything vanished in the hour they were together each Friday. On the fourth Friday, Josephine woke with her head spinning, and the taste of vomit rising in her throat. And she knew.

But she couldn't let Vincenzo see her like this, or he would know too. She pretended to be asleep until he left for the mill. Then she buried her head in the chamber pot and puked. That day, Tommy Petrocelli did not come to her. He didn't come the next week either. He never came again. People said Alfredo died. Some believed his cousin did too. The blond one who had helped out for a while. Soon a new ice man came.

Josephine tried to think of what to do. It had been years since her husband had lain with her. If he learned she was pregnant, he might kill her. Unless he believed it was his. That night, when he heaved himself into bed, Josephine said, "Vincenzo, do you no longer desire your wife?" The words made her sick, but she had no choice.

Immediately his hand forced her legs open. He grunted, like a pig. Luckily it was dark and he couldn't see her crying. She imagined her passionless life, stretching endlessly before her. She wondered if she could leave this place, leave all of her children, and find Tommy Petrocelli? But even as she wished for such a thing, she knew it was impossible. She had no money; she didn't even speak enough English to find him in the world outside this neighborhood.

When Vincenzo climbed on top of her, his weight pressing down on her so that she couldn't breathe, Josephine thought she might be sick. But she only had to count to five, and he was done.

Throwing up into the chamber pot two weeks later, Vincenzo beamed at her from the doorway. "Poof!" he said. "I only have to look at you and you get pregnant." He laughed, proud of himself.

Josephine spent all morning throwing up. When she finally had nothing left, she lay in that hot August heat, imagining this baby inside of her. Tommy's baby. In a way, she would have Tommy with her forever. She tried to picture it, this child. What if this baby had Tommy's blond hair? Other than Jacques LaSalle, no one here had hair so pale. Everyone would know. They would remember how she had kept asking for him. They would remember how he always delivered the ice to her house last, even though she was in the middle of the street. As soon as she let herself imagine it, she realized she had to do something.

Josephine went to see Father Leone. She had a lie all ready to tell him. He brought her into his study and offered her a glass of wine, which she eagerly took. Father Leone had one too. He placed the bottle on the coffee table, and came to sit on the red leather sofa, right beside Josephine.

"You're worried about something?" he said kindly.

Josephine nodded. Adultery and lying to a priest, surely she was headed for hell.

Father Leone placed his hand over hers. "Tell me," he said.

She liked his voice. It was smooth, like the wine he served her. "I'm pregnant again, Father," she said. "But with six children already, and at my age . . . " She shook her head.

The priest refilled her glass. "Go on," he said.

"I just wondered if you knew any families who wanted a baby, who maybe couldn't have one of their own."

"Such a selfless thing to do," he said, squeezing her hand. "I remember your offering to God, Josephine. I think about it often. How selfless you were. But what does Vincenzo say about it?"

"I haven't told him," she said, shaking her head again. "It's complicated."

The priest didn't answer. Josephine gulped at her wine. How foolish she had been to come here. A priest wasn't going to protect a sinner. She should have tried instead to find Tommy. Even without money or English, it might have been possible. Wasn't he her soul mate? The man she loved? She was crying now, and Father Leone lifted her chin and looked right at her, just like he'd done that day in the church.

"Whose baby is it?" he said.

"How could you ask me such a thing?"

"You cannot get help or forgiveness unless I know the truth, Josephine."

Her mind was swimming from wine and early pregnancy, from having lost Tommy, from desperation.

"You don't have to tell me who the father is," the priest said. "But don't lie to me about the situation."

Josephine studied the ruby in the ring the priest wore. It was red and shiny. "Pretty," she said absently, and touched the ruby with her free hand.

"It can be arranged," he said, "for you to have the baby in a hospital. Many women do this now, and if you can convince Vincenzo to send you, then all we do is tell him the baby died. The nuns there will give it to a family who can't have their own baby. No one will ever know."

Josephine was crying harder, pressing her face into Father Leone's jacket. His collar was scratchy against her skin.

"But if you don't tell me the truth . . . " he was saying.

"Fine, fine," Josephine said, "it isn't Vincenzo's. I can't keep this baby; it isn't his."

"This service," the priest said. "There's a fee."

She looked up, surprised. "I don't have money."

"Hmmm," he said. His eyes drifted from her face to her breasts, which had grown even fuller in pregnancy. "Perhaps we can arrange something," he said. He met her eyes again. "Do you understand?"

Josephine stood up. "I can't . . . "

"Of course you can," he said harshly. "You gave yourself over to me so easily that day. Remember? I asked you and you did it."

"For God," she said, foolishly.

"Do you believe that I am a holy man?"

"Of course."

"When you offer yourself to me, aren't you giving yourself to God?"

Josephine hesitated. "I . . . I don't know."

"You don't think I take such things for my own pleasure, do you?"

"No!" she said quickly, even though she didn't know what she thought.

"I have dedicated my entire life to God, haven't I?" he asked her. His voice was kind again.

Out of nowhere, Josephine found herself thinking of the war in Europe. The whole world had gone mad. Isn't that what everyone was saying? Magdalena from down the hill said that soon they were all going to have to speak German, unless we won the war and killed all the Krauts.

Father Leone was waiting patiently, smiling his gentle priest smile. What was left to lose? Josephine wondered. She drank her wine and closed her eyes, but she was not yet to the place where the room was spinning, so she poured more into her glass.

Father Leone laughed. "You like wine, don't you?" he said. "Enjoy it!"

"I do," she said softly.

This glass did it. She lay back on the sofa and the room spun pleasantly. Josephine smiled. Young boys were getting killed every day over there, she thought. For all she knew, the Germans would come here and kill them too. She was going to hell. Father Leone was going to hell. The whole world was coming to an end.

"The war," she said, but she was too drunk to put her thoughts into words.

"Remember that God is grateful to you for giving yourself to him, Josephine," Father Leone whispered. "I just want you to unbutton your dress for me," he said, his voice low and kind. "Like you did that day."

Josephine felt her body fly up to the ceiling and watched herself from some distant spot, unbuttoning the dress, unclasping the bra so that her ample breasts fell free. She watched the way Father Leone's eyes gobbled them first, before he bent to suckle them. This was all he had wanted? she found herself thinking. Just like that day in church. Again, newspaper images of the war in Europe filled her mind. All of those young boys had suckled at their mother's breasts, had grown from their milk, grown into men about to die. Josephine wrapped the priest's curls in her fingers and pulled him closer to her.

"Yes," he whispered. "Give yourself to God."

With one hand he unbuttoned his trousers and for an instant she froze. He had taken a vow of chastity. He couldn't expect her to do *that*, could he? From her place high above the man and woman on the burgundy leather sofa, with the afternoon light streaming amber and cobalt through the stained-glass window, Josephine saw the priest take himself in his own hand, and smoothly slide his penis up and down in his firm grip, all the while sucking her breasts, all the while Josephine pushing him closer to her, nourishing him, until a spasm went through his body. He lifted his mouth from her then, and turned away.

"Father?" she said.

Father Leone took the clean white linen napkin he had placed beneath the wine bottle and cleaned himself with it. Quickly, Josephine clasped her bra and buttoned her dress, worried he might look back at her and see naked breasts. When he did face her again, his face was as serene and holy as always.

"God loves you," he told her. "You are selfless, Josephine. He knows that. He is grateful." Then he touched her forehead and blessed her.

She grabbed his hand and kissed it. "I feel closer to God, Father," she whispered in a hoarse voice.

Later, as she walked home in the late afternoon light, Josephine thought of his mouth on her nipples. For a while on that sofa, she had forgotten he was a servant of God and she had thought of him as a man. Ashamed of herself for these impure thoughts, Josephine considered going back and confessing them to Father Leone. But hadn't he blessed her? Hadn't he told her God was grateful? "If you need anything else," he had said to her, "come back." Her head ached, like the sounds of cannons approaching.

ON VALENTINE'S DAY, a month earlier than she'd expected, Josephine gave birth alone at Saint Mary's Hospital. The baby was a girl, with soft blond hair, different from any of the other babies Josephine had. So tiny, this beautiful baby girl; her last two babies had been so big they'd ripped her so that she couldn't even pee without pain for weeks. But Valentina was small and calm. Worse, when Josephine held her, she felt a surge of love that she had not felt so immediately with any of her other children. She loved this baby with every cell in her body.

"Her name is Valentina," Josephine told the nun. "Today is her day. The day of love."

"Sure," the nun said, "but the parents give them whatever name they want."

"Who are they?" Josephine asked, her voice catching.

"Can't tell you. Sorry. She's going to Vermont, though." The nun lowered her voice. "Very rich family. She's a lucky one. You're doing a selfless thing," the nun said, handing Josephine her daughter wrapped in swaddling.

It was the only time she was allowed to hold her. Valentina opened her eyes and struggled to focus them. But she managed, and looked right up into Josephine's. Josephine's heart tumbled. "I love you," she whispered.

That night, as the hospital slept, Josephine got out of bed and went into the long corridor. At the end, two nuns in white habits sat, sipping tea. The lights cast an odd and ugly green over everything, and the floors moved like the sea beneath it. Josephine had to hold on to the wall as she walked quietly down the hallway toward the nursery. She could see it, halfway between her and the nuns. Behind the long pane of glass, all the babies lay under heaters.

Josephine wanted her baby.

She felt the familiar tingle of her milk coming in, and she wanted to get her baby and bring her to her breast. She could not send this baby, her Valentina, away. That was clear to her. Let Vincenzo kill her. Let everyone whisper about this blond-haired girl. But Josephine was going to keep her. Maybe when she felt stronger—because now she was dizzy and her legs wobbled, but soon she would be strong, back to normal—maybe she would take Valentina and find Tommy. "Look," she would tell him. "Our daughter."

"Mrs. Rimaldi?" one of the nuns said, her head jerked upright so that her wimple looked like wings and Josephine half expected her to take flight, to swoop down the hallway and carry Josephine back to bed.

"I just want to see her," Josephine said.

The two nuns looked at each other. The birdlike one stood. "That's not possible."

Josephine tried again. "I feel my milk coming in. She can nurse now."

The birdlike one was moving toward her, not flying or soaring, but walking deliberately down the hall. "I'm afraid her parents have already come for her, Mrs. Rimaldi. They've taken her home with them. To Vermont."

Where was Vermont? Josephine wondered.

Panic rose in her throat. "But she's so little. She needs my milk."

Look, she wanted to say to Tommy, *look at our daughter.*

The nun stood right in front of her. "I'm sorry," she said.

"If I could just look in the nursery," Josephine begged her, "to be sure she's not there."

But the nun was shaking her head, and with a firm grip on Josephine's arms, she was moving her back toward her room.

"If I could just look," Josephine said, fighting the nun's strong arms.

The second nun appeared, and the two of them wrestled Josephine to the ugly green floor. The second one had a syringe in her hand, and while the bird held Josephine down, struggling, fighting, calling her daughter's name, the second one plunged the needle into Josephine's thigh. Her mouth filled with the taste of metal. The strange green lights above her head pulsated. She felt spit drooling from her mouth. She felt suddenly very hot.

"Can you walk?" someone was asking her.

She was pulled to her feet and dragged along the hallway. Was she moving across the ocean? Josephine wondered. Were they taking her back to the Old Country? Was her mother waiting for her there?

"Almost there," someone said. "Keep your eyes open until we get you into bed again."

She had come so far on her own. It was taking forever to get back.

"Stay awake now, one more minute," someone said firmly.

Across the ocean was home. Across the ocean was war. They lifted her under her arms, up, up, until she was flying now. Then cold all around her. White and cold as ice.

War Stories

As soon as the first American troops arrived in France, Chiara began to pray. She took the white rosary beads that all the little girls of the parish had received for their First Communion from their white satin pouch, kissed the fake silver crucifix that hung at one end, slipped the beads over her head, and prayed. Fingering each bead, silently reciting the Hail Marys, the Our Fathers, the Acts of Contrition, Chiara walked to school, her head bent so no one would see her lips move.

But Elisabetta saw. Four years older, Elisabetta was the tallest Rimaldi girl, the smartest, the most beautiful. And Elisabetta knew these things about herself. She had an air of disdain for everyone else in the family, but especially for Chiara, who was short and ordinary and homely. Elisabetta wanted to become a scientist like Madame Curie; Chiara wanted to be Elisabetta.

"What are you doing?" Elisabetta demanded right in the middle of an especially fervent Our Father.

Chiara kept her head bent, finished the prayer, said, "Nothing." She could feel Elisabetta's eyes on her.

Giulia, who was merely pretty but not smart or tall, said matter-of-factly, "We're rolling gnocchi."

"I know what *we're* doing, you cretin. I asked what *Clara* was doing."

This was yet another annoying habit of Elisabetta's. She called them all by the Americanized versions of their names. We're American, she would say haughtily, not a bunch of guineas right off the boat. So she called Concetta Connie; Isabella Belle; Giulia Julie; Chiara Clara; and she referred to herself as Betsy. She liked to tell them about all the famous Betsys in America. Betsy Williams, the wife of Roger Williams, the founder of Rhode Island. Betsy Ross, the woman who designed and sewed the American flag. Elisabetta knew so much information that Chiara wondered why her head didn't explode, like Mount Vesuvius.

The problem was, Betsy was a cute name, the name of a girl people wanted to be friends with. Someone named Betsy could jump high, and smile easily. But Clara was an ugly name. No one would want to be friends with a Clara. At least Chiara sounded exotic, like a dancer or an opera singer.

"You're praying again, aren't you?" Elisabetta demanded.

Chiara sighed and looked at her sister. She had successfully finished a complete rosary so she could say honestly, "No, I am not praying."

Elisabetta said, "Well, you *were*. You always move your lips when you pray. And when you read," she added, disgusted.

"I hate reading," Giulia said. "And arithmetic. I want to be famous, and when I am, I won't have to read or do fractions ever again."

"That," Elisabetta said, flicking the tines of the fork off the pasta, leaving perfect ridges, "is idiotic."

It must be hard to be Elisabetta, Chiara thought, having to do everything just right. Then Chiara bent her head again, and began another rosary.

WHEN THE SPANISH INFLUENZA swept their neighborhood, taking dozens of people with it, Chiara prayed even harder. Her brother was fighting in France, so she had to pray for him as well as for all the American soldiers. She prayed so much there was hardly time for anything else.

"Why don't you run off and join the convent?" Elisabetta said. "Then you can pray all day and all night."

She said it to be mean, of course, but Chiara thought it was a wonderful idea.

"How do you join?" Chiara asked her.

"How should I know?" Elisabetta said. She was doing complicated algebra problems at the kitchen table, smiling to herself as she solved each one. "Go ask Father Leone."

"Sorry," Chiara said, "I thought you knew everything."

Elisabetta kept scribbling numbers and letters on a piece of paper. "I know everything that matters," she said.

CHIARA, LIKE ALMOST everyone else, was terrified of Father Leone, despite his handsome face and thick, wavy hair. When she had told her mother this, her mother had said she should never be afraid of one of God's servants. He is so holy, her mother had told her, that the pope writes him letters of admiration. This only made Chiara even more humbled and frightened of the priest.

But today, when she climbed the steep stone steps that led to his residence behind the church, she burned with pride instead of fear. Imagine telling the most respected priest in the entire world that you too wanted to become God's servant.

She was surprised when Father Leone himself answered her knock. Usually, one of the parish nuns was in there cleaning or cooking for him. Right then, as the heavy door swung open and Father Leone appeared with dramatic light pouring in from the window behind him, Chiara decided that not only did she want to be a nun, but she wanted to be the nun who took care of Father Leone. What an honor that would be. To wash the floors he walked on and to simmer a rich ragu for him to eat. Even Elisabetta would never have such pleasure.

Father Leone was smiling down at her, waiting. "Yes?" he said finally. "Have you come to stand on my doorstep? Or do you have a problem?"

Chiara spoke in a rush of Italian. "Forgive me for the disturbance," she said, "I'm God's servant Chiara Rimaldi—"

"I know who you are," he said. "Your mother is a selfless woman who gives everything to God."

This shut Chiara up. She never thought of her mother this way. To Chiara, her mother was a woman in a faded cotton dress, always working. She never seemed to be at rest. Even when she sat, she sewed or knit or kneaded. She was not like Magdalena down the hill, who brought her children onto her

lap and sang them silly songs. Or like Catalina next door
who baked her children their own loaves of bread in animal
shapes: cats and horses and rabbits.

She felt Father Leone waiting.

"I want to be a nun," Chiara blurted.

The priest studied her face carefully, and nodded. "How
old are you, Chiara?"

"Eleven," she said. Then she added quickly, "And I'm ready
to leave my family and become a bride of Jesus."

"You must be twelve to become an initiate," he said. "But
I can arrange it for you if you are still serious about this
next year."

"Oh, I will be!" Chiara said. "Even more serious."

He smiled down at her. She thought he must be the tallest
man she'd ever seen.

"You will make a good nun," he said, turning serious. "You
are homely, although in God's eyes everyone is beautiful. So
taking Our Lord Jesus Christ as your husband is very wise."

Chiara thought she might cry from joy. She fingered the
rosary around her neck, praying in gratitude. She didn't even
care that the priest had told her how ugly she was; she knew
this about herself. Her face was flat, as if God had punched
her just before she was born, and her nose was like a pig's
snout. Even her hair was not silky like her sisters'. Instead, it
grew in tight, kinky curls all over her head.

Father Leone kneeled at her side so that he could look
in her eyes. "What are you praying for, child?" he asked
her gently.

"For my brother, Carmine, who is fighting in France, and
for all the American boys there, and for the people dying of

the Spanish Influenza, and for my sister Elisabetta to some-how go to college, and for my sister Giulia to be famous, and for my sister Isabella to not be retarded, and for gratitude that next year you will send me to the convent."

"Those are a lot of prayers."

She nodded solemnly, crossing her fingers behind her back because there were more things she was praying for and leaving them out was a lie of omission.

"Why don't you come here after school on Fridays and help Sister Alma clean my house?"

"Me?" Chiara said.

The priest touched her forehead and said a blessing before closing the door.

But Chiara did not move for a long time. She stood on the priest's doorstep, praying and letting this new blessing fill her: she was special after all.

IN ONE SHORT MONTH, Betsy's life changed. Her mother had always claimed things came in threes. When someone in the neighborhood died, she would warn that two more deaths were coming. When good news arrived, she would watch for two more pieces of luck. Betsy wanted to be a scientist. She didn't believe in superstitions like those that dominated her family and their neighborhood. But in fact, in one week, three things happened that changed Betsy's life.

The first was that the Spanish Influenza ripped through town for a second time and killed her father. She found her father disgusting. He was fat. He ate like a pig, grunting and spilling. He ignored all of his children. And he treated her mother like a servant. When her new baby sister died at birth in February, he'd only shrugged, even though her mother cried and moaned for weeks. So when he got sick, she hardly even paid attention. Her littlest sisters, Belle, the one everyone said was "off" or "not right in the head," and Julie, who was next in age to Betsy, got it the week before. She had not wanted them to die, and had run over a mile to the doctor's to find out what to do for them. No sooner did they pull through, emerging pale and exhausted, than their father got sick. Before she even had time to think about it, he died. More surprised than sad, and never having seen a dead person up close, Betsy went in to stare at his body. She was surprised at how blue his skin was, how his tongue jutted from his mouth, how contorted his face looked.

"From coughing himself to death," her mother explained. Her mother was dry-eyed too, even though out in the kitchen, all of the other kids were sobbing.

"It turned to pneumonia," Betsy said, more interested in the clinical aspects of this than any personal ones.

She expected everything to go on the same as it always had, except without her father around, until her mother announced that he had left them no money and the older girls would have to drop out of school and go to work in the mill.

"Not me," Betsy said. "I'm going to go to college."

"College?" her mother said. "Are you crazy? We need to put food on the table."

The very next day, Belle and Julie brought home papers for their mother to sign, agreeing to let them drop out of school. Belle had stayed back twice already anyway, and Julie liked boys more than studying.

"Where are yours?" her mother said.

Betsy shook her head. "I want to be a scientist. I need to finish high school." She was fifteen years old, a sophomore. Already she'd been voted social committee chairman, won a spot on the JV cheerleading squad. She was a person going places.

"Tomorrow you bring the papers for me to sign."

The next day, Betsy watched Belle and Julie get ready for their first days at the mill. They giggled and whispered as they got dressed, helping each other fix their hair and choose what to wear.

"We'll tell you all about it," Julie promised. "It won't be so bad."

"But you want to be famous," Betsy reminded her.

Julie shrugged. "Maybe a handsome man will fall in love with me. Maybe even the owner of the entire mill."

Belle took two cigarettes from the pack she kept hidden in the top dresser drawer. "I'd rather work than go to school anyway," she said. "Dying was the best thing Papa ever did for me."

Betsy wanted to tell her sister that she would graduate in a year. Then she could get a better job, as a secretary or a stenographer. But Belle was smearing red lipstick on her mouth, trying to look older and sexy.

"You'll see," she told Betsy, "it's going to be fun working."

That afternoon, Betsy had cheerleading practice. Her cartwheels were so strong that the team captain told her she'd definitely be moved up to the varsity team during basketball season. On the way home, Betsy walked as slowly as she possibly could, forming arguments to convince her mother she had to stay in school. But when she walked into the house, instead of the angry atmosphere she was expecting to find, her mother jumped up and kissed her on both cheeks.

"Look," she told her, "look who's come to rescue you."

Sitting at the kitchen table, sipping coffee and anisette, was Father Leone. And grinning beside him was her little sister Clara.

"Rescue me?" Betsy said.

"I told him that you were supposed to be a scientist but Papa left us broke—" Clara began.

"Shh, Chiara," her mother scolded. "Let Father explain."

"He's going to help you get a scholarship!" Clara blurted.

"What?" Betsy said. She dropped onto the floor at the priest's feet.

His strong hands grasped her forearms and lifted her so that they were eye to eye.

"After your sister here explained what was happening, I called the school. They told me you maintain a straight A average," Father Leone said in his smooth voice.

"I do!" Betsy said, in case he needed more evidence.

"I offered to tutor you, in Latin and mathematics, two nights a week. If you continue getting straight A's, it can be arranged for you to get a scholarship to study at Salve Regina College."

"College?" Betsy said. She needed to be certain she understood what she was hearing.

"Of course," the priest said, "in addition to your studies I'll expect you to do some work at the church. Filing, typing. That sort of thing. Nothing is free, child. You must earn what you get."

Betsy was nodding.

Her mother said sharply, "But surely I could do the church work for her, Father?"

"I'll do it, Mama!" Betsy said. It would be just like her mother to ruin this one opportunity for her.

The priest glanced up at her mother, almost dismissively. "You won't have to take care of anything, Mrs. Rimaldi," he said.

"But I will," her mother said evenly. "So she can work on her studies."

Silently, Betsy willed her mother to shut up.

Father Leone rose. He was such a tall man; Betsy had never noticed this when he stood at the pulpit in his flowing purple robes.

"You have enough to do holding a family together alone," he said, patting her mother's hand. Then he helped Betsy to her feet. "We will begin studying Latin next week then, Elisabetta?"

"Betsy," she said, deciding right then that she was going to marry Father Leone.

"Betsy?" he said, laughing. "So you are American through and through," he continued in English.

Later, in bed with her sister, she whispered her plans to Clara.

"You can't marry a priest," Clara said. "It's against the law."

"No, it's not," Betsy said.

"It's against God's law," Clara said.

Betsy closed her eyes but she couldn't sleep. She felt as if her life was finally beginning.

———

THE THIRD THING THAT HAPPENED, and Betsy believed this was the thing that really changed her life, was that her brother, Carmine, came home from the war. His best friend, Angelo Mazzonni, had been killed in action; Carmine, the Army notified them, was shell-shocked. He had been in an Army hospital for months and months, but there was no more they could do for him. None of them knew what to expect, although Belle said someone at the mill said it only meant he would be afraid of loud noises, and maybe he would tremble a little. This did not seem so bad.

But although those problems may have existed, clearly something very bad had happened to Carmine. He looked confused and said crazy things. It was like his brain had been injured, even though the Army assured them he had not suffered any wounds at all. In fact, he had medals, lots of them, for trying to save Angelo and others during battle. When they asked him about his bravery, he looked even more confused.

"Battle?" he said. "France?"

In bed that night they whispered together. How could they tell Carmine that while he was fighting the war, getting shell-shocked, being brave, his girlfriend, Anna Zito, married Nicola Padua and they had a baby on the way.

"Honestly," Belle said, sitting on the windowsill so she could blow the smoke from her cigarette out the window, "I don't think he's going to care about Anna Zito."

"But he loves her!" Julie said.

"I don't think he's shell-shocked," Betsy said, promising

herself to look the symptoms up in the big science dictionary at school. "I think he's brain damaged."

"The Army said 'shell-shocked,'" Julie said. "He just needs some rest."

But the next morning, when their mother carefully brought up Anna Zito's name, Carmine laughed.

"You remember Anna?" their mother said gently.

"That *puttana*," Carmine spat. "Of course I know her. I put my thing in her all the time."

"Carmine!" their mother said.

He shook his head. "Anna Zito is a whore."

The mill wouldn't give him a job, not with the crazy things he said, or the confused look that swept over his face most of the time. But Chiara spoke with Father Leone, and the priest said Carmine could sweep the church, replace the candles and incense, small things like that.

"Good," their mother said. "He can go on Tuesdays, when Elisabetta studies her Latin with Father Leone."

Elisabetta groaned. "Why does he have to come with me? He's creepy!"

"He's your brother and he will go to the church with you," her mother said.

On Tuesday evenings, after supper, Elisabetta and Carmine walked together to the church.

"Anna Zito liked me to fuck her like a dog, from behind," Carmine said.

Elisabetta covered her ears and conjugated Latin verbs in her mind so she wouldn't hear him.

"Anna Zito is a *puttana*," Carmine said as they climbed the steps to the church.

Once inside, he got the broom from the closet and began to
sweep. He was extremely methodical, which was also creepy.
He dragged the big broom up and down the aisle, beginning
against the wall and then up the aisle. Down and up. Elisabetta paused to be sure he was lost in the sweeping before she
hurried into Father Leone's study behind the altar.

Father Leone was always waiting for her at his desk.
He had a glass of red wine and the Latin book opened to
their next lesson. Elisabetta loved his mustache. At night
sometimes she imagined what it would be like to kiss him.
Certainly it would tickle. Her friend Connie at school had
kissed a soldier with a mustache and she said she could taste
soup in it. Father Leone would taste like wine, Elisabetta
thought.

"Always smiling," Father Leone said when he saw her
standing in the doorway.

Kiss me, she thought. *Let me see what your mustache tastes
like.* She hoped that if she thought these thoughts hard enough,
Father Leone would receive them through mental telepathy.
She had read in a science magazine in the school library about
a man who could bend spoons by staring at them.

"What is going on in your pretty head, Betsy?" the priest
said. He leaned back in his chair and she saw that he was
dressed like a normal man: black pants, white shirt. No collar
or crucifixes in sight.

"Do you know about mental telepathy?" she said, taking
her seat across from him.

"Yes," he said slowly. "You mean communicating through
thoughts?"

She nodded. "There is a man in England who can bend silver spoons just by staring at them."

"Ah!" he said. "Shall we try it?"

"Bending spoons?"

"No, mental telepathy. Send me a message and let me see if I can get it."

"Oh, no," Elisabetta said, embarrassed. But then she looked at the priest and with all of her might thought: *Kiss me! Kiss me!*

Father Leone shrugged. "Sorry," he said. "I'm not very good at reading minds, I guess."

Disappointed, she opened her Latin book.

"Sweeping's done," Carmine said from the doorway, startling them both.

"Fine," the priest said. "Scrape the wax from the altar then. Get it all, now, Carmine. Be sure."

Carmine nodded but he didn't leave.

"Is there something else?" Father Leone said impatiently.

"She's a *puttana*," he whispered, pointing to his sister. "Watch out." Then he walked away.

"I'm sorry," Elisabetta said.

"You? No, no, Betsy. It is God who is sorry for making a world where war can do that to men."

Elisabetta studied the priest's face. *I love you*, she thought.

He patted her hand. "God loves us all," he said.

SOMETIMES ON TUESDAYS they all three walked to church after supper: Chiara and Carmine and Elisabetta. Chiara

prayed as they walked, her lips moving, her fingers caress-
ing the rosary beads. She prayed for Carmine to stop being
shell-shocked. She prayed for the end of all war. She prayed
to turn twelve soon so she could become an initiate. This
last would happen in two months; Chiara knew that. But she
prayed anyway.

"In Coney Island I fell in love with a woman," Carmine
said one night.

"No, you didn't," Elisabetta said.

Chiara finished her prayer and said gently to her brother,
"No, Carmine. You were supposed to marry Anna Zito."

"That *puttana?*" He laughed.

Elisabetta rolled her eyes and walked faster, leaving those
two behind her. The week before, Father Leone had said he
was worried about her. You can be a scientist, he had told her,
but you cannot forsake God for science. What have you given
to God? he'd asked her. He had told her that her mother gave
anything God asked. Think about it, Betsy, he'd said.

She had thought about it. Tonight she would tell him that
she put up with a brain-damaged brother for God. She put up
with stupid sisters. She tolerated her mother's lack of affec-
tion. When she became a scientist, she would give her knowl-
edge in God's name. She was pleased with her response.

Father Leone was in his usual place, waiting for her. She
heard Carmine and Chiara come in. She heard the sweeping
begin and Chiara go down the basement stairs, where she
would wash all of the holy linens used in Mass.

Before Father Leone could say anything, Elisabetta gave
him her answer. He smiled as she talked.

"You are intelligent and beautiful and holy, Betsy," he said when she was finished. "You are sixteen now, aren't you?"

She nodded, pleased.

"Then I think you should have a glass of wine with me. First, I will bless it, and we will drink it in honor of God."

She watched him bless the wine and pour two glasses. When she sipped it, she wrinkled her nose and he laughed.

Father Leone got up and closed the door. Standing behind her, he put his hands on her shoulders.

"Do you remember when we tried to do mental telepathy?" he asked her, his voice low.

She remembered everything he had said to her, ever. Everyone believed his handsome, still youthful looks were a gift from God. But she knew he was more than that. He was a man. *I love you, Father Leone*, she thought, sending the words out to him.

"John," he said. "My name is John."

She smiled. He could read her mind. He could. *John*, she thought.

She tried to turn in her seat to face him, but his hands held her in place.

"I believe you were telling me to kiss you that night."

Elisabetta gasped.

"I didn't want to say it because I am a man of God, Betsy, and we do not partake of bodily pleasures. You are such a beautiful girl. Believe me, if I were not a priest—"

"I shouldn't have such thoughts," Elisabetta said, dropping her head. "But I do, Father. At night, especially after we study together, I can't stop imagining it."

"Imagining what?"

"Is this confession?" Elisabetta asked, jerking her head up. "Bless me, Father, for I have sinned—"

His hands reached in front of her and stopped her from making the sign of the cross. "Not confession."

She took a breath. "I imagine you touching me," she said. Would he give her a penance now? How many rosaries for forgiveness of such a sin?

"Where?" he whispered. His mouth was pressed against her ear and she felt the tickle of his mustache.

She didn't want to say it. She couldn't. It was a sin. Elisabetta shook her head.

"Betsy, you can tell me anything."

But she shook her head again. She couldn't *say* it.

Father Leone released her hands and walked around, kneeling at her feet. "I'm sad that you don't trust me. That you don't trust God."

Elisabetta leaned forward. She felt sweat trickle down her arms. She took the priest's face in her hands and whispered in his ear: "Down there. I imagine you touching me down there. I imagine that we do all kinds of dirty things together." She released his face and pushed away from him, running out of his office and down the long aisle of the church, past Carmine sweeping, out the door into the night.

THE NEXT WEEK, Elisabetta said she had a stomachache and couldn't go to study Latin with Father Leone. She pictured him in his office, waiting for her. How long would he sit there? she wondered guiltily. But then Giulia came home, flushed and dreamy, and announced she was getting married. She had met someone at the mill, a foreman, and they wanted to get married next month.

"No," Josephine said. "Out of respect for your father you have to wait one year."

Giulia cried and carried on about love and desire, but their mother wouldn't budge. "Next fall," Josephine said, "we can discuss this."

"Isn't this romantic?" Chiara whispered to Bella.

Bella agreed. But Elisabetta thought it was terrible. "You want to be famous," she reminded her sister.

"No," Giulia said, "I want to marry Mario."

"Enough about Mario!" Josephine said. "No one's getting married until the year is up."

"You're jealous," Chiara whispered, "because you can't marry Father Leone. Ever."

Josephine reached across the kitchen table and grabbed Chiara by the hair, hard. "What did you just say?"

"Nothing," Chiara said.

Josephine turned her attention to Elisabetta. "What has he told you? What has he done?"

Elisabetta thought of the priest's hands on her shoulders, the tickle of his mustache, the way he'd asked her what she'd imagined about them. She thought of what she had confessed. *I imagine that we do all kinds of dirty things together.* She felt her face grow hot.

"Elisabetta?" Josephine said. She stood in front of her beautiful daughter, her mouth dry with fear. He had told her that she was doing these things for God. She had felt holy as he bent and suckled her breasts. She had believed that his flesh was not like other men's.

"Why didn't you go to Latin tonight?" she demanded.

"Stomachache," Elisabetta said, and her stomach was aching now.

Chiara began to pray for forgiveness. She had gotten her sister in trouble by saying her secret. Would she ever get to the safety of the convent? She prayed for the next six weeks to pass swiftly. She prayed to be twelve.

"Mama," Giulia was saying, "we can't wait. We can't."

Josephine pressed her temples with the palms of her hands. So many worries, these daughters gave her. Only Concetta was easy. She worked at the mill. Helped at home. Stayed out of trouble. Her mind flitted back to her baby girl, Valentina. What was it like in Vermont? she wondered. Cold. Snowy. She thought there might be mountains there.

"I want my scholarship," Elisabetta said. "I need to study Latin to get into college."

"Mama, are you listening?" Giulia said. "We can't wait."

Josephine frowned at her.

"Mama," one of them said.

"You've brought shame to this household?" Josephine said to Giulia. Hypocrisy rose in her throat but still she said the words as if she did not know about desire and sin and the babies that come from that.

Giulia bent her head.

"But who is this boy? This Mario?"

Giulia shrugged. "A foreman at the mill," she said again. "I love him."

"He'll marry you?" Josephine said. Tommy Petrocelli's face appeared in her mind.

Giulia nodded, her head bent.

Josephine sighed and looked at Elisabetta. "Go there now. Learn your Latin. Get to college."

"But it's late," Elisabetta said, even though she was grabbing her pink sweater and slipping on her shoes.

"Go to him now," Josephine said. This daughter would get out of here. She had a good head on her shoulders. She would be a scientist, like Madame Curie.

Chiara watched her sister hurrying to the church, to Father Leone, to some future that Chiara could not even begin to imagine. Last Tuesday, Elisabetta had whispered to Chiara in their dark bedroom, "Did you know Father Leone's name is John?" Her sister's words had pierced her. He had chosen Chiara to become a nun. It was Chiara who was special, not Elisabetta. "Giovanni," Chiara had corrected her.

"Go!" Josephine was shouting as Elisabetta gathered her things: Latin book and spiral notebook filled with verb conjugations. "Get away from here! Run to him, Elisabetta. Run!"

Chiara felt frightened and jealous and desperate. She fumbled in her pocket for her rosary beads, but when she found them, she was unsure what to pray for.

Coney Island Dreams

ALL WOMEN WERE *PUTTANAS*. CARMINE KNEW THIS. But still.

Still at night, to calm the images of that day in France in 1918, he summoned Eva Peretsky. Eva Peretsky was only six years ago, right before he left for the war, but she seemed a million years ago. Too much had happened since that weekend in Coney Island and tonight, lying in his bed in his mother's house. He had to work hard to summon her, reach back before the thing that happened in the war. Back to Coney Island. First, Carmine closed his eyes and counted to three, picturing each number clearly before moving on to the next. The straight line of the 1 with its small hook at the top, like the hook at the end of a fishing pole; then the 2, swanlike and elegant; and finally the 3, its curves as round and bulging as Eva Peretsky's breasts.

But he could not think of them yet. No. First he had to count backward: 3, 2, 1. Again picturing each number clearly, the breasts of 3, the swan of 2, the fishing pole 1. Sometimes, he was already growing hard at this point. Sometimes, he had to place his hands beneath his ass to keep from touching himself. He counted backward and his hands twitched, begging for Eva Peretsky.

"Not yet," Carmine sometimes scolded himself out loud. His room was small and narrow, a former storage closet. His bed was also small and narrow, not even really a bed. More like a cot, like the one he'd slept on during Army training. If he thought about Army training, he would think about France, and then he would lose Eva. He made himself take a slow, deep breath, the way the Army doctor had taught him when he came home. He made himself count backward: 3, 2, 1.

Then he imagined a lemon. He imagined a lemon the size of his hand, the hand fighting for release beneath him. He imagined the yellow of that lemon. It was a yellow all its own, not the yellow of butter or egg yolks or Eva Peretsky's hair. It was the yellow of this lemon. Sometimes he could almost smell the citrus over the sour smell of his sheets and his small room. When this happened, Carmine smiled. If he could free his hands, he would have made the sign of the cross in thanks to the Virgin for helping him get this far: Eva Peretsky's hair. But he could not free his hands because he knew where they would go and what they would do and he had not earned that yet. He had not yet worked his way back to Eva Peretsky.

Lemons.

Carmine imagined a knife slicing into the lemon, cutting through its yellow flesh to the skin below. Then he imagined lifting that lemon to his mouth and biting into it. If he had done everything exactly right, the counting, the lemon, the cutting, when he took that bite, his mouth would fill with saliva and the glands behind his jaw would ache and his lips would pucker. And Carmine would smile and release his hands finally and reach for his cock, which was by now hot and throbbing. He could actually feel it throbbing from inside, could feel the blood coursing through it.

Still, he could fail. Sometimes, as soon as he wrapped his hands around his cock, he came, too fast. Then the night would stretch ahead of him with its smells of sweat and dirt and dead bodies left in the sun. Instead of Eva Peretsky, he might remember his buddy Angelo Mazzonni. They had signed up together and traveled by train all the way to Kansas for basic training. Angelo was going to marry Carla Zito, and Carmine was going to marry her cousin Anna. The girls had seen them off at the train and pressed white handkerchiefs soaked in rose water into their hands as the train pulled away. This was to remind the men of them while they were at war.

"Have you kissed her?" Angelo had asked as the train headed west, smack into the sunset with all of its pink and red and orange. Carmine felt both excited and terrified. He thought the train might take them right into the sky. His heart pounded, and he shook his head, lying.

"You might be dead in a few months," Angelo said. "You should have done it." He leaned forward. "If you tell anybody this, I'll cut your throat, but Carla gave me a farewell present."

He pointed to his crotch and grinned. They were eating provolone and salami and good hard bread that their mothers had packed for them. When they unwrapped it, two men already in uniform walking past their seats had said, "Shit, wops, they sell real American food in the next car." The men had laughed, patting each other on the back and shaking their heads. "Stupid wops," one said.

"She took all of it in her mouth," Angelo said, lowering

his voice. His chin was shiny with oil. "She sucked until I exploded."

The strange thing was that Angelo really had exploded, right beside Carmine. His head had opened up like a melon, spitting gray juice and pieces of bone and flesh all over Carmine. Without thinking, Carmine had grabbed his friend's hand, and told him in Italian that he would be all right. When Angelo squeezed his hand, Carmine thought maybe he still had a chance, so he kept talking to him, promising him things. Even when he saw that the thing that he thought was an egg in his lap was actually one of Angelo's eyes; even when he lifted his free hand and wiped brain and blood off his face; even when he realized that what he was looking at was a fragment of Angelo's head—no face, some hair curling around an ear—even then Carmine whispered about Carla waiting at home for him, about the French whores in the next town, about how right then the grapes hung heavy on their vines, ready to be picked.

This was what happened if he came too soon. If he was lucky, if he had done everything right: the counting first, 1, 2, 3, seeing the numbers clearly, then 3, 2, 1; the lemon; the cutting into its flesh; the biting; the salivation; allowing his hands to be set free; grasping his hot cock; then waiting, not coming yet, not moving, nothing but being still; only then did he get to Eva Peretsky.

NO ONE COULD UNDERSTAND why a man like Carmine Rimaldi, a man who had everything, would leave home for Coney Island. Here, in this small village of Italian immigrants in the middle of Rhode Island, no one saw what Carmine saw—that beyond this place lay opportunity. To Carmine, that opportunity was waiting for him in Coney Island. A person, any person, could go to Coney Island and make more money than this entire village could imagine. A person could find shops to open, products to sell, men looking for partners, investments to be made. Coney Island was ocean and beach and glittering lights, and all of it was calling to Carmine Rimaldi.

This was in the summer of 1918. He was about to turn eighteen years old and had just gotten engaged to Anna Zito, arguably the most beautiful girl in the neighborhood. Anna was fifteen, so small that Carmine could lift her one-handed like a barbell, and easily move her up and down, up and down, in the air, Anna screaming the whole time for him to stop. But he knew this thrilled her, just as he knew that when he and Angelo went swimming, the cousins Carla and Anna sitting on a blanket on the stones by the quarry, peeling apples and pears or making sandwiches of mozzarella and tomatoes, she liked how he came out of the water, sleek and wet and cold, and wrapped his arms around her, making her shiver and scream. He had seen her tracing the damp outlines his hands made on her waist and smiling.

Anna Zito, Carmine learned, was a girl who said no when she meant yes; who said stop when she meant go. Maybe all girls were like this. Carmine wasn't sure. He asked Angelo if Carla meant yes when she told him no, but Angelo laughed. "Carla says yes and she means it," he said. "I ask her if I can touch her breasts and she says yes and then she takes my hands and places them, one hand on each breast, and tells me to pinch." Carla's breasts were famously large. Even in a bra with bones and stays, her breasts swayed and rose magnificently.

More than once, Anna had caught Carmine sneaking glances at Carla's breasts, and swatted him and pouted. But they were breasts that demanded attention. The nipples, Angelo had confided to Carmine, were pink. They had both assumed, for reasons neither could explain, that nipples were brown. "And," Angelo had continued, "a big pink circle surrounds the nipples that pucker when you touch them." Whenever Carmine looked at Carla after that, he tried to imagine it: those breasts like dough that has just risen, still warm from lying under the cloth; the big pale pink circles; then the hard nipples, also pink, jutting from them. Then Carmine would put his arm around Anna, and she would slap his knee and say, "No!" which meant he should hold her closer still.

EVERYTHING WAS IN CONEY ISLAND. This was what Carmine told everyone who tried to talk him out of going. In Coney Island, you'd find a wooden ride that plunged thirty feet down a wooden track. You'd find freaks, women with beards and men with feet where their hands should be and giants and midgets and even a person who was both a man and a woman. You'd find fine white sand and the blue Atlantic Ocean and women in woolen swimsuits running along the shore, showing their legs and arms to anyone. On the other side of that ocean, Carmine knew, lay Europe, and a war that would soon beckon American men. It would call him, too, if America didn't get in there and win it, fast. Coney Island could be his only chance for something more, something big.

"Why would I go all the way to Coney Island when any day now, right here, Carla is going to let me put my thing inside her?" Angelo said.

"In Coney Island," Carmine said, "girls will do that without any promises. They *like* to do it."

"Those girls," Angelo said, "are called whores."

Carmine shook his head. "They're not Catholic," he explained. "That's all. Girls who aren't Catholic *like* it. They want to do it all the time." He had no evidence of this, but Carmine believed that Anna's nos and stops came from her fervent belief in Jesus Christ.

"*Puttanas.*" Angelo laughed. "You'll see."

ALL DAY, CARMINE worked on machines that tore fingers from hands or broke arms or sent fumes into the air that made you cough and turned your eyes red. The noise in the mills was loud enough to get inside your head and stay there even after you had gone home. The mill was dark inside, and damp, and by the end of a shift you felt like your back could break and you might lose your mind if you didn't see sunlight.

Carmine had worked in the mills since he was seven years old. The pinky finger on his left hand was flat above the first knuckle from an accident when he was nine. His ears rang on and off all day, even when he was asleep or out of the mill. From where he stood that summer, seventeen years old, a war about to claim him and all the other boys he knew, his only hope was Coney Island.

THE NIGHT BEFORE he left, Carmine took Anna for a walk beside the river. It was eight o'clock, but still light, and the river flowed by them fast and murky from a spring heavy with rain. She let him hold her hand as they walked, and he liked the feel of her small smooth one in his big calloused one. They didn't speak, but Carmine kept sneaking looks at her. She was beautiful; that was for certain. Her hair wasn't curly or straight but fell in thick, luxurious ripples all the way past her shoulders and down her back. Most girls tied their hair into braids or buns, but Anna showed hers off, letting it hang loose like that. Her eyes were so dark that when he stared into them, Carmine couldn't distinguish the pupils from the irises. But everything about her was small. Her tiny waist, her almost boyish breasts, her hands. As he held her hand now, Carmine slowly massaged it, as if he could count each thin bone.

"How do I know that you won't meet a girl in Coney Island and fall in love with her and marry her and never come home?" Anna said finally.

"Because I love you!" Carmine said, surprising both of them. Once he said it, he knew it was true. What else could it be when he thought about her constantly? Dreamed about her? Tried to see her every day, at least once?

"If you love me—"

"I do!" Carmine said, feeling giddy with it. "I do love you."

They had stopped walking and Anna was peering up the length of him, frowning. Shouldn't she be smiling? He loved her. But no, Carmine realized. This was that thing again. Frowning when really she was happy. He bent and lifted her up so that her mouth reached his, and then he kissed her harder than he had ever kissed her before. He kissed her with his mouth open and his tongue finding hers with such delight that he groaned.

Anna pulled away. "Stop!" she said, but Carmine knew that meant go, so he kissed her again, harder still. He knew that the way he held her to him, she could feel his cock straining, and boldly he pressed it against her.

Anna gasped, a small sound of surprise.

For some reason, when she did that, Carmine slowly lowered her to the ground. The river whooshed by them and his ears began to ring with the mechanical sounds of the mill.

"Why would you leave me if you love me?" she said. She had her arms folded across her chest, as if it were cold. But it was a beautiful June night. The moon was yellow and full above them, bright even in the still-light sky.

"In Coney Island," Carmine said, breathless with possibility, "I'll make a fortune and come back and marry you." He could suddenly imagine this: marrying Anna. Kissing her until he grew too old to do it any longer.

"You want to marry me?" she said, hugging herself.

"Yes."

"Are we engaged then?" she asked him. She was fifteen years old and, standing there like that in the dying light, she looked like an absolute child.

"Yes," Carmine said again, marveling at how simple this all was.

"An engagement is a promise," she said.

Carmine considered her words. "Of course."

"So you are promising to come back and marry me?"

He laughed. All he wanted was to kiss her some more. The sky behind her was darkening. Carmine liked dusk, the inky swirls of blue and black that seemed to gobble the sky.

"This is my favorite time of day," he said softly. Usually he was still in the mill at dusk and missed it. Instead, he walked out the big double doors into night.

They had walked far enough that the mill was not in sight. The river made a gentle bend, and they had walked along that elbow of soft grass to this spot. Everything was in bloom. White blossoms covered trees. Buttercups and black-eyed Susans dotted the grass. The air smelled of the river and fresh grass and flowers.

"What's your favorite time of day?" Carmine whispered. He realized he knew nothing about this girl.

"When the sun comes up," she said. "I like lying in bed and having the sun come through the window and warm my skin."

Carmine nodded. He could see her in a bed, with white sheets and a white coverlet, her dark hair spilling everywhere, and warm sunlight touching her.

"I want to make sure you come back," Anna said.

"But I promised," he told her, impatient.

Anna slowly sat on the grass and patted beside her. It was damp from being so close to the river, but he sat anyway.

"If I give myself to you and you don't come back, no one else will have me," she said. "I'll be a *puttana*."

He tried to think of what to say, but Anna was slowly unbuttoning her dress. It was a navy-blue cotton dress with two big pockets, long and shapeless, not a very pretty dress. She wore it often. Carmine watched as she stood and stepped from it. Beneath it she wore white bloomers and a cotton shirt like children wore and long white stockings that came just above her knee. She took those off first, then the bloomers. While she rolled the stockings together and folded the bloomers, Carmine tried not to stare at the thick patch of hair she had. Somewhere in there was what Angelo called the Garden of Eden. Angelo had not yet been there, but he told Carmine that Carla let him reach under her skirt, into her bloomers, and stick his fingers inside. Carmine wondered if this was what he should do now, pull her down beside him and stick his fingers beneath all that hair.

But now she was lifting off the shirt, pulling it over her head, and folding it neatly too. She had no breasts really. Her chest was almost completely flat, with just two bumps, and hard brown nipples poking out at him. He felt like he was dreaming. The moonlight, this offering, his ringing ears, made Carmine dizzy.

"Now you," she said.

Carmine nodded, then stood and unbuttoned his shirt, tossing it onto the grass. When he pulled off his T-shirt, Anna put her hand to her mouth in something like disgust.

"You have so much hair," she said. She studied him like she was a scientist instead of his lover. "I had no idea," she said. Then she looked up at him. "Are all men this way?"

"I think so," he said, suddenly embarrassed by the curly hair that blanketed his chest and stomach and shoulders. What would she say when she saw the rest of him?

She nodded slowly as if considering this.

Carmine took off his shoes and socks, then his pants, not pausing as she had to fold and place them carefully. He was only thinking of what he was about to have. The Garden of Eden. At last, he took off his own knickers and stood before her. He was proud of his dick, hard and full, ready.

Her mouth opened slightly as she stared openly at it. "It's so ugly," she said finally. He thought she might cry. Or change her mind. So he quickly took her hands and brought her down to the ground with him.

"You don't have to look at it," he whispered.

This seemed to make her feel better. Unsure of what to do next, Carmine pinched her nipples the way Angelo told him Anna liked for him to do.

"Ouch!" Anna said. "Don't do that."

Angelo had described the Garden of Eden as wet, so wet that his fingers moved in and out of it with a great slippery ease. But Carmine was having trouble entering Anna. He poked gently at the dry, tight hole he'd found between her legs.

"I don't like this," she whispered, and he glanced at her face for the first time and wondered how long she had been crying.

Surely if he didn't get in there fast she was going to change her mind. Anna was whimpering now, murmuring, "This is terrible, I hate this, I hate you," but Carmine kept pushing until something seemed to let go, and that wonderful wetness that Angelo had promised him was waiting there, flooded over him.

Truly, this was the most wonderful thing Carmine had ever felt. The warmth, the wetness, the flesh beneath him. He could, if he lay right on top of her, feel her hard nipples reaching up toward him. She was sobbing and he wished she would stop, but he didn't say anything. He was too overwhelmed with this feeling. He heard her voice as if from far away telling him to hurry or to stop, please. But she was vanishing. It was just him and this place. Then he heard his own groaning and he pulled himself out of her just in time. The smell of rust and water and dirt filled him, and slowly he remembered she was there. He leaned over and kissed her softly on her mouth, tasting her tears.

"You have to really love someone to do that," she said, her voice quivering.

"What if I have a baby?" she said. She was shaking now, her voice high and shrill.

"No," he told her. "That's why I came outside of you. The seeds have to go inside for a baby. After we get married," he said, his voice proud, "I'll come inside and we'll have babies."

Still, Anna couldn't stop crying. The sky had turned completely dark, and there were no stars in it tonight.

As they dressed and walked back toward home, both of their legs trembling, Carmine wondered how he could leave now that he had this, and go to Coney Island. If he stayed, he could do this once, twice, even more every day. If he stayed, they could get married soon—next month! Sooner!—and he would be able to sleep with her every night, going to the Garden of Eden over and over. Nothing else mattered when he was in there. The mill, the noise, the darkness. Everything disappeared.

He was surprised to see people moving about in ordinary ways when they reached town. Men sat outside the barber shop, playing cards and drinking wine. On front porches, women fanned themselves, cleaned green beans, shelled peas, drank strong coffee. The sounds of children playing rang through the streets. A dog barked. Carmine saw all of these things, heard these sounds as if for the first time. He had never felt so alive. He squeezed Anna's hand and was pleased when she squeezed his back.

"Let's tell my parents we're engaged," she said. "Let's tell everyone."

"Now?" he said, surprised.

She looked at him, her eyes hard. "Now," she said.

Carmine said, "Of course, of course." Inside, he could expect hugs and slaps on the back, shots of anisette and the beginnings of plans.

He watched Anna run up the cement stairs to her house. "Come on," she called to him over her shoulder.

He followed her up the stairs, through the front door. Tomorrow, he would go to Coney Island.

...

IF HE DID everything just right, then he earned Eva Peretsky.

"I'm here," he would whisper, and her face would appear in front of him in his small, dark room. He would hold on to his penis firmly but not move yet. First, he would spend the night with Eva.

"I can see that," she'd say. He loved her voice. It was husky, like Greta Garbo's, and her Russian accent made sharp cuts in the air between them. She said all of her *w*'s like *v*'s. *You vill like this*, she'd say. *I vant you*, she'd whisper.

"Eva," he'd whisper into the dark.

Sometimes, he got this far only to lose everything and almost frantically pull at himself until he came. Then he'd have the whole night to wipe Angelo's brains and skull off his face. He'd have the whole night to pick his way out of that trench and step over body parts: arms still in jacket sleeves, boots with jagged legs protruding from them, and the stench of blood and dead people everywhere. His doctor told him to breathe in this particular pattern. To breathe and say, "Hoo, hoo, hoo," in short hard exhales when his memories got too powerful. But once he stepped out of that trench, he couldn't find his way home, no matter how he breathed or what he did.

That was why he had to keep Eva with him as long as possible.

"Eva," he'd whisper.

And when he had done everything just right, she climbed into bed beside him, and held him in her arms, and whispered, "I am right here."

THE AIR ON CONEY ISLAND smelled of fried food, salt, summer. When Carmine stepped from the train onto the boardwalk, that smell almost knocked him over. It made him whoop. People stopped to stare at him, a man dressed in black pants, a black shirt, and a black fedora, in this beautiful warm sunshine. A man who gazed at the ocean and whooped, loud. He didn't care if they stared at him. He was there to make his fortune.

By the end of the day, he had met a Greek named Steve, who rented him a cart to set up on the boardwalk, where he could sell hot dogs. These weren't ordinary hot dogs. These were Coney Islanders. Smaller than a regular hot dog, served in a steamed bun, and topped with a sauce made of ground hamburger meat and spices. Everyone who visited Coney Island had to try a Coney Islander.

And Carmine began to think, as he stood the next day in the bright sunshine, selling hot dogs from his red-and-white striped cart, that everyone came to Coney Island. Women in fancy cotton summer dresses, holding parasols, walked past him. Children in short pants, rolling big hoops down the boardwalk, begged for a hot dog, and parents always agreed. Men in striped bathing suits, with enormous black mustaches, came still wet from the water and ate two or three at a time. Even the freaks came out of their tent to buy Coney Islanders.

By the end of the week, Carmine had more money than he had made in a month at the mill. He sent a telegraph to Angelo: MONEY FALLS FROM THE SKY HERE. STOP. ENOUGH FOR BOTH OF US. STOP. BUSINESS OPPORTUNITY AWAITS YOU. STOP. He sent one to Anna: I MISS YOU. STOP. I LOVE YOU. STOP. HOPE WEDDING PLANS ARE COMING ALONG FINE. STOP. None of what he wrote to Anna was true. He didn't miss her. In fact, he never even thought of her the entire month, except to think of what they had done by the river the night before he left. That he missed. That he loved. And if marrying her was how to keep getting it, he would keep his promise and return.

At night, in the bars along the boardwalk, Carmine sat and listened to the men talking about the war. In no time, they predicted, we would be sending troops to Europe. We had to stop the Germans, or pretty soon we'd all be eating sauerkraut and wearing lederhosen. Carmine listened and drank his whiskey. "What do you think, wop?" they asked him. Carmine said, "I think Coney Island is heaven," he'd say, and he'd order another whiskey and listen to the waves pounding the shore.

HE MET EVA PERETSKY on the fifth of August. She bought three hot dogs from him. Then came back for three more. Still later, she came back again. Her hair was blond and straight and her light-blue eyes were slanted like a cat's. She had sharp, high cheekbones, long legs, big hands that looked like they had known hard work.

"Vat does a girl do to get the hot dog man to notice her?" she asked him that third time. He liked the way she said "Vat."

"I mean," she said, "I cannot eat any more hot dogs today." She smiled at him. Her lips were long and pink. Carmine thought about what it would be like to kiss them.

"Can you eat a steak?" Carmine said.

She tilted her head back to better study him in the sunlight. "Yes," she said.

"Meet me here at eight and I'll buy you the biggest steak you've ever seen."

She laughed and told him he had better be there at eight. She was very, very hungry for steak.

This was fate. Carmine knew it. The fifth of August happened to be his birthday, and on the very day he turned eighteen, a beautiful blond woman fell right into his life. He had known that Coney Island held everything he could want. Opportunity. Ocean. Sunshine. And now this.

At eight fifteen, Eva came walking up the boardwalk. She wore a pale-blue dress that showed off her slender hips and long legs. Her breasts seemed to be fighting the fabric that held them in, pressing against it and tugging the buttons there slightly apart. She wore high heels. And red lipstick. And a silver bracelet hugged her wrist. When she came up beside him, Carmine smelled her perfume—a cloying, heavy scent.

They walked across the street and down two blocks to the best steakhouse in Coney Island. Eva slipped her arm into his comfortably, chattering the whole way there. She was a widow, she told him. Her husband had been killed three years ago in the war. She had come here alone, with no money, and they almost sent her back because she had pneumonia and lice and malnutrition. But she had convinced them to let her in, and she had been in Coney Island ever since. She was twenty-one years old, she said. "But I feel much older," she added, averting her eyes.

Outside the restaurant, he took her by the arms and turned her so that she was facing him. He liked that she was tall and he could look at her, eye to eye.

"It's my birthday," Carmine told her. "Tonight we celebrate. We order the biggest steaks they have and we drink French wine—"

She was laughing now, and her cheeks were pink with excitement. "And we have the dessert at the end?" she said.

"Yes! The dessert at the end," Carmine said.

Already, stars were popping out in the sky. When the restaurant door opened, sounds of people having fun shot through the air. Carmine pulled Eva toward him and kissed her right on the lips, quickly, boldly.

But she didn't act surprised. She said, "Tonight we celebrate because the war is coming and men are dying and it is your birthday." Then she reached up and kissed him, soft and long on the mouth.

She tasted like lipstick and onions, an intoxicating combination. Carmine prodded her mouth open and slipped his tongue inside and Eva responded with her tongue, teasing.

"I watch you, Hot Dog Man," she whispered. "Every day for month of July. I watch you selling your hot dogs. So handsome. So strong. You are from where? Africa?"

He laughed, keeping his mouth on hers. "Italy," he said.

"So exotic," she said.

Then she straightened her dress and smoothed her hair. She took his arm again, and together they walked inside.

AFTER THE STEAK DINNERS and the bottle of French wine, and another bottle of French wine, and the desserts, and dancing together slow and close, after she ordered shots of vodka for them and he ordered two small glasses of anisette—"Too sweet!" she said, wrinkling her nose—they stumbled back out into the street, drunk and laughing.

"Ah!" she said. "It is ten forty-five and in one hour your birthday will be over and we will not be able to celebrate anymore."

Carmine threw his arm around her shoulders and held her close to his side. "One hour and fifteen minutes," he said.

"I have a bottle of vodka in my flat. We will toast your birthday," she said.

They walked past other couples arm in arm, past men kissing women against the sides of houses. The air here smelled different, like cabbage and spices he could not name. Russian filled the air, a language like none he had ever heard before. Italian, Carmine thought, sounded beautiful. Like a song. This sounded like people clearing phlegm from their throats. Down an alley, up a staircase to the second-floor apartment, both of them tripping and stumbling and laughing at their drunkenness.

Eva had trouble unlocking the door, so Carmine took the keys from her and managed to open it. The apartment was small, just one shabby room with a few pieces of furniture, and then a second room behind it with a bed and a pole with clothes hanging from it. This was where Eva led him, pushing him gently down onto the bed.

"I get vodka," she said.

She disappeared into the front room, and he heard her bang into something and curse. Carmine lay back against the pillows, which were surprisingly plump and soft. He liked the way his head sunk into them, reminding him of the fluffy clouds that he liked to watch float over the sea from the boardwalk. He told her this when she came back with the bottle of vodka.

"Goose down," she said, leaning back against the pillows beside him. She opened the bottle and took a drink directly from it, then passed it to him.

"Now you have just one hour," she said. "Then," she rubbed her hands together, "done."

Carmine took a big swallow of the vodka, and then lifted his head from the pillows to better look at her.

"You will kiss me now more, yes?" she said.

He laughed. "Yes," he said.

Until tonight, he had known only Anna, with her crying and his pushing at her. But this was different. They kissed for a very long time, slowly removing their clothes. First he reached under her dress and unfastened her garters, rolling down her stockings, slipping them off, pausing to explore her long, broad feet and toes. Then she unbuttoned his shirt, and her fingers traced his ribs and his nipples, and she nuzzled her face into his hairy chest. For a very long time, they kissed and touched, both of them wearing just their underclothes. She paused to take a drink of vodka, and when he went to kiss her again, she emptied it from her mouth to his.

When her bra came off, he poured vodka on her nipples and sucked them dry. Her breathing, fast and shallow, made him even more exited. Soon they were both naked, and licking places on each other that Carmine had never known two people could examine so intimately. But he couldn't stop exploring her. And her tongue on him made him groan so loudly that she laughed and put one of the fluffy pillows over his mouth.

She surprised him again when he moved to finally climb on top of her and she pushed him back down, mounting him instead. She easily slipped his penis inside of her, and began to rock back and forth in a steady rhythm, moaning.

"Here I am," she said.

Carmine didn't know what she meant, but then she threw her head back, her rocking increasing and her moans growing louder. "Here I am," she said again.

He felt her whole body shudder and her nipples beneath his fingers grow hard.

Laughing, she brought her face close to his. "I come," she said. "Yes?"

Carmine bit his lip. *She* came? A girl could come?

"Now you have turn," she said, and she rolled off of him and got on all fours, sticking her ass in the air.

Carmine kneeled behind her, his hands reaching for the Garden of Eden. So wet, so hot, he lingered there, rubbing her. Her breathing was changing again. "Yes," she said. "Here I am." His fingers kept rubbing her and soon she shuddered again, pressing his hand to her wetness.

"Italians good men, yes?" she whispered. "I come again with my Italian man."

Confused, Carmine finally slid back into her. He couldn't believe how each position felt so different, each one better than the last one. She moved with him, and he thought of Anna's resistance. But then he forgot Anna altogether. He pressed his mouth to her ear. "Here I am," he whispered.

———

"TELL ME," Eva said to him when he could finally conjure her.

"My friend Angelo," he began. And she whispered, "Tell me everything, my Italian."

She was the only one who understood. Maybe because her own husband had died in the war. Maybe because of what they had done with each other. But if he did everything exactly right, and she appeared in his small room, and he lay perfectly still, he could tell her everything and she would listen. And then she would release his hand from his penis, and she would begin to kiss him, and slowly, slowly, they would make love together, pleasing each other until, finally, he could sleep.

HE DIDN'T HAVE to work for the next two days. So Carmine stayed there with her. Unlike Anna, she couldn't get enough. "Are you ready again?" she would ask him. "Have you ever tried this before?"

Carmine knew he would not go back to Anna. He would sell his hot dogs on the boardwalk of Coney Island. He would buy Eva steak dinners and vodka. He would make her frittatas and ravioli. He would find things she had never done before. They would do them together. He would stay in this room on the second floor and he would let that war be fought without him. Carmine had come to Coney Island for opportunity, and her name was Eva Peretsky.

On the third day, as he was dressing to leave, he caught

sight of Eva in the mirror. She was sitting naked in bed, smoking a cigarette, watching him.

"Should I just come over at seven?" he said. "Or do you want to meet me on the boardwalk? I can bring you for real Italian food."

That was when he saw she was crying. Not like Anna cried, but quietly.

"I'm sorry. I am done with you now," she said.

Carmine turned to face her. "What?"

"This war, it so bad and it kill my husband. And probably it kill you, too. But even that, I don't care. I just wanted to see if I could feel alive again."

"What are you talking about?" Carmine said, kneeling beside her on the bed.

"You good Italian lover," she said. "Thank you."

He grabbed her by the hair, hard. "What are you telling me? You used me? You're giving me the bum's rush?"

"Bum's rush," she said, as if filing it away.

He yanked her hair even harder. "I'm coming back here tonight. I'm taking you for a real Italian dinner."

But Eva just shook her head. "I'm not alive. I'm dead too. Like Ivan."

Her hair felt smooth in his hands. "Please," he said.

She shook herself free of him and stood. "I go to toilet," she said. "You please go."

He watched her walk away from him. He sat on the bed, trying to think. After a while, he stood and walked out the door, down the stairs. An old woman stirring something on the stove of the first-floor apartment glared at him.

That night he went back, past that same woman at the stove, taking the steps two at a time. Surely he could change Eva's mind. She was grief-stricken; he understood that. But he had made her feel alive. Inside, her clothes were tossed around the rooms, her bed was unmade, but Eva was not there. He waited, finally falling asleep on those cloudlike pillows. But when he woke in the morning, he was still alone.

The old woman at the stove called to him as he sat outside on the stairs trying to figure out what to do next.

"She won't come back," the woman said, peering up at him through the open slats.

"She has to come back," he said, hating how weak he sounded.

The woman climbed the steps toward him. She smelled sour, like cabbage and boiled meat.

"I know this girl," she said softly. "Her heart is broken into so many pieces and now she's broken your heart. That's how the world goes."

Carmine licked his lips and glanced in the direction of the ocean. All he could see from here were rooftops, but he knew it was out there, glittering in the hot August sun.

"Boy?" she said, as if trying to wake him from a deep sleep. "Boy!"

He looked at her pasty, saggy face, hating her.

"Eva is my daughter. She told me to let her know when you go away finally."

Carmine got to his feet and grabbed the woman roughly by her shoulders, shaking her. "Tell me where she is," he said. He shook her harder. "Tell me!"

She shrugged away from him, and made her way back down the stairs.

Carmine thought about chasing her, making her tell him how he could find Eva. But there was something in the woman, a resignation, a sadness so deep that he understood her hopelessness.

THE THING TO DO was to go to fight the war. But still.

Back at home, Anna waiting for him so expectantly that he almost hated her. He enlisted with Angelo. They would save the world. But all he could think of was Eva Peretsky, those slanted blue eyes, that silky blond hair, her pale skin so smooth and translucent that the veins were like road maps, blue and complicated.

His homecoming was also a farewell. His mother made large pans of eggplant parmesan, his favorite, and baked ziti, and sausage and peppers. Carmine went to the liquor store to buy vodka, but the man there only frowned.

"That Russky stuff?" he said. "Don't carry it."

He came in late to his own party. His mother and Anna stood in the kitchen together, heads bent, as they stuffed figs with walnuts and roasted chestnuts. A crowd had already gathered. He saw Angelo with Carla, her face puffy from kissing or crying or both; he saw his sister Giulia looking fat and tired, pregnant perhaps?; he saw the neighbors, all of them crowded in there, shoving food into their faces.

Anna looked up at him.

"Why don't you go in?" she said.

He shrugged, unable to answer. "Do you want to come for a walk?" he asked her. Something like fear crept across her face. "I just need air."

"Air?" his mother said. "You just got here. You go and talk to everyone and take a walk later."

Anna waited to see what he would do. He felt so tired that he wanted to curl up and sleep, until after the war, maybe. Or after his wedding, which had been put on hold until he came back. He wondered if he left here and went back to Coney Island if he could find Eva Peretsky, if she would take him back into her arms. Sometimes he felt he had dreamed her.

"What are you waiting for?" his mother said, without turning around. She elbowed Anna. "Go in there with him. You're going to be his wife."

Anna took off the apron she was wearing, and touched his elbow, urging him forward. He'd known these people forever, but when he walked into the room, they all seemed like strangers. Anna stood on tiptoe but still had to tug on him to bend down.

"After," she whispered in his ear, "we can do it if you want."

Carmine nodded.

He didn't want to. But how could he tell her that he was a different person from the boy he had been on the riverbank just a couple months ago?

She grabbed his hand and held on tight, pulling him into the crowd.

THE NIGHT BEFORE HE LEFT, they went down to the river, to the same spot. It was colder now, and already dark.

"Come here," he whispered. It was so easy to lift her onto him that he did it in one motion.

"Don't you want to do it?" she said.

"Like this," he told her.

To his surprise, he entered her without any problem.

Anna gasped. "It hurts like this," she said.

"No," he said. "Relax." He tried to get her to rock back and forth on him. But she started to cry again. Carmine thought of Eva Peretsky, the way she'd thrown her head back and moved on him. "Just bounce on it," he said impatiently. "It will make you feel good."

"What am I?" Anna said. "A whore? It doesn't feel good. I hate it."

"It isn't bad to like it," he said. "I want you to like it too."

"What happened to you in Coney Island?"

He looked at her face and imagined she was Eva Peretsky. "Come here," he said, pulling her face down to meet his. He kissed her, and tried on his own to simulate that movement that had made Eva say, "I am here." He clutched onto Anna's ass, trying to get her to that same place. But she didn't. When he came, he thought of Eva, and groaned so loud that Anna told him to shut up.

The next morning, as he lay in bed, he heard her calling him. Carmine went to the window and saw Anna, still in her nightdress, shivering. She had the same brown sweater on as before, and her shoes and stockings. The sky was still dark, with distant hints of pink and red. He pulled on his pants and a shirt and met her outside under the cherry tree. He lit a cigarette and offered her one, but she shook her head.

"Please don't die," she said.

"I won't," he told her. She was the type of girl who took comfort in empty promises like this. Girls around the world were asking this same thing of men, knowing there was no choice in it. Perhaps Eva had asked her husband not to die, but he had anyway, killing her, too.

"Promise?" Anna said.

Carmine nodded.

"I thought," Anna said, working out a snarl in her hair, "I thought you might want to do it one more time before you go. Men like it, I know that."

It struck him that perhaps she believed he would die, to offer herself again like this.

Carmine took her face in his hands and kissed her. He knew a man and woman could kiss for hours. He knew that kissing built passion. Maybe if he kissed her until the sun came up fully, she would enjoy it too. But she was fidgeting, eager to get it done.

He unbuttoned her sweater and reached his hand inside her nightgown to touch her breasts.

He pushed her against the cherry tree too roughly, and bent her over, moving his hand under her nightgown. There. The Garden of Eden. He found the spot and began to rub, slowly and methodically.

She protested, but he kept up the same rhythm. He felt her growing wet. He heard her breathing come in small, short breaths. Carmine pressed against her and kept rubbing.

"Stop," she said, and as soon as she said it, he felt it, that shiver running right through her. She pressed against his hand, as if begging for more.

"What's wrong with you?" he heard her say. "What happened to you on Coney Island?"

Smiling, Carmine pushed into her.

EVA TOOK HIM in her hands and began to move up and down. Carmine closed his eyes and gave a final thrust, coming at last.

"Eva," he said.

He reached out for her, but nothing was there.

"Eva?" he said, hearing the panic rise in his voice. Sticky and hot and wet, he got out of bed. The sun had started to rise. He could see it from here.

In the hallway, he saw his niece, Francesca. So many people lived in this house. So many women. He hated them all.

"*Puttana*," he snarled at her.

She wrinkled her face as if she might cry.

"*Puttana*," he said again, softer now.

His mother appeared, pushing the girl out of his way. "*Basta*, Carmine," she told him. "Enough."

He went downstairs to the sink and began to wash the brains and bones and bits of skin from his face. He scrubbed with the rough towel and the fat bar of soap. But no matter how hard he tried, he couldn't get clean.

Moonlight in Vermont

VERMONT COMES FROM THE FRENCH—*VERT MONT.* Green mountain. Josephine knows this because her daughter, Elisabetta, the one so smart that she got to go to college, where she slept with her English professor, got pregnant, dropped out to marry him, and became a faculty wife, tells her things like this. Elisabetta lives in Iowa now. Iowa, which was named for the Iowa River, which was named for the Ayuhwa Indian tribe, which the English called the Ioway, which means *one who puts to sleep.*

"This is an appropriate name for Iowa, Ma," Elisabetta writes to her. "It is dull, dull, dull here."

Elisabetta calls herself Betsy, her husband Kip and her son Eugene. The boy peers out at Josephine from a black-and-white photograph, its edges cut in a zigzag pattern like someone put garden shears to them. He is too skinny. His black glasses appear to be taped together on one side. He is holding a rabbit or a fat cat, Josephine can't be certain. Behind him, a lot of grass and a barn in the distance. This is Iowa, the place that puts you to sleep.

But Vermont. Green Mountain. Josephine goes there to

visit her daughter Chiara, the one who is becoming a nun. This is how she has come to think of her daughters. Concetta, the responsible one who has moved her family in with Josephine; Giulia, the one who can't stop having babies even though her husband is not a good provider; Isabella, the slow one who married a man who is also not quite right; Valentina, the one she lost, the daughter she gave away.

Is it a coincidence that of all the convents where Chiara could have been placed, she ended up at this one near Montpelier, Vermont? Montpelier, which means nothing except that it is the capital of Vermont. When Josephine got the letter from Chiara telling her where she was being sent, Josephine thought it was a sign. The daughter she gave away, the one lost to her, her Valentina, is somewhere in Vermont. That is all she knows about the girl, but surely it is no accident that Chiara is there too. Surely Josephine is meant to find her daughter.

"IOWA IS CALLED the Hawkeye State," Elisabetta tells Josephine. "After the scout, Hawkeye, in James Fenimore Cooper's *The Last of the Mohicans.*"

They are on a train to Vermont for Chiara's graduation from postulate to novice. Elisabetta has come home, without Eugene or Kip, for an unspecified amount of time, claiming vaguely that she wants to accompany her mother on this trip. It is early autumn and as they travel north the leaves are more vivid, scarlet and persimmon and gold.

"Do you think children who grow up in Vermont are happy?" Josephine asks.

Elisabetta gives her a quizzical look. "As happy as any-where, I suppose," she says.

She pours herself another small glass of apricot brandy from the flask she keeps in her purse and stares out the window at the landscape rolling slowly by.

"It looks a lot like Iowa here," she says in a resigned way.

"They have fresh cheese in Vermont," Josephine says. "And green mountains. And maple syrup right from the trees."

"I guess," Elisabetta says, as if she has stopped listening.

When the college learned that Kip had gotten a student pregnant, he was let go. But he keeps finding new positions, first in North Dakota and then in New Mexico and Tennessee and now Iowa. *Because he's an adjunct,* Elisabetta told her mother angrily when Josephine asked her why they were always moving here and there and not staying still. *He can't find a tenure-track position after what happened.* Josephine had no idea what any of this meant, but she'd nodded thoughtfully and said, *Ah, I see.*

"Are there any Italians in Vermont?" Josephine asks.

Elisabetta doesn't look at her. She gives her thin shoulders a little shrug and says, "I don't know. Probably not."

Every day, Josephine tries to not think about her lost daughter. But every day she finds herself unable to do this. She wonders if the girl is tall, if she eluded the outbreak of infantile paralysis last summer, if she likes to read or draw or climb trees. She wonders if the girl even knows that she, Josephine, exists. Or does she believe she is the true daughter of this woman who took her home from a hospital in Providence before Josephine got to kiss her good-bye?

Once, Josephine took the streetcar to Providence and

walked almost two miles to that hospital. She waited while they found someone who spoke Italian, and then she told her story to this blank-faced stranger, this doctor in a rumpled suit, this man who listened without hearing.

"Records like this," he said finally, his Italian awkward and halting, "are sealed." He made a motion with his hands like he was zipping something shut. *"Capito?"* he said.

"Then unseal them," Josephine told him. "I am her mother."

The man frowned and Josephine could almost see him translating in his brain.

"Uh . . . " he said. "Actually, you're not."

Josephine took a step back, away from him. How could he say this? She had carried that baby inside her, felt the first butterfly-wing flutterings of life, pushed her out into the world.

"I want to speak to someone who understands Italian," she said, because surely this man in his wrinkled suit did not.

"You see," he said, "you signed the papers. You gave her up. You—"

"Stop saying *you* did this and *you* did that!" Josephine said, raising her arms in the air and flailing them about. "I made a mistake! I want her back!"

"You can't," he said, his eyes growing wide. "You gave her up."

With each accusation he made, Josephine grew wilder. She pushed him. He was a small man, a nothing man. She pushed him again and this time he lost his balance.

"Where is she?" Josephine screamed.

When he didn't answer, she fell on top of him, her fists landing on his shoulders.

"Where is she?" she screamed over and over.

Two men came, maybe policemen, she wasn't sure, and they lifted her up so that her legs kicked at the air and her hands fell on nothing.

"Just get her out of here," the doctor who spoke terrible Italian said as he got to his feet and smoothed his suit.

"Crazy wop," one of the men said, laughing.

"Oh, they're crazy," the other one said, gripping Josephine harder than was necessary. "That's for sure."

Later she found four angry bruises above her collarbone where he'd held on to her so tightly. She watched them turn from purple to green and then yellow until they faded away. But sometimes, even after they were gone, Josephine thought she could still see their imprint there, like the man had marked her.

"HOW MANY PEOPLE LIVE IN VERMONT?" Josephine asks Elisabetta.

The train is almost in Montpelier. They have been on it for a long time, changing in Boston and eating the provolone and salami and fresh bread that Josephine packed. Elisabetta has only nibbled, wrinkling her nose at the sharp smell of the cheese and steadily sipping her apricot brandy.

"Not a lot," Elisabetta says. Her eyes have grown heavy-lidded and her mouth looks puffy.

Josephine smiles. Maybe she would walk down the street in Montpelier, Vermont, and catch sight of a six-year-old girl, who looks like her, a girl on a bicycle, smiling with her hair blowing in the breeze. And then Josephine would walk up to that girl and say: *You are mine.*

"What's funny?" Elisabetta asks, frowning.

She's had a book open on her lap for a long time now, but she hasn't even glanced at it. The book has a blue cover with a woman's eyes looking out from it. When Josephine asked what the book was, Elisabetta said: Only the most brilliant book published this year. And when Josephine sounded out the title—*The Great Gat-sby*—Elisabetta rolled her eyes at her mother.

"I'm imagining wonderful things," Josephine says.

Elisabetta grunts. "Such as?"

But Josephine just shakes her head.

Or maybe, she thinks as the train slows, the girl would look nothing like her. Maybe she looks like her father. Even thinking this makes Josephine's heart lurch. What would it be like to see that face again?

Elisabetta stumbles slightly as she stands to get their valises from the compartment. The bottle of apricot brandy is empty, rolling about on the floor.

Josephine picks up the book. "You forgot this," she says, holding it out.

But Elisabetta waves her away. "It's too depressing," she says. "Leave it."

The eyes on the book stare out at Josephine. It seems wrong to leave it there.

"What?" Elisabetta says mockingly. "Are you going to read it?"

"You said it was brilliant," Josephine reminds her.

"I changed my mind. All right?"

By the flush on her daughter's cheeks and the thin layer of sweat on her forehead, Josephine sees that she is drunk. She thinks back to the night Elisabetta arrived home, how she tripped coming up the stairs. And then last night, she fell asleep on the sofa, early, her mouth open, snoring lightly.

They are in the aisle now, moving with the other passengers toward the door.

"Elisabetta," Josephine says softly, placing her hand on her daughter's shoulder.

Elisabetta turns around, shaking her mother's hand from her.

"Betsy," she hisses. "I told you it's Betsy."

"Betsy," Josephine says. It comes out more like *Bitsy* when she says it. An ugly name, she thinks. Foolish-sounding. "You drank that whole bottle of brandy?" she asks.

"It wasn't full," Elisabetta says.

Their eyes meet briefly before Elisabetta continues down the aisle, the valise banging angrily against the seats she passes. The lies between them settle on Josephine. This is what happens, she thinks. Years pass. Wrongs are committed. Secrets take hold and the only way to protect yourself is to lie. A mother hopes her children don't have to hide things from her. She watches Elisabetta's green wool coat in front of her, the pleated back and fine workmanship in the stitches. She's unhappy, Josephine realizes. The thought surprises her. This is the child who she knew was going to become something. Even as a little girl, Elisabetta was orderly, motivated. She used to write a little newspaper every week, full of stories about the neighborhood, with illustrations she drew accompanying them. Josephine imagined she might become a writer or a scientist. Someone important. Someone special.

The urge to take her daughter in her arms overcomes her. But she knows that Elisabetta would resist such an impulse. She never hid how much Josephine and her sisters and brother embarrassed her. One Christmas she went all by herself to the five and dime and bought a bottle of cheap perfume for Josephine. She wrapped it in shiny blue paper and tied it with silver ribbon. Wear it, Mama, she'd said when Josephine opened it. Wear it every day. That was when Josephine understood that she repulsed her in some way. She'd done it too, for Elisabetta. She'd sprayed a big spritz of the overly floral perfume on herself each morning. But Elisabetta never seemed to notice.

Josephine follows her daughter out of the train, carefully stepping down the steps onto the platform. It is cold here in Vermont, much colder than back home. The air cuts through her thin coat and makes her shiver. How did a mother keep a baby warm in the winter in such a cold place? She thinks of all the children she swaddled in blankets she'd knit for them. Even now she can feel the weight of them in her arms. But this daughter she never held, who had wrapped her in soft wool and held her close enough to let her own warmth spread to her?

THE CONVENT IS STUCCO with ivy climbing on it. Inside, arched doorways, high ceilings, the smells of candles and bleach. No sounds, except a distant door shutting, perhaps soft voices.

Josephine sits up straight, her purse in her lap. Elisabetta slumps beside her, asleep or passed out, Josephine does not know which, her head gently bobbing. So pretty, this daughter was. So smart. But now she looks smudged, like God took his thumb and tried to erase her. Footsteps approach, heavy and rushed. The door opens and there is Chiara, in her black habit and thick stockings and black shoes. This one, unattractive as a girl, looks almost pretty as a nun, her hair hidden beneath the wimple so that all you see is her face, round and smooth, her brown eyes framed in long lashes.

Behind her is an older nun, stern-faced and bespectacled. Neither of them moves toward Josephine, so she gets to her feet and approaches them.

"No physical contact," the older nun says.

Josephine struggles to understand.

The nun puts a possessive hand on Chiara's shoulder. "She belongs to God now," she says.

Chiara smiles. "Isn't it wonderful, Mama?" she says. "Sister Gregory is my mentor. She stays by my side almost all day and night."

The older nun is frowning. "A long trip?" she says.

Josephine follows her gaze to where Elisabetta slouches on the bench.

"Very long," she says.

The three women stare at Elisabetta in an uncomfortable silence.

"Elisabetta," Josephine says finally, her voice sharper than she intends.

Slowly, Elisabetta opens her eyes and looks around, confused.

"Chiara is here to greet us," Josephine says, unable to take the edge out of her voice.

Elisabetta licks her lips, shifts her heavy-lidded eyes from face to face as if she is trying to place everyone.

Sister Gregory makes a clucking noise. *Like a hen,* Josephine thinks, and as she thinks it she decides that the nun even looks like a hen with her big, round bottom and narrow chest, the soft folds of her neck above her habit trembling slightly.

"We'll go to our motel," Josephine says firmly, taking charge now. "And we will see you tomorrow morning at the chapel."

"You can take this with you," Sister Gregory says, holding out a large sack. "It has all of her worldly goods in it," she explains as Josephine takes it from her. "She won't be needing any of it any longer."

Chiara beams at this.

Josephine resists the urge to open the sack and see what her daughter has given up. She doesn't need to look really; she knows Chiara has given up everything. *For God,* she reminds herself. But that thought doesn't comfort her.

THEY EAT DINNER in a small café on the main street in Montpelier. Elisabetta has ordered something called an open-faced sandwich—turkey smothered in gravy on top of two pieces of toast. It looks nothing like an open face.

"Elisabetta," Josephine begins.

"Betsy," she says in a tired voice.

"Why are you so . . ." Josephine struggles for the right word. Unhappy? Angry?

"How should I be?" she says before Josephine finishes. "I am trying to finish my degree, but we have to keep moving because Kip can't keep his pants on."

Josephine frowns. Can't keep his pants on?

"Oh," Elisabetta moans, "I'm such an idiot."

Josephine chews the stringy pot roast, considering what to say. But her mind stays blank.

"I should have married John Leone," Elisabetta says unbelievably.

"Father Leone? How could you have married a priest?"

"I could have," Elisabetta says in her drunken sleepy voice. "I had my chance."

"Blasphemy," Josephine mutters, and she makes a rapid sign of the cross.

Outside the window, beneath a streetlamp, a family walks past. The father is tall and lean and wears a red knit hat with a pom-pom on top. The mother has a long, blond braid down her back, and giant fuzzy earmuffs, and she holds the hand of a girl in a powder-blue coat. A light snow begins to fall, and Josephine feels like she is watching a movie of a family walking down a street in the snow in Vermont.

The girl stops, and slowly turns and faces the café. Josephine holds her breath. The girl seems to be looking right at her. Josephine stares back. *I am here*, she thinks, willing her words to leave the café and float out into the street, where they could settle on the girl.

"A pretty moon," Elisabetta says in that way she has that seems like she is talking to herself and not Josephine.

Still, Josephine nods. The moon is a perfect crescent, her favorite, silver in the blue-black sky.

Now the girl smiles. *At me*, Josephine thinks. *She is smiling at me.* Her heart lurches and she gets to her feet. Without thinking she is moving toward the door, and then she is out the door, standing in the cold night air.

But the family has continued walking, and the father is saying in a loud voice with a strange accent, "That's a good one. Tell it again."

The girl's high-pitched voice drifts in the air. "Why shouldn't turkeys do math?"

Turkeys? Math? Josephine starts walking after them.

"Because if they add five plus three, they get eight!" the girl says, and the three of them burst into a fit of giggles.

The street is slippery with snow, slowing Josephine down. At the corner, they have vanished. She looks in every direction but the streets are empty. Did she imagine them? Did she imagine that girl staring at her, finding her in the café window?

"Valentina?" she says softly.

Elisabetta runs up behind her. "What the hell?" she says when she reaches her mother.

"I thought I knew them," Josephine tells her.

"Knew them?" Elisabetta shakes her head, confused. "Like you know people in Vermont?"

Josephine could not know it that night, but for many years to come, whenever she visited Chiara in Vermont, she would chase girls like this one, girls of a certain age. She would lean in closer to hear them talk. She would memorize their faces, their clothes, the sounds of their voices. She would search crowds at Masses and train depots until she found one who might be hers. But in the end, they always disappeared, swallowed up as if they never existed in the first place. Perhaps this was the fate of mothers who lose their children: they spend the rest of their lives trying to find them, even though they know it is impossible. But isn't that faith? Isn't that hope? That maybe one of them will pause under a perfect moon on a snowy night and, when she hears her mother's voice, will turn toward it?

Part Two

1938–1956

Dear Mussolini

"Duce," Francesca's grandmother began.

Rat face. Francesca wrote. *Turd.*

Her grandmother folded her hands, brown-spotted and blue-veined, into her lap and considered. She wore a thin cotton dress, black, and beneath it a white slip, white bloomers, a white camisole. Over it she wore an apron in a gaudy floral pattern. Francesca hated her. She had lost several teeth, and as she spoke air whistled through the spaces.

"I am writing to tell you of my gratitude and the gratitude of the Italians who are here in America, away from the homeland that you will once again make strong . . ." her grandmother dictated.

Josephine only spoke very basic English. Although she had been in America for over thirty years, she still mixed up please and thank you, still looked like she was drowning when she tried to piece together an entire sentence. Even her grandmother's Italian embarrassed Francesca, with its dropped final vowels and bastardized words.

You Fascist pig, Francesca wrote. *We living under the democracy of the United States of America despise you . . .*

It was warm for April, and Francesca sweated under her wool sweater. She wished she could take it off and run bare-chested through the yard, the way she used to when she was a little girl. Now she was fifteen years old. She had been kissed by four boys; all of them shorter than she was. One of them, Bruno Piazza from down the hill, loved her. She hated him. She hated every boy she had kissed.

Her grandmother's voice droned on, blending with the bees that buzzed around their heads, dictating her letter of loyalty to Il Duce.

Francesca sighed.

"Your devoted servant," her grandmother said.

May you burn in hell, Francesca wrote.

"Josephine Rimaldi." Her grandmother grinned at her, not even caring about her missing teeth, or the long, silver hairs on her chin. She picked up the small sharp knife in her lap and began to cut a pear that had fallen to the ground.

"Do you know you're supposed to wash that?" Francesca told her in English. "The ground is full of germs."

"Bella," her grandmother said, not understanding. *"Grazie."*

"You stupid old woman," Francesca said in English.

"Eh," her grandmother said, shrugging.

Francesca folded the letter into thirds and put it into an envelope. On the front she wrote, as she always did:

Benito Mussolini
Italia

On the back, she wrote her grandmother's name and Natick, Rhode Island.

"Go mail it," her grandmother said. Juice from the pear dribbled out the corner of her mouth.

Relieved, Francesca stood to go. Robert Torre mailed all the letters back to the Old Country. His store was at the bottom of the hill, near the mill, a long enough walk to get some of this nervous energy out of Francesca. On the way to Torre's, she would pass Bruno's house, and Michele's, another boy she sometimes kissed. Maybe she would see one of them and they would walk together to the river first. She would lie beside them and let them kiss her, let their tobacco-tasting tongues explore inside her mouth, and their hands grope at her. Today she would take off her shirt, surprising whichever boy she ran into, and let them touch her breasts. Touch only, not kiss. These were things that the ancient priest, Father Leone, would not understand, these lines girls drew, the way girls felt desire too.

Her uncle came into the yard.

"Hi, Uncle Carmine," she said, trying not to sound nervous.

"You *puttana*, going to get laid?" he asked, a terrible thing to say to his fifteen-year-old niece, but ever since Anna Zito married someone else he called almost every girl a *puttana*.

Francesca held up the letter. "Going to mail this to Mussolini," she said, and quickly closed the gate behind her.

FRANCESCA'S SISTER, MARY, always made a point of finding something beautiful here. If Mary were walking beside her right now, she would say, "Look at the pink blossoms on that cherry tree!" She would stop at the Galluccis' to admire their new shrine to the Virgin Mary, taking the time to open

its glass door, to gasp at the lovely face of the Madonna, perhaps even to light a candle at her feet. Mary would know
whose cat these drunken-looking kittens zigzagging on the
street belonged to and that Old Man Conti's wine was ready
to drink. Mary, who was twelve, loved everything about this
town. She loved everything as much as Francesca hated it.

"Where would you go if you left?" Mary asked, but only at
night when the two of them lay together on the iron bed they
shared upstairs. The ceilings slanted so that they could reach
up and touch them easily, something Francesca often did,
pressing her fingertips against the eggshell-colored paint as
if she could break through to the roof and beyond.

"I don't know," Francesca answered. She was embarrassed
that she knew so little of the world that she could not even
name a place to run to.

"Providence?" Mary asked.

"No!" Providence was awful, a jumble of carts and ped-
dlers and shouting, without any of the exciting things a city
might offer. Francesca had gone there once with her father, to
buy cheese.

"Back to the Old Country?" Mary asked. She wouldn't
stop until she had an answer, and Francesca had no answer
to give her.

"Yes," Francesca whispered. "I would go to Italy and be
Duce's mistress."

Mary giggled. "Then you'd have to take Nonna with you
so she can be his mistress too."

Later, after Mary would fall asleep, Francesca would press
her fingertips to the ceiling, pushing, pushing, unable to move
anything even a little.

———

NO ONE WAS OUT TODAY except Francesca. Poor Bruno, she thought as she approached Torre's store. Tomorrow she might not feel the same way, she might keep her breasts to herself. She saw the men from the neighborhood across the street. They had set up tables on the sidewalk in front of the store. The acrid smell of cigars already reached her, the medicinal smell of their homemade wine sitting in glass jugs on the sidewalk. The men were playing cards, laughing, shouting in Italian. She saw her own father among them, gambling away their money, money they needed for Mary's new glasses and pencils for them to do their homework.

In the distance she heard the whirring of a car engine. Automobiles were no longer strange on the street here even though most people couldn't afford them. Walking, Francesca always had to sidestep horse shit. But the DiGiornos didn't have a car and they still held a certain fascination for her. She paused to watch it pass. A bottle-green Ford.

To her surprise, the car stopped and a man's voice called out, "Excuse me?"

Francesca looked around, but she was the only one on the street except the men a half block away. Swallowing hard, she walked toward the automobile. She was aware of how she must have looked in her dull wool sweater, too heavy for such a warm day, and the thick black boots and unevenly hemmed skirt. Still, she smoothed her hair, trying to flatten the strands that insisted on springing up.

She peered into the car. The driver wasn't a man. He was a boy, not much older than she was. His hair was so blond it seemed almost white in the sunlight and his face looked pink, like a baby's.

"I'm looking for Jerry Piazza. Do you know him?"

Francesca shook her head. The letter to Mussolini grew damp in her sweaty hands.

The boy sighed, exasperated. "Do you speak English?" he asked her.

Insulted, she said, "Yes, I speak English." She was trembling. She smelled mint, as if it grew in the backseat of that car.

"Sorry," he said. "You never know. There's so many wops in this part of town."

She could've said something about how ignorant he was, how he should try to call one of those men across the street wop and see what happened. One of those men was, in fact, Gennaro—Jerry—Piazza.

ON THE FEAST DAY of the Virgin, the men of the town took the statue from the church and wheeled it through the streets on the giant platform they built new each year. The girls covered the platform with roses, working all morning, their fingers bloodied from thorns. Then they joined the throngs of people in the street, pressing against each other to throw coins at the Virgin as she passed. The old women, dressed in black, walked slowly behind the Virgin, praying, their voices so soft they sounded as if they were humming.

Francesca did not like this part of the feast. It was hot and the men always grabbed at the teenage girls in the crowd. Already her thighs were bruised from their pinches.

She looked at her sister, Mary, beside her, shouting, *"Ave*

Maria! Ave Maria!" and throwing her own pennies and nickels at the passing wagon.

Francesca turned and fought her way out of the crowd, away from the parade. After the Virgin and the old ladies there would be a band and some floats and the littlest girls dressed up like miniature madonnas. Today there was also going to be a march for Mussolini, the local men who were Fascists would hold a banner with Il Duce's face on it and march, singing the Fascist anthem. Her grandmother had taught it to her and Mary, and no doubt Mary would want to stay until the very end to sing it. But Francesca had had enough.

She cut through the Contis' yard to the street beyond, which was deserted, and pulled a cigarette out of her pocket. It was half-smoked, discarded by her uncle Carmine earlier. That was how Francesca got all her cigarettes. At least today she was dressed for the warm weather in a pale-yellow short-sleeved dress that her mother had sewn for her. It buttoned down the front and had a wide, sailor-style collar. Really, the dress was for a child, a younger girl, but the fabric was so thin and soft that Francesca was happy to have it. She kicked off her shoes and rolled down her stockings, then leaned against the stone wall that marked the end of the Contis' yard.

With her eyes closed, she tried to think of what people in other places were doing today. In the newspaper she had seen a picture of San Francisco, where there was going to be a World's Fair. She did not know what people who lived in San Francisco did, though her father had once told her about a terrible earthquake there, and Antonio the fish man had once been a fish man there. Fish and earthquakes, Francesca thought, trying to put them together into some sort of life.

Hands covered her eyes and she knew right away it was Bruno. He had probably followed her.

"Guess who?" Bruno said. Most of the people their age did not have the accents of their parents; but Bruno did. His family went back and forth, never satisfied in either place.

"Bruno," she said flatly.

He released his hands and laughed. "I'm going to kiss you," he said.

She shrugged. It didn't matter to her if he kissed her or not.

His lips were on hers, hungry, his tongue pushing its way into her mouth. Almost immediately it happened; Francesca seemed to fly out of her body and into the air between this short squat boy and this girl in the yellow dress. The boy's hands, square and thick, were running up and down the girl's body and Francesca felt nothing. Bruno was breathing heavier.

What would he do, she wondered, if she sat up and unbuttoned her dress to her waist and let him touch her breasts?

The band was playing "The Star-Spangled Banner" badly. Too much brass.

Francesca pushed Bruno away from her and began to unbutton her dress. She would've liked covered buttons, but they were too expensive. Instead, her mother had sewn on big, smooth black ones from an old dress of Nonna's. They slipped easily through the buttonholes. This smooth, quick action brought a jolt of electricity to Francesca, the one she had when she wasn't with Bruno, or any boy. It was a hum she wanted to keep going, to have a boy push forward like an accelerator in an automobile. A boy, she thought, could take her somewhere special if only he could keep that feeling going in her.

She unhooked her bra and shrugged it off her shoulders, letting her breasts fall free. Her breasts were large and full, and Bruno, when he beheld them, gasped. The hot, sticky air on her bare skin made her want to be touched even more, and it was Francesca who grabbed Bruno's hands and placed them on her breasts. Almost immediately, she became that observer again, the one watching. How foolish they looked, Francesca thought. The boy's hands as if they were kneading dough for pizza. The girl's new dress in a rumpled heap around her waist.

The Fascists were singing. Soon the parade would be over and the streets would fill with people on their way to the church and the *festa* on its grounds.

Francesca, wanting to finish her cigarette, to get rid of Bruno, let him suck on her breasts briefly. He made loud slurping noises that disturbed her. When she roughly pulled him away, clutching his thick hair, he looked up at her, his mouth wet from his own spit.

"I'm going to marry you," he said gruffly. "I'm going to marry you and do this to you every night."

Those words in her ears made her cry uncontrollably as she stumbled home, trying to avoid the crowds of people returning to their houses for the food they would bring to the *festa*. Without a plan, she thought, her breasts sore from Bruno's clumsiness. What hope did she have for anything different from the very life he had predicted? She was ashamed that she was so ignorant that she did not even know where else to go. She did not want to fall into a crevice in the earth and get swallowed up in San Francisco. She did not want to farm land in the Old Country. And she did not want this life.

When she walked into the kitchen at home, she stood in the doorway and looked at the dark wallpaper and badly laid floor, and heard the Italian words buzzing through the room, as if they were not in America. Her grandmother, smiling proudly, held a small sign with Mussolini's face on it attached to a basket. The basket was brimming with gold. Francesca moved closer. She recognized earrings, crosses, thick chains, and on top, Nonna's wedding ring. To be certain, Francesca looked at the woman's left hand. Bare.

Her uncle Carmine was grinning at her as he added gold pins and his Army medals to the basket.

"What's going on?" Francesca asked in English.

Her mother said, "There's a drive at the church. Gold for Italy. Duce has asked all Italians to send their gold for the good of Italy."

Pressing her hands together, Nonna said happily in Italian, "Duce will make Italy strong again so we can all go home."

Francesca took a step back, and then another, until she was standing at the door. All that gold, she thought, all that gold could buy their way out of here, could buy Mary her glasses, could be used as a down payment for one of the larger stone houses being built in town, on the flat land away from the mill and the river.

"What are you, crazy?" she shouted. "We have nothing and you send these valuables to a dictator? A Fascist who's killing people in the streets?"

Nonna frowned. "Eh?"

"*Tu sei pazza,*" Francesca said. "You're crazy."

The old woman's face crumpled.

"You and Mussolini are crazy!" Francesca shouted. "We need that gold. We have nothing here. You stupid, stupid people."

She ran out of the house, leaving them behind, all of their faces blank. She wished she could keep running until she reached the ocean. She had never seen the ocean, though she knew it was not too far from here. Francesca tried to picture a map, to see what lay beyond this town, but she could not find its shape.

In the distance she could hear the sounds of the *festa*. Music and laughter and Italian and French; the French Canadians always came to the Italian parties. But she had run the long way, and was on the dark road leading away from town.

A car passed, then stopped, backed up, and stopped again, this time beside her.

She immediately recognized the blond boy driving.

"Are you all right?" he said.

"Yes," she lied. She put her hand to her chest to slow her pounding heart. "I'm on my way home."

He studied her face. "You look familiar."

She smiled and shrugged, hoping her face did not have the red blotches it sometimes got when she cried.

"I guess you live back there," he said, pointing in the direction of her house.

"No," Francesca said. "I live this way." She pointed too, toward the newer houses made of stone, the ones where the town's doctor and undertaker and some of the teachers lived.

The boy laughed. "I took you for one of those wops," he

said. "The ones that work as slaves at the mill down there. Stupid guineas."

Francesca forced a laugh.

"Well," he said, "hop in. I'll give you a lift."

He leaned across the seat and opened the door for her, extending his arm to help pull her up. Inside the car smelled of leather and mint and something else, something foreign that Francesca could not identify.

"Name's Mac," the boy said.

"Priscilla," Francesca told him, giving the most American name she knew. In Mrs. Miller's English class they had read *The Courtship of Miles Standish*, and it had seemed to Francesca that Priscilla was the most wonderful woman ever.

"Priscilla?" he said laughing. "That's a mouthful."

She could feel him giving her sidelong glances.

"Hey," he said finally, "there's a big wop festival at their church. There'll be great food to be sure. Want to go? With me?"

Francesca gripped the edge of the seat hard, digging her nails into the soft leather. "No," she said. "I don't like that sort of thing." She did not want him to go away. "But I'll go for a ride with you."

"Okay," he said.

Francesca began to tell him things, how her father was a dentist and her mother had infantile paralysis and was confined to her bed now. She told him that she had been to San Francisco and would like to go back. The whole while she talked, that humming grew in her gut. Mac told her things too. He lived in East Greenwich and went to the Catholic boys' school there. His mother wanted him to become a priest but he knew he would end up breaking her heart and doing something else.

"I like pretty girls too much," he said. "Like you. I guess I'll just have to be a lawyer like my father."

She was glad it was too dark for him to see her blush. None of the boys from the neighborhood, not even the ones who had kissed her, or Bruno who had sucked on her breasts, had ever told her she was pretty.

Mac stopped the car and the night was completely still. There did not seem to be any air.

"Where are we?" Francesca whispered.

"Lake Mackinac."

"Oh," she said. She had never heard of it. But now that she knew they were near water she could hear it lapping against the shore. "Funny," she said, "just today I was thinking of how much I'd like to go to the ocean."

"This is better," Mac said. "Not so wild. Safer."

"Hm," Francesca managed. How could she tell him that she wanted that other, wilder thing? That her body ached for something unnamable, unreachable?

"If I kissed you, would you slap my face?" Mac asked her.

She thought of how Michele had started kissing her one Christmas Eve after they'd gone into her yard to beat the fig trees that hadn't bloomed that year. She still had a bit of cookie in her mouth and he had not even bothered to let her swallow first.

"You may kiss me," Francesca said.

Mac laughed softly. "You're so regal," he whispered. "You're like a princess."

Then he had his soft lips on hers and he was prodding at

her mouth with his tongue and Francesca was not leaving her body. She was in it. That surge of electricity kept humming inside her. Anything could happen with this boy, she realized. She thought of the name of the town where he lived and decided it was far enough away for her to go.

"I think I could kiss you forever," Mac whispered into her ear.

It took everything she had in her to say, "We'll have to see about that." And for her to make him stop and take her home.

This time on the ride she sat so close to him that she could feel the muscles in his legs when he moved the pedals.

"Stop here," she told him when they reached the fork in the road where he had first picked her up.

"I can't leave you here," he said. "It's late."

"My father would kill me if he thought I was with a boy. He thinks I'm at my friend's house studying, which was where I was coming from."

"I'll only let you out if I can see you again."

She pretended to consider this. "Monday night?" she said.

"Three whole days away? No. It has to be sooner."

Francesca shook her head. "I'll be right here on Monday night at nine o'clock."

She didn't let him kiss her again. She slid across the seat and out of his car, dizzy.

BY THE TIME she walked in the direction of the new houses and then backtracked to the church, the *festa* was almost over. The men were drunk and sloppy on their homemade wine. Arms linked, they swayed and sang together in Italian, some of them growing weepy as they sang. The women were sitting together, holding sleeping babies or sipping grappa. Some of the children still played, kicking the ball around the grass. Everyone Francesca's age had gone, found private spots in the alley and fields that made up this part of town. She imagined those boys, Bruno and Michele, with their rough hands and clumsy kisses; the girls wanting something from them that they could not name.

On the table near the statue of the Virgin sat baskets heaped with the town's gold. Posters of Mussolini were lined up everywhere like soldiers. Francesca stepped back, into the shadows, watching these people she would leave behind. These Catholics, these immigrants, these Fascists— displaced, lonely, scared. And her heart, for the first time she could remember, filled with a love so strong for them that her arms reached out for an embrace she was already too far away to give.

Waiting for Churchill

FROM THE WINDOW OF HIS STUDY UPSTAIRS, NIGEL
Smith watches his daughter-in-law leave every morning. The
girl, Martha, dressed like a man: pants, button-down shirt,
thick shoes. Only her hair, blond and wavy, falling loose to
her collarbone, gave away her gender. She walks with a light
but determined step. In another time and place, not London
1943, she would be a girl going somewhere. Even with the
windows closed, Nigel can smell war in the air around London. It smells of fire, of dust, of blood.

"Ask her where she goes," his wife says.

He promises he will. But he never does.

*She is a child on her parents' farm in Vermont. It is autumn.
October. The leaves are just changing color, mostly at the
tops of trees. Fistfuls of red, bright yellow, orange. Martha
can smell the apples, ripe, ready to be picked. Macintosh.
Golden Delicious. Granny Smith. Around the trees the air
is heavy with the smell of rotting leaves, fruit going bad, the*

earth. But the apples, when she holds one to her nose, smell clean. They are so crisp that when she bites into one she can't hear anything but its crispness.

Tonight, Diana has made lamb. It is tough, dry. But there is mint sauce and roasted potatoes. The girl has brought home apples, shiny red ones that looked obscene when she held them out to Nigel. Then she went into the kitchen and began to peel and slice them, working hard, her face wrinkled with concentration.

As always, dinner is silent. There is the scraping of forks and knives against china. The clock ticking. Nothing more. Until the girl breaks the silence. She always does.

"You worked hard on this lamb, didn't you Diana?" she says. Nigel's wife cringes at the familiarity, not even Mrs. Smith, but Diana.

"Do you know what my mother back in Vermont used to do? She would sear the meat first with garlic and rosemary. That infused the meat. She always made a moist, tasty lamb." Martha smiled then, as if she hadn't just insulted her mother-in-law.

Diana stops chewing and looks at Martha, this stranger in her home, this interloper when she most needs to be alone and private in grief.

"Wait until you taste the apple pie I've baked," Martha continues cheerfully. "I've been saving flour for weeks to have enough. Aren't rations just the worst possible thing?"

No, Diana thinks, but doesn't say it. They all know the worst possible thing because it happened to them.

Martha sighs and leans back in her chair. "Robin loved my apple pie," she says.

His name seems to hang there, bouncing between them, a light thing, a magical thing.

Nigel clears his throat. The dry lamb is caught there, unable to be swallowed.

Martha gets to her feet and clears the plates of uneaten food. She brings out the pie. Holding it out to them like a gift. It is so high, and lightly baked with a fluted crust and the smell of apples and cinnamon, nutmeg and cloves, an exotic thing really.

She gives them each a fat wedge of it, the steam escaping, rushing the aroma into the air. Diana wants to hate this girl's pie, but the taste is so alive that she cannot hate it. She must eat it. She cries as she eats it, but she cannot stop.

NIGEL GETS THE news of the war from the radio and from his friend John who comes to visit every Tuesday for tea.

They know war, these men. They'd fought in the last one together. John was with Nigel when he lost his leg. He stayed with him, holding a cloth to the place where Nigel's leg had been to keep him from bleeding to death. When a man has done that for you, he is in your life forever.

Today with the tea, Nigel serves slivers of what is left of the girl's pie. "Apple pie, eh?" John says. "That's what Americans eat, isn't it? And hot dogs?"

He tells Nigel the news. Germany is winning this war. There is no doubt about that.

———

AT NIGHT SHE PLAYS the same record over and over.

Missed the Saturday dance . . . heard they crowded the floor . . .

"Why doesn't she go home?" Diana asks from her side of the bed. She has a book open but she is not even pretending to read it. "Back to Vermont?"

Nigel is facing the wall. "I don't know," he says.

"I don't want her here," Diana says with conviction.

Nigel doesn't answer.

"Did she say where it is she goes every morning?" Diana asks him.

"No."

"Did you ask her?"

"I will," he says. "I promise."

IN HIS STUDY the next morning, Nigel takes off the artificial leg. It irritates the stump that is left from his real leg. He gets blisters, sores, an ache that nothing can take away. But with it off, and a few glasses of sherry, and some salve on it, he can almost forget the pain.

He watches Martha bound down the stairs, hair flying. Always off in the same direction. He rubs the thing that is missing. It is tender there, but he rubs gently.

There are fields at the farm. Endless fields of hay stacked in neat bundles and clover everywhere. The grass smells sweet. Martha presses her face right into it, feels the wet dirt and the soft grass, pushes her face into it and breathes deeply.

—

FROM THE BENCH where Martha waits she always sees the same woman walking through the park. At first, Martha thought she was old with her white, wild hair and her blotchy face. But now she realizes that the woman is probably no more than fifty. Her eyes are the blue of the autumn sky in Vermont—deep and clear.

"Winston Churchill is the father of my child," the woman tells anyone who will listen. "He's the father of my daughter, Poppy. I only want what's mine."

Martha brings the woman an apple.

"I'm waiting for him to come out," the woman says, polishing the apple on her thin cotton skirt. "Then I'll say, remember me? Remember the weekend we spent in the cottage by the sea? Well, we have a daughter. I'll say, I only want what's mine."

Later, Martha sees the apple, shiny but uneaten, lying under a tree.

DIANA HAS PREPARED a light supper. Cold slices of leftover lamb. A salad. But she tells Nigel she won't be joining them. Some nights it is more than she can manage to make her way downstairs to the dining room.

"Do you think Winston Churchill would have an illegitimate child?" Martha asks Nigel. She is cutting her meat into tiny pieces.

"I don't know," Nigel says, baffled and embarrassed.

"He's half-American, you know," she says.

"Of course I know that," Nigel says. "He's our prime minister."

She leans wickedly close to him. Her eyes are green with flecks of gold, like a precious stone of some kind. "Did you know his mother invented the Manhattan?" she asks him.

Nigel frowns. "The Manhattan?" he repeats.

"Oh," she says, grabbing his hands. "It's the most wonderful cocktail. I'll make us some! That's what I'll do!"

"I don't know," he says.

"Just wait," she says, closing her eyes, still holding on to his hands. "You'll love a Manhattan." She opens her eyes. "We won't tell Diana."

"No," Nigel says.

"It will be our secret," Martha says. She winks at him. Such a fun-loving girl, a happy-go-lucky girl. He sees why his son married her. He still doesn't understand why Robin didn't tell them, why he didn't bring her home himself. But he sees Robin loving her. That much is clear.

NIGEL SUPPOSES HE SPENDS too much time drunk. It isn't the drunkenness of his youth, when he and his friends would spend hours at the pubs, drinking and boisterous, singing, loud. This is a somnambulant drunkenness. It makes everything fuzzy and soft. It makes everything pleasant. It slows his thinking and reactions; he knows that. But it's worth it for the gentle humming it brings deep in his brain.

He watches the girl leave and wonders in his drunkenness

if tonight she will bring home the Manhattans, like she promised. It is morning. It is May. He is drunk. The girl walks with her bouncy American steps down the gray London streets.

MARTHA SITS ON THE BENCH and eats some bread and cheese. She waits.

"Winston Churchill is the father of my daughter," the woman says loudly. "I only want what is mine."

WEEKS PASS. Nigel waits. But the girl does not bring him secret cocktails.

She is in Vermont. It is fall. The air carries a chill that gets into your bones. Martha sleeps under four blankets, sinking into the feather bed. Her mother reads her Robert Louis Stevenson, A Child's Garden of Verses. *She closes her eyes and her mother's voice lulls her to sleep.*

Since they got word about Robin, Diana has not let Nigel touch her. But tonight he feels her hand slide down his pajama bottoms. She takes him, soft and small, into her hand and works and works but he cannot grow hard. There is an ache where his leg used to be, a deep ache. He thinks he might cry from what he has lost and the pain it brings him now, even after all this time. Diana pumps and pumps his poor soft thing. When she gives up, he makes his way on his one good leg to the front room and sits in his pajamas and drinks another glass of sherry.

From behind the closed door of the girl's room he hears that song.

Missed the Saturday dance . . . Heard they crowded the floor . . .

THEN, WHEN HE has finally given up hope that Martha will come to him, she slips into his study. Nigel does not want her to see him like this. He has on only his boxer shorts and his shirt. His artificial leg leans against one wall like a sentry. The stump where his leg used to be is bright red and covered with fresh sores.

But he cannot get up and hide it from her. She is here and is holding a pitcher of amber liquid with ice and cherries in it. In her other hand, she has two cocktail glasses.

"Try to get some bourbon in this town," she says, laughing. She tries not to look at his stump.

She pours them each a drink, then hands him one. When they clink glasses, she says, "To Winston Churchill!"

"To Winston Churchill," Nigel says. The drink is delicious, sweet but sharp. "Very good," he says.

"What happened to you?" she asks, glancing at it.

"War," he says. "The last one."

She is a good drinker, this girl. A party girl, Nigel thinks after she refills their glasses.

"Where did you meet him?" Nigel asks her.

"At a dance," she says. "He was in uniform. So handsome," she says, her eyes and her voice both fading. But then she turns bright again. "Like his father."

Nigel has that foggy pleasure in his brain. The girl is muted somehow. The sound of her voice distant.

She moves toward him, reaches out a tentative hand.

He sits perfectly still.

She runs her fingers across the stump lightly. "So smooth," she says, surprised. "Like a baby."

Her fingers linger there.

Nigel thinks of his son. Robin knew this girl intimately, privately. She holds some key to him that Nigel would never have had if she had not appeared in April on their doorstep. He knows that his wife wants her gone, but how can they let her leave and take the last bits of Robin from them?

"Where do you go every morning?" Nigel asks her. The bourbon has numbed his tongue. It burns in his gut.

"I'm waiting to talk to Winston Churchill," she says.

Her mother holds her on her lap while she kneads the bread. She tells her how you know the dough is ready. She has Martha press her little finger into the wet dough. See how it springs back? her mother says. Martha watches as the small dent her finger left disappears, and the dough is once again smooth and whole.

"If we could only get enough flour," Martha tells them at dinner one night, "I would bake the most delicious bread. It's all in the kneading, you know."

It is almost June and still the air is damp and chilly. Nigel longs for the sunshine. He longs to throw open the windows and smell the warmth of it. Instead, the cold air smells, still, of war.

Nigel wants to please the girl. "Really?" he says, although

he doesn't care about any of it—bread or apples. "It's in the kneading, is it?"

Diana is frowning. She concentrates on dissecting the fish on the platter. She slices it and reveals its spine. She lifts the bone from it whole.

"Lovely," Nigel says. It is lovely too, he thinks. The shape of it. The sturdiness. Long ago he loved the sciences, biology most of all. He refills his wineglass, splashing some on the tablecloth. It is white, thank heavens. White wine with fish.

Diana holds a serving of the fish toward Martha, who lifts her plate to receive it.

"You weren't married to him," Diana says, her gray eyes leveled at the girl. "Did you think I wouldn't check? Did you think I would simply believe you?"

Martha looks up, surprised, her fork held in midair.

"Robin," Diana says, and Nigel is certain he has not heard his wife say their son's name since they got word last winter, It sounds strangled in her throat. "You were not his wife."

Martha puts a bite of fish into her mouth and chews slowly. "No," she admits. "Not the way you mean."

Diana laughs. "The way I mean? There is only one sort of wife. The other . . . " She lets her voice trail off.

The girl continues to eat her dinner. The overcooked green beans, the dry fish.

Nigel watches her, this girl who is not his daughter-in-law after all but instead was what? His son's lover? Whore? He presses his fingertips into his temples, trying to clear the fog in his head.

"You have to leave," Diana is saying. "You have to get out of our house. Go back to America. Or not. I don't care where you go. But you must leave here."

Martha continues to eat. She says between bites, "I met him at a dance. So handsome. So British." This makes her laugh. "He came by my flat the next morning and asked if I'd like to take a ride with him. He said he would be going off to fight soon. He was trying to get a lot of living in. Just in case, he said. I don't think I was away from him again, until he left. I came here because I didn't know where else to go. Who else had loved him? Who else had known him, really?"

Nigel's heart goes out to the girl. He says, "Surely you would have been his wife. . . . " When he sees the hurt look on her face, he corrects himself. "His legal wife, if he'd come back. We'd be sitting here, the four of us, with fresh-baked bread and lots of butter."

Martha smiles at him, gratefully, he thinks.

"We don't know any such thing," Diana says. "He never once mentioned you to us. Why would he? Young men who go off to war need to have pleasures that make them feel alive. They need to have relations with a woman. It makes them feel invincible. If he had come home, he would be here without you. Without your bread. We would never know you even existed."

"You're wrong," Martha says, her face set with determination.

ALL SHE HAS is one green valise, a small square thing. He watches from his window as she walks away from him, down the street, the suitcase bumping against her. There is a light rain falling. The air carries a chill unusual in early June.

Nigel imagines opening a window and calling for her to come back. We'll drink Manhattans, he'll say. He can almost hear her footsteps on the stairs and see her bright face in this dim room. The bourbon on her breath, the cool touch of her fingers. Shakily, Nigel pours himself a sherry and lifts it to his lips. It is ten o'clock in the morning. His day stretches before him, endless, cold, lonely.

WHEN DIANA GOES into Robin's room, where the girl had the nerve to stay all those months, she finds the record still on the phonograph. Carefully, she lifts it like it is a precious thing and smashes it against the sharp edge of the night-stand. It cracks easily. She lifts it again and again, each time bringing it down with as much force as she can muster, until it is nothing. Nothing but shards. A useless broken thing.

MARTHA SITS ON THE BENCH, shivering slightly in her trench coat. Her valise is at her feet. She has no idea what she will do next. There is nowhere for her to go. She thinks of Robin, his face with the chiseled good looks of a movie star. His voice, so clipped and British; she used to mimic it to entertain him. She thinks of how he touched her there, and there; his lips on hers, so hungry and fierce; all the ways he entered her, his hands on her waist, his body over hers, under hers, behind hers. She cannot imagine that body cold, without life. She cannot imagine those lips silenced, empty.

Martha watches as the big black car comes to a stop across the street.

She hears footsteps running and a voice: "Winston Churchill, you are the father of my baby!"

Martha gets to her feet, leaves the valise behind, and walks quietly toward the car. Its doors fly open and men in dark suits and dark hats and faces cast dark with worry, emerge.

Winston Churchill gets out last. Martha is right in front of him.

"Mr. Churchill," she says.

He looks up. His face is soft with a round nose and big jowls. His eyes narrow, seeking some recognition of her.

"Mr. Churchill," she says again.

Behind her the woman screams, "I only want what is mine!"

Martha looks into Winston Churchill's face and tries to say what is in her heart. How she loved a man who went to war and will not come home. How she seeks comfort any way she can. How she needs refuge from the things in the world that are killing young men like hers.

Without thinking about what she is doing, she goes to Winston Churchill and hugs him. Startled, he takes her into his arms. He murmurs something that she cannot understand. All she can do is smell the wet wool of his coat, his strong aftershave, and oddly the crisp smell of apples and bread baking. One of the other men comes between them, but not before Mr. Churchill has patted her back and offered some words of kindness.

Then she pushes away from him and is left standing as he

disappears with all the men in black suits and hats into the building.

Martha does not move. She lifts her face to the rain. It is gray here. The bombers are on their way. Martha opens her arms, the arms that have held great men, and finally weeps.

La Vigilia

CONNIE STANDS ON THE FRONT STEPS OF HER CHILD-hood home, refusing to move forward. Her husband, Vincent, stands close behind her, breathing heavily in the cold air. He sounds like a dragon, or something about to explode. Like a geyser, Connie thinks. Like Old Faithful. Even thinking about Old Faithful fuels her anger. On the list of things she and Vincent were supposed to do but never have, visiting Old Faithful is number two, right after a honeymoon in Niagara Falls. Instead, they drove as far as Seekonk—only thirty minutes from the hall where her family still sat drinking wine and eating egg biscuits and *wandi*. Vincent had stopped at the first motel he saw. So eager to take her virginity finally, he did not even wait for her to remove her pale-green going-away suit and put on her Champagne-colored negligee. Right then, she should have known. She should have picked up her American Tourister matching luggage and gone to Niagara Falls herself. Now, six years later, it was too late. Connie would never see Old Faithful. Or Niagara Falls. Or do any of the things on her ever-growing list of disappointments.

"I'm fucking freezing, Connie," Vincent says between snorts, which finally propels her forward.

"Davy," Connie says, nudging her five-year-old son, "ring the bell."

But Davy can't reach it. He stands on booted tiptoes and stretches his mittened hand upward.

Connie sighs, worried that Davy will be a short man like his father, worried that this trip home for Christmas will be just one more misguided decision.

"Jesus," Vincent says, and leans against Connie to ring the doorbell himself.

He doesn't move away from her when he is done. Instead, he presses against her back, making sure she feels that even in the below-freezing temperature, even beneath his long wool coat and gray flannel trousers and white boxer shorts, he has a hard-on. As if he has accomplished something special.

"Jesus," Connie says.

Davy turns his beautiful face up toward Connie and smiles his perfect baby-teeth smile.

"Happy birthday, Jesus!" he says, and Connie's heart swells with love and pride. Davy is smart. He is beautiful. Despite being conceived on that very night in that terrible motel in Seekonk, Davy is the very thing Connie has always wanted for herself: Davy is special.

The door finally opens, and with it comes a strong smell of fish. Tonight, Christmas Eve, is the *festa dei sette pesci*, the Feast of the Seven Fishes, a reminder to Connie of everything she tried to flee when she married Vincent and moved to Connecticut six years ago. The *festa dei sette pesci* screams immigrant, *guinea, wop*. The smell of fish and the dread at this step backward in her life make Connie's stomach do a little flip.

Her sister Gloria stands at the open door wearing a sweater that makes her breasts look as pointy as ice-cream cones and a skirt that hugs her ass. Peeking out from behind that ass is Gloria's daughter, Cammie, her hair in Shirley Temple ringlets and her dress a frilly white confection.

Cammie looks like she belongs on top of a cake, Connie thinks, even as she plasters a fake grin on her face and says, "Look at Cammie! So beautiful!" The girl, Connie decides, will have a hook nose like her father.

"Don't just stand there like guests," Gloria says, standing back to let them in.

Even then, as Davy goes inside, Vincent doesn't move right away. He has his hands on Connie's waist and he gives her the tiniest shove with his erection before releasing her. Like a teenager, he loves that thing. *I've got a chubby*, he whispers in her ear in bed at night. *A woody. A Johnson. Little Vinny*, he calls it. *Little V.*

Still grinning, Connie steps into the kitchen. The smells of fish and perfume and coffee percolating on the stove make her dizzy. All the faces looming toward her with their bright lipsticked lips flapping, their breath of cigarette smoke and anisette cookies, suffocate her.

The next thing Connie knows, she is going down hard onto the green-and-yellow linoleum squares, and someone—maybe her mother?—is shouting *She's fainting! Oh my God!* And then she is down, flat, her head throbbing and spinning at the same time, the sharp ammonia smell of smelling salts burning her nose.

She opens her eyes and tries to make sense of what she sees: Her sister Gloria with those ridiculous tits, her skinny arched brows frowning. Her sister Angie with what Connie hopes is a red wig and not her own hair, sprayed into a strange stiff flip, her eyes lined in heavy black liner and a fake black beauty mark beside her very red lips. Her sister Anna, so pregnant she can hardly kneel without toppling over. Little Cammie, wide-eyed, banana curls bobbing. Her own Davy, his face scrunched up the way he does when he tries not to cry. The smelling salts have been jammed up her nose by her mother, who is kneeling beside her frowning, her faded flowered apron splattered with grease. On the other side, Vincent kneels beside her. Was he smiling? Was that asshole smiling?

Vincent looks up at everyone and announces, "I guess this confirms it. She's knocked-up again."

Immediately, everyone's worry turns to squeals of happiness.

Connie watches their faces transform. Now they are smiling and their frowns are disappearing. Even her mother is smiling at her, stroking her cheek. She looks at Vincent, smug and proud, trying to decide whether he should be happy or not.

"What's knocked-up, Mama?" Davy says in a breathy voice. "You mean knocked down? Like, you got knocked down to the floor?"

Connie opens her mouth to answer him, but instead of

words what comes out is a loud, painful cry that sounds like the cry their cocker spaniel Ziti made when he got hit by a car last fall. Even after Connie is lifted to the green couch and covered in a hand-crocheted afghan; even after Connie's mouth is long closed, she still hears her own awful cry, echoing.

FOR THE PREVIOUS five Christmases, since Connie married Vincent Palazzo, she stayed home in their small white Cape in Middletown, Connecticut. She did not make seven fishes on Christmas Eve; she made a rib roast and roasted potatoes and string beans amandine. On Christmas morning she served Vincent and Davy French toast and maple bacon. Her family did not eat in the kitchen, they ate in the dining room on the china she bought piece by piece with S & H Green Stamps that she dutifully pasted into a book, filling one after another so that she could get the matching gravy boat and teacups and salad plates—all creamy white with a border of tiny off-white raised flowers. All perfect.

When Connie first met Vincent, she believed he was a man who was going places. By that time, everyone considered Connie a spinster. Twenty-five, without even a prospect of a husband. Twenty-five and a virgin. The only men who asked her out were older, widowers or bachelors with odd habits.

Then Vincent walked into the office where Connie worked in the secretarial pool with his case of Royal typewriters and Connie felt something she had never felt before. An almost unpleasant tug in her groin. It made her squirm in her seat. Vincent—dark-olive skin and green eyes that bulged like a bullfrog's; stiff, shoe-polish-black hair that she would learn only after they were married was a toupee that sat on a mannequin head at night; short, just her height, and round like a barrel—Vincent sat across from her waiting to see the procurer of office supplies and Connie squirmed. She wished she'd curled her hair, freshened her lipstick, worn the sweater with the pearl buttons that looked so flattering.

He smiled at her, showing a row of white teeth as small as baby's teeth.

"How do you like that Remington?" he said, his voice smooth and silky, a voice you wanted to touch.

Connie cleared her throat. "My what?" she asked.

He pointed his chin in the direction of her typewriter. "The Remington," he said.

She realized her fingers, which had been busily typing when he appeared, had sunk into the keys like melted wax.

"It's a fine typewriter," she managed to say. Then she blurted, "I graduated from Katherine Gibbs, top in my class."

Vincent nodded approvingly. "Very impressive," he said. "Did you learn on a Remington?"

That tug in her groin. It was all she could focus on. An image of the rows of girls—*Katie Gibbs girls*—in their business-smart clothes, fingers sailing across the keys: *the quick brown fox jumps over the lazy dog.*

"I'm a Royal man," Vincent said, leaning closer to her.

She caught a whiff of cologne, strong and spicy.

"Yes," Connie said, putting her hands in her lap as if that might subdue the tugging. She noticed his hat resting on one of his knees, black with a small red feather in the ribbon.

"Just got promoted to manager at the factory over in Connecticut," he said proudly.

His boasting, his confidence, only made the tug stronger. She found herself leaning toward him too.

He winked at her. "I'm on my way," he said, pointing his forefinger upward.

Every cell in her body was shouting, *Take me with you!* She wished he could read her mind.

The procurer's door opened. He beckoned Vincent Palazzo in.

Connie watched Vincent Palazzo walk away without looking back. She thought she might cry when the procurer closed his office door. Taking deep breaths, she went into the ladies' room, grateful to find it empty. Inside a stall, she leaned with her back against the door, wondering what would become of her. She imagined a life with her mother, the two of them crocheting at night, sipping an apricot brandy before bed. She imagined never feeling that tug again, that elusive something that her sister Angie seemed to feel all the time. Angie, who came home with smeared lipstick and a bruised mouth, smelling briny. Younger than Connie by seven years, she'd already broken off three engagements.

Connie knew she should wash her face, apply powder and lipstick, comb her hair. But instead, almost cautiously, she lifted her skirt and rubbed herself, lightly, over her girdle. That tugging, that yearning, would not go away. When she closed her eyes, the image of Vincent Palazzo filled her mind and she could almost smell his cologne again. She rubbed a bit harder, surprised at the way her hips lifted toward her hand. Damn girdle, Connie thought, gripped unexpectedly by the desire to push her hand against her flesh. For an instant, she thought she had urinated on herself. She was wet, and breathing in short gasps.

Somehow she managed to squeeze one hand down her girdle, her fingers reaching, reaching, and then rubbing and rubbing, her eyes closed so that she could picture Vincent Palazzo, and then her breath quickening until something happened, something like falling off a rooftop. Something Connie had never felt before, or even considered feeling.

On wobbly legs she managed to get back to her desk.

Vincent Palazzo stood there, twirling his hat on one finger and whistling "Sentimental Journey."

"There you are!" he said. "I almost gave up hope."

Connie tried to smile. Could he tell what she had been doing by the way she looked? She would have to go to confession, right after work, she decided. Surely she had broken a commandment. But which one?

"You like Chinese?" he was saying.

She nodded.

"I like the chicken wings at the Ming Garden. And the chow mein. You like chow mein?"

Vincent Palazzo was asking her out, Connie realized. On a date.

She stood straighter. "Yes, Mr. Palazzo, I do like chow mein. And pork fried rice."

He grinned. "Good then. I'll see you Friday at six."

He walked off, whistling "Sentimental Journey" again.

I am going to marry that man, Connie thought as she watched his bowlegged strut. I am going to marry that man and move to Connecticut and never ever come back here again.

She smiled, sat at her desk, lifted her fingers above the typewriter keys, and typed.

———

"THE BACCALA," CONNIE'S MOTHER SAYS, "needs to be soaked three times." She holds up her thumb and the two fingers beside it. "For the Father, the Son, and the Holy Ghost."

Davy nods solemnly.

Even though one of the many changes Connie has made in her life includes not going to church, Davy holds a fascination for religion, and Jesus in particular. Vincent does the obligatory Catholic duties: Palm Sunday, Easter Mass, and—until this year—midnight Mass on Christmas Eve. But enough of the kids at the St. Alphonsus kindergarten practice their faith that Davy has gleaned some of the details.

"Is the Holy Spirit related to the Holy Ghost?" he asks his grandmother as she begins to flour the smelts.

"They're all God," she answers.

Davy looks confused but doesn't pursue it.

Connie, thick tongued and fuzzy headed, joins them at the table. Silently, she counts the fish spread out there in various stages of preparation. Baccala, smelts, snail salad, octopus, marinated eel, anchovies.

"Six," she says, after she's counted again. "There's only six."

"I've got shrimps in the icebox," her mother says primly.

Connie supposes that her mother will never forgive her for moving away and not coming home to visit. Until now. To her mother, it is probably too late. But to Connie, she has come only out of desperation. The flush of joy over a new grandchild has already faded as her mother remembers the disrespect Connie has shown her.

"Why do we need six fishes?" Davy asks. He has put

his hand over his nose and mouth to block out the strong fish smell.

His grandmother shakes her head sadly. "This one, he knows nothing."

"We eat seven fishes on Christmas Eve," Connie explains. "One for . . . " She hesitates. "I almost said one for each apostle, but that's wrong."

For the first time since she's arrived, her mother looks right at Connie, her face so full of disappointment and disapproval that Connie has to catch her breath.

"So," her mother says evenly, "you follow a man to some fancy job and buy some fancy house and pretend you're American, and you actually turn into an American?"

"Ma, I am American," Connie says. She can feel Davy's eyes on her. "Italian-American," she adds.

Her mother takes hold of the rubbery white octopus and splays it on the table, slicing it with quick knife strokes.

The slap of the octopus against the enamel cuts through the silence.

"You know Vincent lost that job, Ma," Connie says quietly.

"Daddy is unemployed," Davy says with pride.

Connie's mother hesitates, the knife in midair.

"I thought he got a job with—"

"That didn't work out either," Connie says.

"And this is the time you decide to get pregnant?" her mother says. "Is that what they taught you at that fancy secretarial school I paid for? I used to have to borrow from the other kids' lunch money for your bus fare to Providence."

"I didn't decide," Connie mumbles.

She wants to tell her mother that this is why she has not

come home. Her own disappointment with her life is big enough for all of them. She wants to tell her how sometimes, when she watches Vincent feed his fat bullfrog face, she prays that he will choke. How when she finds him asleep on the sofa late in the afternoon, she watches to see if he is still breathing, and is always angry when his chest rises and falls in perfect rhythm.

"Mommy works for Dr. DiMarco," Davy says through his fingers.

Her mother's head snaps to attention.

"You work? I'm glad your grandmother is spending Christmas with Sister Chiara this year. What would she think?"

"In the doctor's office," Connie says, trying to sound casual. "A few days a week while Davy's at school."

"Vincent stays home, and *you* work?"

Connie's glance flits to Davy, and then back to her mother. But her mother doesn't take the hint.

"What kind of wife . . . what kind of mother . . . works?" her mother says.

"Dr. DiMarco looks like Montgomery Clift," Davy says.

She frowns, but doesn't look away. Connie can feel her cheeks turn red.

Connie picks up the bowl of smelts that still need to be fried and takes them over to the stove, where a pot of hot oil waits. Through the window, she can see her husband drinking homemade wine with Angie's husband, Pat, and Gloria's husband, Rocky. The men have cigars clenched in their fingers and Vincent is holding court, talking and gesturing, happy to have an audience. She wonders what he is bragging about. His woody? Her pregnancy? The car they can't afford payments on?

She drops a handful of smelts into the bubbling oil. It splatters, burning her hands and arms.

"Montgomery Clift is a famous actor," Davy is saying. "Mommy's favorite actor, right, Mommy?"

The smelts sizzle. Connie fights back nausea as their acrid smell fills her nostrils.

Behind her, her mother slaps the octopus down hard, slicing it into small pieces.

"Mama G," Davy says, oblivious to the tension that fills the kitchen, "why are there seven fishes?"

"For the Holy Blessed Sacraments," his grandmother tells him. "Your mother should remember that."

THREE MORNINGS A WEEK, after Connie drops Davy off at kindergarten, she drives across town to Dr. DiMarco's office. He has given her what he calls *Mother's hours,* working just while Davy is in school. She wears a white uniform that shows off her small waist, unbuttoned just enough so that if Dr. DiMarco wanted to, he could glimpse the white lace of her bra, the swell of her breasts. Connie hopes he is sneaking looks at them, at her. He is movie-star handsome, with thick, dark hair and a high forehead, thick black eyebrows above piercing black eyes.

The diplomas that hang behind her in the office are from Williams College and Yale Medical School. Fancy schools. Connie imagines Williams College, which she knows absolutely nothing about, as a beautiful place with brick ivy-covered buildings and smart, handsome men debating great ideas on brick-lined paths. She imagines pink dogwoods in bloom, and bright azalea bushes, and a clock tower that chimes on the hour. Davy will go there, Connie has decided. Davy will go to Williams College just like Dr. DiMarco.

Sometimes, Connie spends the ride from Davy's school to Dr. DiMarco's office planning how she will seduce him. Maybe she will call him into one of the examining rooms on the pretense of something in a patient's file and when he enters she will slowly unbutton the buttons on her uniform and take his hands and place them on her breasts. Or perhaps she should offer to cover for Bea, who works on Tuesday nights when the office stays open till eight. After all the patients were gone, Connie and Dr. DiMarco would be left alone in the office. It would be dark out, and just the two of them would be there with the hum of the fluorescent lights and the smell of ammonia and cough syrup.

So far, Connie has not executed any of her plans. Dr. DiMarco's wife, Becky, Doris Day—blond and cute, calls several times a day just to say, *Love ya.* Every time Connie has to take one of Becky's calls, her chest fills with such jealousy that she can't breathe. How did Becky get so lucky? How did Becky get born into a family with a dentist father and a mother who bred golden retrievers? How did she get to go to Mount Holyoke, an all-girls college that is maybe even more beautiful than Williams? Connie hates Becky, hates her turned-up nose and tanned cheeks and the tennis skirt she seems to have on every time she stops by the office.

One day Connie went so far as to call Dr. DiMarco into

an examining room under false pretenses. She held a manila file in her hands. She'd unbuttoned her buttons one lower than usual.

Dr. DiMarco did not seem to notice the extra button.

Connie glanced down at the file to see who it belonged to.

"The Pattersons," she said. "They're ninety days late with their bill."

He frowned. "Gee, that doesn't sound like Peggy, does it?"

Connie shook her head. Her throat had gone dry from being so close to Dr. DiMarco and she couldn't speak.

"Let me think. She brought Billy in for tonsillitis—"

"Whooping cough," Connie managed.

Dr. DiMarco nodded. "And Peggy had—"

"Gallstones. Or you thought she might have gallstones but the X-ray showed her gallbladder was clear," Connie said. She had so much to give him, so much information, so much of herself. Surely he must see that?

Dr. DiMarco smiled at her. "What would I do without you, Connie?" he said.

"Fall apart," she said, shifting so that he could definitely see the white lace of her bra, surprising herself with her boldness.

This was flirting, wasn't it? Connie thought. No one had ever really flirted with her before. But this must be it, the smiles, the joking, the double entendres.

"I'm sure it was just an oversight," Dr. DiMarco said. "Thanks, Connie, for being so efficient."

Then he was gone. Just like that.

Connie felt her heart tumbling around beneath her ribs. She waited until she heard his deep voice greeting Pamela

Sylvestri and her three kids, waited until she heard the door of that examining room close. Then she went and locked the door of the room she was in.

Alone in the room, with the colorful posters of the digestive system and respiratory system on the wall, Connie unbuttoned her uniform the rest of the way. She kicked off the white rubber-soled shoes and rolled down her girdle. Then she climbed up on the examining table, spread her legs, and closed her eyes, her own hands running up the warm length of her body, lightly pinching her nipples, imagining that it was Dr. DiMarco touching her, imagining him reaching his hands between her legs like she was doing to herself now, imagining he was whispering to her, *What would I do without you, Connie?*

This was her shame. She was a sinner. Three days a week, in Dr. DiMarco's office, she found herself doing this. In the bathroom. In an examining room. Once even in her car in the parking lot. Touching herself like this, so often, so desperately, was a sin. And wanting it to be Dr. DiMarco broke the tenth commandment: *Thou shalt not covet thy neighbor's house; nor his wife, nor anything that is thy neighbor's.* Worse, she would break the seventh commandment readily: *Thou shalt not commit adultery.*

When she got home on the nights she worked, as she made pork chops with mashed potatoes and peas with pearl onions and Davy practiced writing his letters, his careful *a*'s over and over on the yellow papers with the wide blue dotted lines, and Vincent came up behind her whispering, *Little V wants a date,* Connie thought about those stolen moments, that tug, that yearning that took over her body. She thought about Dr. DiMarco and how life with him would be, how different everything would be.

DINNER BEGINS without Vincent. No one can find him.

Vincent arrives just as Mama G starts to serve the spaghetti with anchovies. He sits down without apologizing and fills his plate high with smelts and eel and octopus and fried shrimp and *baccala*, then holds it aloft for Mama G to add the spaghetti with anchovies.

"Now I see how you keep your girlish figure," Pat says. His own belly is big enough to hang over his belt, and to quiver when he talks or takes a breath.

Vincent laughs and raises his jelly glass of wine. *"Salute,* my brother-in-law. To our girlish figures."

Mama G has left some spaghetti plain for the kids, but Cammie refuses it.

"I'll take it with the anchovies, Mama G," she says proudly.

Mama G beams, pinching the girl's cheeks. *"Figlia mia,"* she says, and kisses the top of Cammie's ringleted head.

It seems they will never stop eating, Connie thinks, even though she touches almost nothing. The platters keep getting emptied and refilled. Vincent and Pat drink too much wine and grow sloppy and silly. The metallic taste of vomit fills Connie's mouth. When they get home, she will have Dr. DiMarco do a pregnancy test. No, she decides as quickly as she thinks this. She will go to Dr. Caprio. Somehow, the thought of Dr. DiMarco knowing she is pregnant embarrasses her.

Connie glances up at the clock.

"Amahl and the Night Visitors," she says, getting to her feet.

Standing so fast makes her dizzy and she clutches the edge of the table, the plastic her mother has placed over the polyester tablecloth decorated with fake-looking poinsettias beneath it crinkling.

Angie stares into a small gold hand mirror, applying fresh dark-magenta lipstick. "Amahl?" she repeats.

"The opera," Connie says. "It's going to be on television in a few minutes."

"Yeah," Pat says, "that's just what I want to do. Watch a friggin' opera."

"I've got your opera right here swinging," Rocky says.

Unexpectedly, tears fill Connie's eyes. She wants to go home. Now. Back to her small white Cape in Connecticut and her dreams of Dr. DiMarco falling in love with her. She wants to take Davy away from these people, who do not even seem to notice how special he is. But when she looks at her husband, it is clear he is too drunk to drive in the dark all the way to Connecticut.

The opera is just beginning when Connie sits in her mother's worn easy chair, the powder-blue upholstery fraying at the seams. She runs her hands over it, as if she can fix it.

Anna comes in too, but she is not interested in *Amahl and the Night Visitors*. She just needs to put her swollen feet up on the little footstool.

"He wants five kids," she says, almost boastful. "I am going to be pregnant for the next ten years."

The little boy, Amahl, is trying to convince his mother that there are three kings at their door. The mother keeps asking, *"What shall I do with this boy? What shall I do?"*

"Mother, Mother, Mother, come with me," the boy sings in the

sweetest voice Connie has ever heard. *"I want to be sure you see what I see . . . "*

The boy's name is Chet Allen, and watching him Connie realizes that Davy could be on television just like Chet Allen. She thinks of him in his kindergarten play back in October, how he came onstage in a floppy chef's hat and white apron, holding a tray of baked goods and singing, *"Have you seen the muffin man?"* He had sung louder and more clearly than any of the other children.

Connie leans forward.

"I was a shepherd," Amahl is singing, his voice pure and high. *"I had a warm goat who gave me warm, sweet milk . . . "*

Others have come into the living room. The air is filling with the smells of perfume and cigars and sweat and wine. But Connie can only stare at Chet Allen.

"Cammie's going to do a little performance," Gloria says. "A little song and dance."

Davy climbs on Connie's lap and she holds him tight.

"See that boy on TV?" she whispers to Davy. "You can do that. You can be that boy."

Davy has his thumb in his mouth, sucking quietly.

"Watch the boy," she says.

Vincent sits on the arm of the easy chair, holding a grease-stained bag.

"For you," he says, offering it to Connie.

"What is it?"

He smiles crookedly and takes a white Chinese-food container from the bag.

"Pork fried rice," he says. "From Ming Garden."

"But when—"

"I went and got it before dinner. I figured all that fish might upset your stomach."

He is holding the container out to her, but Connie doesn't take it. On the television, Amahl's mother is agreeing to let him go with the three kings.

Mama G puts on the too-bright overhead light.

"Come on in, Cammie," she calls into the kitchen.

Cammie bursts in, dressed in a sea of sparkles. Her cheeks are rouged, her lashes thick with mascara, her lips reddened and shiny with lipstick. Even her tights sparkle as she tap dances to the center of the room. In her hands she holds a shiny red baton with white rubber tips. She holds it as if it weighs nothing at all, throwing it in the air easily and catching it without even looking.

"*On the good ship Lollipop,*" Cammie sings in a squeaky loud voice, "*it's a sweet trip to the candy shop . . .* "

Her feet tap across the floor, the baton flies into the air, and is caught again and again.

Cammie points the baton right at Davy: "*. . . and there you are, happy landings on a chocolate bar.*"

Chet Allen is singing. He is with the kings. He is following that star.

"Look," Connie whispers to her son. "Watch that boy."

Around her, her family is applauding. They are on their feet, surrounding Cammie, clapping and clapping until Connie thinks she cannot take it, not one more minute of it.

"Watch him, Davy," she says, her voice cracking as she presses her beautiful son close to her, holding on to him as tightly as she can. "Watch him."

Husbands

SHE SAW THEM EVERYWHERE. ON OVERHILL DRIVE, Maplewood Street, Linden Way. Mowing lawns, walking dogs, pulling cars in and out of garages. She saw them in backyards and driveways, on sidewalks and cul-de-sacs. Early in the morning they tucked newspapers under their arms; placed cigarettes between their lips; adjusted hats, ties, glasses, watches, wedding rings. Jangled car keys, whistled, waved good-bye. In the morning, they drove away. The ones who worked in factories, hospitals, fire stations, police stations came back by four. But most returned at five o'clock, six o'clock, sometimes even seven. Car doors slammed, children ran outside to get swooped into arms. Martinis were stirred and tables set. The blue glow of television news filled the neighborhood. The husbands were home. Husbands were everywhere. But none of them belonged to Francie Partridge.

She'd had one once, long enough ago now to make him seem like a dream. He had been tall and broad-shouldered, with a cowlick, and a scar under his chin from getting hit with a hockey stick. When she got the news that he'd been killed in France, in a place called Normandy, she'd thought about him all the time. She could feel the pressure of his lips on hers, remember his minty scent. All she could do at first, really, was think of him, as if she might be able to memorize every detail. But she hadn't been able to. He faded, grew small and faraway like a picture in a library book. Now, ten years later, weeks passed without her thinking of him at all.

Francie was meandering dreamily through the A&P produce section and a man strode past her. He walked purposefully, like he had somewhere to go. Francie saw him, saw his wide back and the sandy hair in need of a trim, his long legs and a certain way he held his head and she remembered her dead husband. The memory made her woozy, made her grip the edge of the display of Golden Delicious apples. She thought she might faint, right there in the A&P. Francie closed her eyes, ready for anything except the pair of strong arms that caught her. Yellow apples tumbled to the floor.

A man said, "Whoa there," and Francie looked into the bright blue eyes of the person who had caused all this in the first place. Up close, he looked nothing like her husband. Her heart slowed. Her stomach settled. She took a few deep breaths. The man smelled like just baked pie. His name tag said: ART CUMMINGS, BAKERY MANAGER.

Francie smiled up at him.

"You okay?" he asked, not letting her go.

She was aware of a crowd around them. She saw the frowning face of Margaret Lefleur. Margaret lived on Maplewood, right where it intersected Francie's own street, Mayflower Lane.

"A dizzy spell," Francie said lightly. "It's passed now."

"You sure?" Art Cummings asked.

She wished he wouldn't let go of her. She wished, in that instant, that he would walk up her driveway tonight, slip his keys into her front door, and call to her that he was home. A dog that she did not own, a cocker spaniel or a Scottie, would run to meet him, and she would step into the living room with a pitcher of martinis for the two of them. Art Cummings would kiss her lightly on the cheek, ask her what smelled so good, follow her to the gold sofa, and sit beside her.

"Ma'am?" he was saying.

Margaret Lefleur stepped forward. "Do you need me to drive you home?" she was asking.

She stuck her pale round face right in Francie's, so close that Francie could smell the tuna salad Margaret must have had for lunch.

"She lives right by us," Margaret explained to the crowd.

"Really," Francie said, straightening, "I'm fine."

Art Cummings released her. He studied her to be certain.

"Thank you," she said.

Someone started to pick up all the bruised apples. Art nodded at her, satisfied. When he raised his hand to his head in a kind of salute, she saw a plain gold wedding band on his left ring finger.

"Anchors aweigh," Francie said. But everyone had dispersed as quickly as they'd gathered. She was standing there, alone.

MANY OF THE HUSBANDS had been in the war too. Paul Lefleur had lost his arm in the Pacific and walked around on hot summer weekends in a sleeveless T-shirt, showing off his stump. Some of the men limped, or had bad nerves. Some of the men walked the streets of Meadowbrook Plat at night, unable to sleep; the war gave them bad dreams, guilty consciences, insomnia.

One summer night, Francie was in her backyard deadheading her lilacs when Mike Macomber from two doors down appeared out of the shadows. Mike was tall and wiry, like a baseball player, with pale blond hair tinged green from chlorine. Francie could see his yard from her back steps, but she'd never been invited over. His wife, Elaine, had a pinched, anxious face, like she was waiting for bad news.

"You nearly gave me a heart attack," Francie said that night Mike showed up.

"Sorry," he said without a hint of apology. "Once Jack Paar's over, there isn't much left to do."

"Where's Elaine? Isn't she watching Jack Paar with you?" Francie said. She was peeved at this interruption and she didn't try to hide it.

Mike laughed and sat in one of her woven plastic chairs. That weave would leave crisscrosses all over the backs of his legs, Francie knew. Mike lit up a cigarette and offered it to her, but she shook her head no and went back to her lilacs.

"Pretty," he said just when she'd forgotten he was there.

She turned to him.

"The lilacs," he said.

"They're hard to take care of," Francie said. She had struggled with these lilacs since she'd bought the house in '51. Her grandmother had told her that lilacs need sun and pruning and attention. She'd said it like Francie was incapable of making lilac bushes bloom, and that made Francie even more determined.

"They smell so pretty," Mike said. "Like France."

Francie sighed and sat in the chair next to him. She took his half-smoked cigarette from his slender fingers and put it in her mouth. After she inhaled and blew the smoke out in a slow, long breath, she said, "That's where my husband died. Normandy."

It used to be that she would grow teary when she said those words: "husband" and "died" and "Normandy." She used to tell anyone who would listen how the military officer who came to tell her the news had cut himself shaving that morning and had a small piece of tissue stuck on his cheek, dotted with blood. She used to add how her mother had fainted at the news, how her grandmother had yelled at the officer in Italian, lunging for him as if he had killed Mac himself.

But Francie had stood still and calm. The garlic her grandmother had been browning in olive oil burned as she stood there accepting the news, and the acrid smell filled the room. She could hear the hot oil splattering. Then she thanked the officer, led him to the door, and watched him walk away. That was when Francie began to shake. It started deep inside her and radiated out—giant, uncontrollable shaking. Her arms and legs jumped, her head shook so hard on her shoulders that her grandmother thought she was having a seizure and jammed a wadded up handkerchief into Francie's mouth so she wouldn't swallow her tongue. Francie took another drag from Mike's cigarette, then lifted the bottle of anisette she'd brought outside with her and poured a shot glass full.

"Here," she said, offering it to him.

Mike drank it in one long swallow, then coughed.

"What the hell?" he said, sputtering. He wiped his mouth with the back of his hand.

Francie laughed and refilled the glass. She took a sip, then held it out to him. "You sip it," she said.

He did as she told him.

"Anisette," she explained. "It's good in coffee on cold days. Or in snow."

"Snow?" he said, grinning at her.

"You collect freshly fallen snow and add coffee and anisette to it. You eat it with a spoon."

"Crazy wop," he said, chuckling.

Francie smudged the butt of the cigarette in the big green ashtray she kept outside. She took another sip of the anisette and looked at her lilacs in the moonlight. They hung in heavy clusters, like ripe things ready to be picked. Tomorrow she would bring some to her grandmother.

"I was there," Mike said, just when she'd almost forgotten about him again. "France. And then Italy."

Francie nodded. She didn't care about Mike Macomber or his war stories. She hoped he wouldn't tell her anything.

Mike lit another cigarette and handed it to her. This time she took it.

"I'm sorry about your husband," Mike said.

"I hardly remember him anymore," Francie said, and saying it out loud filled her with such sadness that she began to cry.

"No," Mike said, spilling anisette as he jumped up. "It's too painful to remember. That's all."

But Francie shook her head. She struggled for something particular about him, something to hold on to, something more than a cowlick or long legs or a scar so small it didn't even matter.

Mike was shushing her. A woman crying made men nervous. Francie knew that. "I'm sorry," she said.

"No, no," Mike was saying. He said it like he was pleading for something.

All of the wives in Meadowbrook were fair-skinned, round-faced, flat-chested. They got their hair cut and dried and dyed and sprayed every Saturday. They had small waists cinched smaller with belts. They wore charm bracelets that tinkled when they moved. Francie had thought when she first saw them that they were exotic birds. But she was the exotic one, with her dark curls that could not be tamed, and her olive skin and her large breasts that came to two perfect points under her sweaters. Her hips were wide, her eyes were black, her nose was sharp with a small bump at the bridge. "You Eye-talians," Elaine Macomber always said as a way of explanation for the way Francie looked or smelled or walked. "Why, look at you in that skirt!" Elaine would say in her hushed, nervous voice. "You Eye-talians sure have the hourglass figure, don't you?"

In this moment, with an almost full moon and the intoxicating suffocating lilacs in bloom and the taste of licorice mingling with smoke and salty tears on her lips and Mike Macomber so blond and tall reaching to comfort her, Francie ached for her husband.

Later, alone in her bed, she would blame that ache for letting Elaine Macomber's husband take her into his arms—all pointy, sharp elbows and small, tight muscles—and kissing her. His tongue was lazy and fat. His fingers long and slender. Long ago, before her little pale blue house here, before her husband, back when she was a girl called Francesca, Francie used to let boys kiss her all the time. She used to let them feel her up. She didn't care. And she didn't care now. Francie smiled into Mike's kisses.

"Why are you smiling?" he whispered.

But how could she explain that letting him kiss her here in her backyard was somehow giving her a power that she had forgotten she'd had. It was like finding herself again. When they tumbled onto the grass, it was wet with dew. Francie felt it soaking her blouse and skirt. It was May, warm in the daytime but chilly at night. Francie shivered, and Mike mistook it for pleasure, for permission. She heard the sound of his zipper unzipping, let him reach under her skirt and pull down her panties, let him bunch up her skirt and put his thing inside. She had not done this with anyone except her husband; she had not done this since he died. It felt unfamiliar and oddly pleasant.

Mike whispered, "I've never done this with an Eye-talian." He sounded out of control. "So different," he murmured, and she almost laughed. She'd heard once that Orientals' slits were horizontal instead of like everyone else's. But were Italians different down there?

"So much hair," Mike was saying. "So much."

He threw his head back, teeth clenched, his face in the moonlight as pale as a ghost. The lights in all the houses on Mayflower Lane and Maplewood Street and Overhill Drive, all of them were off, the houses dark, the husbands snoring softly beside their wives.

FRANCIE PARTRIDGE GREW up Francesca Caserta less than a mile from Meadowbrook Plat. As she navigated the familiar path home, her car filled with the lilacs she had gathered for her grandmother, Francie felt like she was driving a long distance, traveling to a place far away. Once she passed the French church, where the French Canadians went to Mass, she entered the Italian part of town. Instantly, everything looked different. Vegetable gardens replaced backyards; shrines to the Virgin Mary stood in place of barbecue grills or patio furniture; fig trees and cherry trees dotted yards instead of leafy maples and elms. People sat on front steps and sidewalks. Men at folding tables at the edge of the street played cards, smoked cigars, drank homemade wine. Everyone was yelling—fighting, calling children, talking too loud. Francie hated it here. Hated the noise, the smells, the plastic Virgins watching her.

After her husband died, she had stayed here with her family until she'd saved enough money to buy the house in Meadowbrook Plat. Once, that land really had been a meadow, large and green and dotted with buttercups and black-eyed Susans. The brook still ran through the neighborhood, back near the older houses. Those houses were two stories, made of brick or painted yellow.

But Francie wanted one of the newer ones, away from the brook and the woods that still bordered the plat. She wanted to live in the crisscross of streets, in a house no one had lived in before, with shiny wood floors and Formica countertops speckled gold.

The house was called a ranch, and it made Francie think of open spaces somewhere out west, of rolling hills and towering trees. It was robin's-egg blue, with black shutters. My nest, Francie thought when she saw it. The garage was attached and she could drive her car into it, open a door, and step directly into her kitchen. That small action delighted her each time she did it. Everywhere she could, Francie planted flowers. Along one side of the house, where her mother would have put tomatoes, zucchini, green beans, eggplant, Francie grew pansies, petunias, violets. In the backyard, her lilacs and roses and peonies.

Francie filled her arms with those lilacs and made her way up the cracked sidewalk toward her grandmother.

"Francesca!" she heard, and grimaced. It was her sister, Mary, pregnant again, waddling toward her with her arms outstretched.

"Don't crush the lilacs," Francie said, turning away from Mary's hug.

"Look at those!" Mary cooed. "Did you grow them? You couldn't!"

Mary's son, Alfred, had followed her out. He was dressed in a saggy grayish diaper and nothing else. Staring from the screen door was her daughter, Joanne. Francie tried to like Joanne. She bought her pretty things, patent leather shoes and a furry white muff last Christmas, but the girl was too shy and dull. She wanted plastic baby dolls and old-fashioned dresses all stiff and scratchy.

"Where's Nonna?" Francie asked. She knew she was supposed to fawn over the children, tell Mary how beautiful they were. She was supposed to pay attention to her sister's bulging stomach, ask how she was feeling and when she was due. But Francie didn't care about these things. And she wanted to go back to her little blue house and put an album on her stereo, maybe Patsy Cline, who sang so painfully about love.

"In the garden," Mary said. She walked beside Francie, scooping up her son.

Mary had married Michele, one of Francie's old boyfriends. He always stared at Francie's breasts, maybe remembering them from when they were teenagers. He was doing it now, looking at her chest hard like he had Superman's eyes that could see right through the olive-green cotton of her dress. Michele was short and dark and sweaty, with his hair greased back and a cigar clenched between his teeth.

"Francesca," he said. Unlike her sister, he didn't let her escape his hug. Lilac blossoms scattered to the ground when she pulled away from him. "When you going to find a husband, huh?" he said, grinning.

"Maybe I've found one," she said.

"Oh! Really?" Mary said.

"He's lucky," Michele said. "Whoever he is. Is he from the neighborhood?"

Francie smiled as if she were keeping a secret, and hurried to where her grandmother stood hoeing manure. The smell, strong and sour, made Francie gag.

"Figlia mia," her grandmother said, dropping the hoe and pinching both of Francie's cheeks hard.

"I brought these for you," Francie said. She was aware of

Mary and Michele and Alfred watching her. "Take them," Francie said harshly.

Her grandmother held out her arms and Francie dumped the flowers into them.

"Silly girl," she said in Italian. "What am I supposed to do with a pile of lilacs?"

"Put them in a vase," Francie yelled at her, knowing that there were no vases in the house. "Throw them away! I don't care!"

Her grandmother shrugged, and let the flowers fall to the ground. Carefully, she stepped over them, and went back to hoeing the dirt and manure.

"They're beautiful, Francesca," her sister said as Francie walked past her. "Really."

"Hey!" Michele called after her. "When are we going to meet this future husband of yours? Eh?"

Francie got into her car. Joanne was still standing at the screen door, staring out at her. Behind Joanne, Francie's mother, Concetta, appeared, frowning. Mary was running as best she could with her huge belly and Alfred in her arms.

"You're not leaving, are you?" she was saying. "Mama made egg biscuits."

Francie put the car in gear and drove away, toward home.

WHEN FRANCIE FIRST moved into her robin's-egg-blue ranch house in Meadowbrook Plat, she knew she was different. No husband. No children. The only Italian in a neighborhood of Irish and French and Polish families. These women's foreign ancestry was far enough back that they had become a pleasant American blur—no accents, no strange-smelling spices or food with names difficult to pronounce. Their children were all Debbies and Kathys and Lindas; Michaels and Stevens and Bobbys. They did not keep rabbits in their backyards or grow vines with tomatoes and grapes or cover their good furniture with sheets of plastic. Their houses smelled of cinnamon. Their yards were mowed, sculpted, tended, uncluttered. She wanted to be one of them, but they were not inviting her in.

So Francie invited them. She spent a long Saturday afternoon handwriting invitations. *Come for Tea!* Carefully, she traced small teacups and teapots from a magazine onto tracing paper and then onto each invitation. She had read in *Good Housekeeping* about how to give a tea party, and she tore the article from the magazine and did everything it described, step-by-step. The recipes were time consuming and confusing. She only knew how to make the things her mother had taught her—red sauce and meatballs, *braciole*, polenta with kale. But now she was mashing bananas for banana bread, topping Ritz crackers with orange cheese and half an olive held on with a toothpick wearing fancy colored cellophane. She made ham and mayonnaise sandwiches on white bread, then cut them into shapes with cookie cutters: flowers, stars, and hearts.

When the doorbell rang, she was sweaty and tired. But the dining-room table where she had never sat, where she had imagined fancy dinner parties or bridge games, was set with a yellow tablecloth and platters of sandwiches, devilled eggs dusted with paprika, banana bread, and Waldorf salad. She had never even bought mayonnaise before, and now it was in almost everything she'd made, the smell sickeningly sweet and cloying.

Francie smoothed her skirt and checked that she did not have lipstick on her teeth. Then she opened the door wide to let in, finally, that gaggle of laughing women. They pushed into the house, thrusting a bouquet of daffodils into her hands, all of them talking at once. She tried to keep them straight, but they all had the same stiff hairdos, the same coral lipstick and blank faces. The women gushed at her table, admired her living-room ensemble, peeked into both bedrooms and what they referred to as the powder room. They sniffed and touched and poked like unruly children.

"Why," one of them said, "is this the tea party from *Good Housekeeping*?"

And another added, disappointed, "We thought you'd make us some spaghetti and meatballs. We thought you'd use garlic."

One of the women wrinkled her nose. "You just can't get the smell of garlic out of a house, can you?" And the other women looked at Francie and nodded sympathetically.

They ate everything, complimenting her on each dish. Francie couldn't bear to eat any of these mayonnaised things. She vowed to throw the jar out as soon as they left, which they did quickly, begging off to meet the school bus. They thanked her and as a group walked out the door. Francie watched from her picture window as they walked away, touching each other's arms, heads bent together, laughing. At her? she wondered. They did not reciprocate by inviting her to their houses. She saw them gathering on doorsteps across the neighborhood. She still waved as she passed them, and sometimes one of them waved back.

WHEN FRANCIE PULLED into her driveway, she found Elaine Macomber standing nervously on her front steps. Francie considered driving away, but it was too late. Elaine had heard the engine and was looking straight at Francie.

"Elaine," Francie said as she got out of the car and walked toward the woman whose husband she'd had sex with twelve hours earlier. Francie swallowed hard and forced a polite smile.

Elaine didn't meet her halfway, the way a person would. She just stood on the top step, wringing her hands.

"Do you want to come in?" Francie said. She had to squeeze close to Elaine to get the door unlocked and she could smell the woman's flowery perfume.

"No, no, that's not necessary," Elaine said. Instead of looking at Francie, she looked in the direction of her own house, two doors down. It was a ranch too, white and red. "Mike thought I should come by."

Francie pushed the door open and stepped with relief into her cool house. The floors were shining and the porcelain figures stood guard, one on each side of the mantel. In between, where she had once imagined photographs, there was nothing. She did not have any to put there.

"He wants me to invite you to a pool party next Saturday at our house. The Lefleurs are coming, and the Podaskis and the MacGuires and, well, just about the whole street."

Francie looked right into Elaine's beady eyes. She thought of Elaine's husband with his head thrown back and his jaw clenched tight, and she smiled. "That would be lovely," Francie said. "Thank you."

FRANCIE PURPOSELY WORE a low-cut red blouse to the party, and a skirt that showed her wide hips. She kept her legs bare, something that she knew would keep the wives talking all night. She watched the others arrive from her back stairs. All those women in their sweater sets or blouses with Peter Pan collars, their full skirts and tiny belts to emphasize their tiny waists. She waited until they all had drinks in their hands and then she walked down the street, through the gate that led to the Macombers' backyard and the pool. Francie saw the women take her in, the swell of her breasts and the dip of the *V* in the blouse. She smiled warmly at them all, pressed their soft pale hands into hers.

Mike came over and offered her a drink. There were stingers and there were grasshoppers. She didn't know what either of these were, but saw Elaine drinking something green.

"A stinger," she said, as if she knew what she was getting into. Francie followed Mike to the outdoor bar, where the silver pitchers of cocktails sat sweating. All of the husbands were there, and she could feel the wives watching her. The rule was to stay with the women and let a man fetch your cocktail. The rule was to talk to the wives.

"Francie's husband was killed in Normandy," Mike said.

Francie nodded at Paul Lefleur with his empty shirt sleeve

pinned up to the shoulder. She looked at Stanley Podaski and
Matt MacGuire and Bill Handy, all of them veterans.

Elaine came over and put her hand on Francie's shoulder.
"You should come and help us bring out the salad and things,"
she said.

Later, after more stingers and big undercooked steaks
and vanilla ice cream with crème de menthe on top, Stanley
Podaski said, "I'm sorry about your husband, Francie. Fucking Krauts. Fucking war."

Stan was thick-necked and red faced, a solid man who
would be fat someday when he lost all this muscle. He was
short, about Francie's height, and she could see the red of his
scalp through his blond hair. His wife, Dottie, was pregnant
and sat smugly with her hands folded over her round belly.

Again Francie tried to remember her husband, but he was
blurrier than ever.

"I should walk you home," Stan said.

Francie laughed. "It's only two houses away," she said.

But she did leave soon after. The men beginning to tell
their war stories and the women sitting on chairs by the
pool, talking about their children. Unnoticed, Francie walked
home. She would write a thank-you note to Elaine and put
it in their mailbox tomorrow. She had read in a magazine
how to write thank-you notes: only three lines, the article had
said. The first line complimented the hostess. The second line
complimented the event. The final line said thank you.

Sitting at her kitchen table with its red enamel top,
slightly drunk, Francie wrote the note: *Dear Elaine, You really
know how to throw a party! Those steaks were delicious! Thank*

you so much for having me. She was pleased with her note, and read it again out loud. But a soft knock on the kitchen door interrupted her. Stan Podaski was standing there when she opened it.

"Just making sure you got home safe," he said. He swayed slightly, drunk.

"Maybe you need some coffee?" Francie said. She had put the percolator on for herself anyway. "Come on."

She held his arm to steady him and he walked in heavily.

"Go sit in the living room and I'll bring you a cup," she told him.

From her kitchen window she could see that the party was not yet over. She poured them each a cup of black coffee and brought them into the living room on a tray.

"Ever since I came back," Stan said, "I drink too much. I can't help myself. It makes me forget things, you know? Dottie doesn't get it. Just don't think about it, she says. But how do you stop thinking about it?" He shook his head. "She's not the sharpest knife in the drawer," he added.

Francie sipped her coffee. She wished she had cigarettes. She liked smoking around men. It felt sexy and important.

"Do you have a cigarette?" she asked, and Stan pulled a pack from his pocket.

"Keep it," he said.

Francie lit a cigarette, smoothing the cellophane on the red pack.

"You don't get over killing people," Stan was saying.

"Shhh," Francie said. She didn't want to hear any war stories.

"You don't get over—"

She leaned over and kissed him full on the mouth to shut him up. Stan didn't act surprised. Francie realized this was why he was here. She wondered if Mike had told him about the other night. She supposed this should make her angry, but instead she had that powerful feeling again. All of these husbands wanted her. They did not want their placid, bland wives with their flat chests, their pregnant bellies, their coiffed hair. They wanted someone who had suffered, like they had. They wanted someone exotic. They wanted her.

Francie pulled off her sweater and her bra. She pulled off her panties and unzipped his pants. He was thick and pink there too and she smiled knowing this. She straddled him, facing him, grasping at him to fit inside her.

Dottie Podaski's husband moaned, loud. This time, Francie was the wild one. She was wild with what she could have, with what she could do. She was wild for these husbands, every one of them. She tried to remember her husband, doing this with him.

Husbands. By fall Francie had had almost every one of them. They came to her unable to sleep, drunk, crying over what they had seen and done. Paul Lefleur would not have sex with her but very politely asked if she would blow him. She did, kneeling at his feet on her shiny hardwood floors, his one arm moving her head, the sleeve of the other flapping against her face. Matt MacGuire said he loved her. He came on Sunday mornings before church and then Francie made sure to be outside when the family drove past on their way to St. Joseph's nine o'clock Mass, all of his little daughters dressed in matching dresses, bows in their hair, his wife, Helen, smiling smugly out the window at Francie. The funny thing was, after each one, the wife showed up to invite her to this or that. She went to parties all the time now, as if by inviting her the wives would never suspect. If something was going on, surely the husbands would not insist she be invited. A new rule, Francie thought.

Late at night. Francie on Stan Podaski's lap. The neighborhood asleep. Tears on Stan's cheeks because he was a killer, a murderer. She tried to remember her husband. His weight on her, yes. And once, in his car by a lake, he had brought her onto his lap just like this. She remembered the steering wheel digging into her back, the shift against her hip. His face, blurry still, had once been close like this.

"Yes," she said, clutching Stan's thick shoulders.

And she saw it for an instant, her husband's beautiful face.

Part Three

1970–1974

Crooning with Dino

AIDA CARUSO LOVES TWO THINGS.

First and above all else, she loves Dean Martin. Every Thursday night she sits smack in front of the Zenith in the living room and waits for Dino to jump onto the piano, swirling a cocktail and waving a cigarette as he sings, looking straight at her.

Second, she loves the boy in the white VW Bug. The boy has pale blond hair that hangs straight to his collarbone, a Barney Rubble nose, sometimes a scraggly patch of hair on his chin. She guesses he is a lot older than her, maybe even eighteen or twenty. Certainly too old to notice a fourteen-year-old.

He drives down the hill in front of her house and around the corner every afternoon at five. Aida watches from the small window at the top of the steps that lead to the three bedrooms in her house. Her weekly chore is to dust the glass dishes and vases and the wooden figurines that line the stairs on a shelf. They are ugly things, the vases and dishes all orange or gold, useless and fragile. Her father had bought the figurines in Haiti when he was in the Navy. They are of women with pointy breasts and men in loincloths. They collect dust in the elbows and knees, along the shoulders and fingers and feet.

She hates them, hates dusting them. But this afternoon, the Thursday before her sister's wedding, Aida likes sitting alone at the top of the stairs, a half-naked man in her lap, a dishrag in her hand, the noise of her loud aunts and uncles and parents and grandmother and great-grandmother all drifting up from below her as she waits for the boy in the white VW to come down the hill.

"Aida!" her mother yells. Her mother only yells. She cannot speak in a normal voice; none of her family can. When one of her aunts telephones her mother, Aida can hear everything she says from across the room. "Aida!" her mother yells again. Then: "That girl gives me *agita*. Her head is in the clouds all day."

"She's a dreamer," her aunt Gloria says. "Like my Cammie."

Aida straightens. Her cousin Carmela—*Cammie*—dreamed of being famous and now she has her own show in Las Vegas. Now she drives a convertible. For all Aida knows, Cammie has met the Rat Pack. All of them. Frank and Sammy and even Dino.

"Cammie isn't a dreamer," Aida's mother says. "She's a doer. Isn't she in Vegas? Isn't she at Caesar's Palace? You don't get there by staring out windows."

Aida catches a glimpse of white in the distance and hears the egg beater engine of a VW. Her heart quickens. She presses her face to the window, feels the tiny squares of the screen denting her flesh. The white Bug comes into view. He drives slowly down the hill, his own car window down, one arm casually draped outside it. As he turns the corner she sees the golden hairs on his chin; he isn't shaving again. A sign of what? she wonders. Heartache? Laziness? Debauchery? She is not exactly sure what debauchery is, but she imagines it as something sophisticated—a rumpled tuxedo, martinis and cigarettes, late nights. With warm weather finally here, and all the windows thrown open, she can actually hear music coming from his car. She recognizes the song as one her sister, Terry, plays over and over: "Suite: Judy Blue Eyes": It's about sadness and regret and loneliness. Oh! Aida thinks. He *is* heartbroken. She wonders if she can somehow mend him, or if he can mend her. "Yes!" Aida calls out the window. "Yes!"

The car slows. Stops. The boy looks around, as if he's heard her. He even looks up, right in her direction. But he does not see her there, her face pressed to the window, yearning.

DOWNSTAIRS, THERE IS CHAOS. Noise and chaos. Chicken breasts split open, waiting to be stuffed. Manicotti cooling. Ricotta and eggs being mixed together in Mama Jo's biggest bowl. Mama Jo herself elbow-deep in ground beef and eggs and parsley and garlic and breadcrumbs. The aunts are sitting, smoking, wrapping candy in yellow tulle and tying the small bundles with white ribbon. Platters of egg biscuits, wine biscuits, *wandi* fill the counter. Aida feels dizzy from the smells: cheese, smoke, hair spray, powdered sugar, something frying in oil.

"Finally!" her mother says. A cigarette dangles from her lips, the ash twitching precariously above the manicotti. She hands Aida a package of prosciutto, all waxy paper and pale pink flesh. "Roll."

Aida peels off a thin piece of the ham and pops it into her mouth. She doesn't chew right away. Instead, she lets the saltiness fill her mouth and nose, the ham dissolve slightly.

Aunt Gloria smacks her on the arm. "It's for the people!"

Aida swallows. She is immediately thirsty. "I'm a person," she says, and takes another piece.

Aunt Gloria takes the prosciutto away from Aida, shaking her head. Right away Aunt Connie hands her a platter of fried eggplant. "Go help Aunt Angie," she says.

The air is blue with smoke. Aida sighs.

"Eh?" Mama Jo says, nudging Aida with her elbow. "I fried all those eggplants myself. My legs are killing me. You know the boy's family? They don't peel their eggplant. Tastes sour." Her face wrinkles up in disgust. "I had to spit it out."

"The boy" is what Mama Jo calls Eddie, the groom-to-be. He is nineteen years old, skinny, long. Long nose, long hair, long legs. He reminds Aida of Gumby, though she's never told her sister this.

Mama Jo nudges her again. "You buy eggplant, you always buy the female. Eh?" She wags a finger thick with meatball mixture at Aida. "Female."

Someone smacks Aida in the back of her head. *"Stunare!"* her mother says, taking the platter from her. "Why are you just standing here?"

"I don't care about this stupid wedding," Aida says, because no one is listening anyway.

It is true. Her sister, Terry, is nineteen years old and works answering phones at Chip Finley's Ford down the street.

Eddie fixes cars there. To Aida, the fact that they are getting married makes her queasy. They should go to South America; they should hike the Appalachian Trail; they should go to college, even junior college; they should learn to cook on a wok, sail a boat, play the guitar. They should do anything but get married and work at Chip Finley's Ford and stay in this town until they die.

She sees Aunt Gloria stuffing the manicotti.

"Cammie coming to the wedding?" Aida asks, hopeful.

"She's trying," Aunt Gloria says. "That girl's busy. When you're in show business, you don't just leave everything. The show must go on, right?"

Aida watches her cigarette bounce as she talks. They are all going to die of cancer, she thinks. Every one of them.

The door bursts open and Terry and Eddie, followed by their best man and maid of honor, practically fall inside. They giggle and hold each other while everyone except Aida beams at them.

"Oh, man," Eddie says, and heads straight for the cookies. He pops them in his mouth whole, one after another.

"Save some for the people," someone says.

Eddie laughs and tosses a few cookies to Frankie, the best man.

"Wow," Terry says, slowly surveying the room. The food, the relatives, the tiny bundles of dressed-up candy. "Someone getting married?" She laughs hard at her own joke.

Aida glances at the cuckoo clock on the wall. Her father bought it in Germany when he was in the Navy, and it is the one thing of all the souvenirs he bought that she likes. She does not know anyone else with a cuckoo clock. It seems exotic and fancy. While she looks at it, admiring the carved scene of birds and trees, the ivory face, the cuckoo shoots out and jerkily cuckoos once. It is five thirty. Hours before Dean Martin comes on. She plans on hiding in her parents' bedroom to watch it on the portable television in there.

Terry has kissed everyone hello, everyone except Aida. She wraps her skinny arm around her and kisses her cheek.

"Hello, little sister," she says.

Her eyes are red and heavy lidded. Aida smells the too-sweet smell of marijuana, which is what Terry and Eddie do in their spare time. Aida found them behind the garage last fall, and threatened to call the police. It was illegal. It led to harder drugs, like heroin. But Terry had grabbed her arm hard and said, "Keep your fucking mouth shut, Aida. If you're a good little girl maybe we'll give you some."

"I don't want drugs!" Aida had said, horrified.

Ever since then, she's caught them smoking it in the car, in the basement, even in Terry's room with a blue bath towel— one of the good ones—rolled under the door. It is all that they do, and it makes Aida alternately sad and angry. For her bridal shower, she bought her sister a book called *Wok Cookery*, believing that maybe if she found something new, something she liked, she wouldn't have to get high all the time. "Wow," Terry had said in her thick stoned voice when she opened it, "Chicken with Cashews."

The phone rings and Aida runs to answer it.

She hears static and then, "Auntie Anna? Auntie Anna?"

"This is Aida," Aida says.

"Little Aida? It's Cousin Cammie."

Aida puts a finger in one ear to hear better. She imagines

this voice cutting through the hot desert air, traveling across mountains and rivers and cities to her ear.

"Cammie!" Aida says it like a sigh.

"Listen, doll," Cammie says, "I'm on my way. I think I'll be able to make it in time for the wedding. If I drive straight through."

"What?" Aida says. "You're *driving*?" Why wouldn't someone in show business fly from Las Vegas?

"I've got my little red convertible, my cooler filled with ice-cold Fresca. It's heavenly," Cammie tells her.

"Okay," Aida says.

"I'm scared of flying anyway. Did you hear about that Eastern Airlines plane that crashed in some lake near New Orleans?"

"Uh-huh," Aida says, though she has not heard of any such thing.

"No thank you," Cammie says.

There is a strange sound, then the phone goes dead briefly.

"Out of change, babe," Cammie says before it goes dead again.

Suddenly Aida has something to look forward to. Maybe she can go back to Las Vegas with Cammie. Maybe she can be her assistant. Aida smiles, hugging herself. Her mother is yelling to her: "Aida, get your skinny ass in here and help." But Aida doesn't move. Instead, she stands alone with her good news.

AIDA WONDERS IF Cammie knows Jeannie, Dean Martin's beautiful blond wife. Last night he said, "Jeannie, baby, don't wait up," and Aida got goose bumps. She imagines Jeannie in a sleek modern house with white furniture and a big stone fireplace and, outside, a piano-shaped swimming pool. Some movie star has a pool like that, she just can't remember who. If she were Jeannie, she would wait up. She would spray on Jean Naté and wear a little babydoll pajama set like the one Terry got at her bridal shower. Her goose bumps rise up again, all along her arms.

ON HER BEDROOM DOOR, wrapped in plastic, hangs her ugly yellow chiana junior bridesmaid's dress. Terry thinks it is sophisticated, but to Aida it looks like a cheap prom dress. Her sister's dress is also chiana—white, even though she isn't a virgin. Aida stares at the dress, hating it.

Downstairs: noise. They are getting ready for the rehearsal at the church, and then the dinner here afterward. Eddie's entire family is coming. They don't peel their eggplants. They put a crust on their Easter *pastera*. They don't do anything right.

"Aida!" her mother yells.

Aida sighs and gets off the bed. Her body weighs three tons. The rehearsal dinner dress sticks to her in the early summer heat. It is black and covered with bright-yellow sunflowers, like a tablecloth. It seems the role of a junior bridesmaid is to be humiliated so that the bride shines. In Las Vegas she will wear bikinis and cover-ups in lime green and hot pink. She will smell of baby oil and iodine, like the older girls at the beach. This idea makes Aida smile as she goes down the stairs, past all of her father's ugly souvenirs.

The souvenirs are all they have left of him. When she was

six, there was a blizzard and school got canceled. Her father went out to shovel the snow and died of a heart attack, just like that. Boom! No warning. To Aida, he is just Old Spice and Vitalis, a scratchy wool sailor's uniform, a pile of worthless figurines and clocks and colorful money from faraway places. Sirens still make her feel like she can't breathe. Snow days still make her sad.

"The Queen of Sheba," her mother says. "Finally."

Terry's rehearsal dress is short and yellow with a matching bolero jacket. She looks like a jaundiced matador.

"You're all wrinkled," Aunt Connie says, disgusted.

Aida shrugs. Her great-grandmother, Mama Jo, pulls her aside and whispers harshly in her ear. "If those people bring any food into this house, don't eat it. You hear me?"

"All right," Aida promises.

Mama Jo pinches her arm. "Don't eat it," she says again.

People are gathering their matching purses—yellow, blue, red. They primp their hair and twirl their lipstick from their cylinders, the poppy and crimson and coral emerging.

"Let Aida wear some," Aunt Gloria says.

"No!" her grandmother, Mama G, says. "She's a little girl. She'll look like a *puttana!*"

"Don't be ridiculous," Aunt Gloria says, coming at Aida with her hot-pink lipstick wielded like a sword.

Aida steps back. No one wears this thick matte lipstick anymore. Girls her age wear plum-flavored lip gloss or Yardley Good Night Slicker all pale pink, almost white. "That's okay," she says.

But Aunt Gloria grabs her shoulders and holds her in

place, then smears lipstick across her bottom lip. It's oily and tastes like crayons.

"Do this," Aunt Gloria tells her, and presses her own hot-pink lips together.

Aida does the same, miserable.

"Look at you," Aunt Gloria says, grinning, her breath sour with cigarettes and Mama Jo's homemade wine. "Your whole face opens right up."

"Hey," Aida says. "Any word from Cammie?"

"She called from Chicago," Aunt Gloria says. "Who knows? She might just make it. You know she could have flown to Paris, France, with Howard Hughes but she said no, I got to go to my cousin Teresa's wedding."

Aida frowns. "But she's afraid to fly, right?"

Already, Aunt Gloria has grown bored with her. She blinks her heavily mascaraed eyes and yells, "Terry! You need a little lipstick, honey."

From somewhere in the distance, Aida hears a bell ring, muffled amid the shouting. She listens until she hears it again. Someone is at the door. Cammie, she thinks. She wants to open it, to see Cammie first. Maybe she can talk to her right away about leaving with her. Maybe they can make a plan.

Aida opens the front door and gasps. Standing right there, inches from her, is the boy in the white VW Bug. His nose is sunburned and he looks hot in his heavy blue jeans and army-green pocket T-shirt.

Immediately, Aida covers her mouth with its hot pink lips. She is meeting the second love of her life wearing an ugly dress covered with too-bright sunflowers and hot-pink old-lady lipstick. She considers closing the door and running upstairs. But it's too late. The boy is talking. At least, his lips are moving but Aida seems to have gone deaf. She can't hear anything except a buzzing in her ears.

The boy points to his car, which is parked on the sidewalk in front of their house, almost exactly in the spot where her father dropped dead.

Her hearing slowly returns. From behind her comes the sound of her mother yelling, "Is someone at the door?"

The boy is frowning at her. "Your phone? Okay?"

Somehow Aida makes sense of this. The car is broken down. He needs to call somebody.

Stupidly, she nods. She wants to tell him that she is not like the people he is about to meet. That she never wears ugly dresses with bright sunflowers or pink lipstick. *I am not who you think*, she screams in her head. But all she does is step aside and let the boy in. As he passes her, she catches a whiff of something familiar, but she cannot name it.

"Close the door!" her mother yells. "You're letting the bugs in."

Aida lets the screen door slam shut behind her. She sits on the front steps, trying not to cry.

"Get up!" Mama Jo yells through the window. "You'll get piles sitting on the cement like that."

"I don't care," Aida mumbles. She feels the weight of loss heavy on her chest. The boy will never love her. He will think her foolish and ugly and unlovable. His car sits neglected in front of her. Aida imagines all the snow that fell that day her father died. When her mother found him, she screamed so loud that Aida ran to the upstairs window to see what was wrong. Far beneath her, her father lay in the snow, his rubber boots black against it and her mother kneeling beside him in her pale-pink rubber curlers and green chenille bathrobe. They looked small from where Aida stood, like dolls.

Slowly, Aida gets up and walks over to the boy's car. She opens the door and gets in the passenger's side. The car smells like sweat and something else. She inhales. Marijuana. The whole world is stoned, Aida thinks, that weight pressing on her even harder.

Crickets sing in the evening air. Soon, people start filing out of the house, a flurry of bright colors under the street-light. The boy gets in the car and looks at her.

"Uh," he says. "I've got to wait here for the guy with the jumper cables."

Aida nods.

"Your mother said it's okay," he adds.

Her name pierces the still air: "Aida!" her mother yells. "Aida!"

The boy leans across her and goose bumps rise on her arms and legs and neck. He opens the door and without a word, speechless, dumb, Aida climbs out and follows the sound of her mother's voice.

SHE LIVED THROUGH IT. The rehearsal at the church, walking down the aisle on the arm of Eddie's stringy-haired brother Billy, again and again; the dinner afterward with Eddie's family not eating her family's food and her family not eating theirs; the wedding itself, the church so hot Mama Jo had to be taken out for air; Phyllis Cardi singing "Sunrise, Sunset" slowly and off-key; her sister stumbling when she climbed the three steps to the altar; the suffocating smells of flowers and wax and perfume; the boring priest; the boring ceremony; the flurry of joy when Eddie and Terry emerged from the church and everyone threw rice at them and snapped photographs. She lived through it all in her yellow chiana gown and dyed-to-match sandals.

Somehow, by the time they get to Club 400 for the reception, Aida feels let down, as if she had expected more, or at least expected something. Whiskey sours flow from a fountain and platters of greasy hors d'oeuvres swirl around her. The banquet hall, with its heavy maroon drapes and chairs is funereal, Aida thinks. The pale-yellow tablecloths and napkins against the dark maroon make her seasick and she steps outside.

In the parking lot a woman gets out of a red convertible and teeters toward Aida on turquoise high heels.

Aida steps into the sunlight and squints. "Cammie?" she says.

Her cousin's hair is so big and platinum blond that Aida can only think of Jayne Mansfield. When Cammie left she had wavy brown hair. Now she is a person under a big bubble of blond hair.

"Cammie?" Aida says again, softer this time.

The face under the hair might be Cammie's, but the breasts beneath the head are not. These are like bubbles too, big and round, about to burst from her low-cut turquoise dress. Aida has never seen breasts like these. Not in person, anyway. After the breasts, past the wiggling hips, are legs—miles of them. Tanned and endless legs.

Men are stopping. Men are fanning themselves with wedding invitations or handkerchiefs. Men cannot do anything but stare at Cammie.

"Doll," she says when she finally reaches Aida, "I need a drink."

Up close, there is still not much left of Cammie. The nose is smaller. The face is tanned. The pouty lips are wet and red.

"There's a whiskey-sour fountain inside," Aida manages to say.

Cammie throws her head back and laughs. "Maybe I'll jump in it later," she says, "but for now I need a real drink."

Aida follows her cousin inside. Busboys clutch their bins of dirty dishes to watch Cammie sashay by. Aida is embarrassed and proud to be walking behind such a creature. She supposes everyone in Las Vegas is this unbelievable. They must all be tall and tanned and busty. If she goes there with Cammie, perhaps she will return reborn into something like this. The idea thrills her. The idea terrifies her.

In the dark lounge, Cammie leans across the bar and orders a scotch and soda. The bartender openly stares at her breasts, which lay on top of the bar like an offering.

"Doll," Cammie says to Aida, "you want a Fresca or something?"

"A Shirley Temple?" Aida says, her voice small and soft.

"And a Shirley Temple," Cammie says to the bartender. "Extra cherries."

A slow smile crosses his face and a flush of red rises from his cheeks to the scalp beneath his thinning hair.

"You bet," he says.

When he places the drinks on the bar, he says, "These are on the house."

Cammie stands up tall, her hair and breasts making a bubbly silhouette. "Why! Really! Thank you so much." She glances at the little black name tag above his shirt pocket. "Fred," she adds.

She opens her gold purse and takes out a prescription bottle of pills, downing a few with her drink.

"Are you sick?" Aida says.

"Oh, no. These help me stay awake. After that long drive."

Cammie takes Aida's hand and wiggles her way out of the lounge. Even without turning around, Aida knows the bartender is watching. His eyes are like lasers, shooting into them.

"What a creep, huh?" Cammie says.

Aida is surprised. "But he gave us free drinks."

Cammie cups her breasts in her hands. They fill them and overflow until Aida is certain they are going to pop out.

"I paid a thousand bucks for these babies and I haven't paid for anything else since."

A waiter passing by stumbles at the sight of Cammie. She puts her empty drink on his tray and says in her breathless voice, "A scotch and soda. Tell Fred it's for Cammie."

"You bet," the waiter says.

"Where the hell's this wedding?" Cammie says, taking Aida's hand again.

Like she is walking on air, on bubbles, on nothing, Aida glides beside Cammie into the Stardust Room.

———

IT IS LATER, much later, before Aida is alone with Cammie again. They have had the soup with the escarole and miniature meatballs, the antipasto, the green salad, the ziti, the roasted chicken with potatoes and green beans amandine, the spumoni. There has been dancing to Frank Sinatra, to the Beatles, to the Rolling Stones. Terry and Eddie danced their first dance as man and wife to "And I Love Her." Aida watched as her sister, her lipstick smeared, her eyelids heavy above red eyes, hung on to Eddie's neck and Eddie kind of moved her around the dance floor. Too many whiskey sours, too many trips outside with her bridesmaids to smoke joints, had left the bride unable to walk or dance without Eddie's help. The aunts and Mama Jo and Mama G and Aida's mother took it for love. "Look at those two," everyone was whispering. "Can't wait for their wedding night."

The cake still needs to be cut and the garter removed and the bouquet thrown, but Terry's maid of honor, Celeste, is trying to get the bride straightened up enough to perform her duties.

The band begins to play "That's Amore" and a sigh passes through the Stardust Room. Everyone finds their husband or wife or lover and takes to the dance floor, leaving Aida and Cammie alone at last.

"Do you know him?" Aida asks. "Dean Martin?"

Cammie blows a few perfect *O*'s of smoke before she answers. "Oh, sure. He's always in Vegas."

Aida looks into her cousin's eyes, which are so bright they seem to be lit from somewhere deep inside her. Her legs shake up and down, up and down as she moves from cigarette to drink to cigarette.

"But do you actually *know* him?" Aida asks.

The bubble of platinum hair bobs up and down. "He's come to my show a bunch of times."

"He has?" Aida says. "Oh God, Cammie, I want to go to Vegas."

Cammie stubs out her half-smoked cigarette and finishes her millionth scotch and soda. "Sure you do," she says, distracted. "This place makes me want to jump out of my skin," she says, not looking at Aida.

Everyone on the dance floor sings along with the band: *"Ting-a-ling-a-ling, ting-a-ling-a-ling . . . "*

"What's he like?" Aida says. "Is he funny? Is he suave?"

"Oh, yeah. Sexy," Cammie says. She plays with the clasp on her purse, snapping it open and shut, open and shut.

When she takes out her bottle of pills, Aida says, "You seem pretty awake. Do you need more of those?"

"These here are different," Cammie says. "They calm me down."

"Uh-huh," Aida says, frowning.

The waiter places a fresh drink in font of Cammie. "From Fred," he says.

"You tell Fred that if he gets me drunk he's going to have to drive me home."

"He forgot my Shirley Temple," Aida says.

Cammie doesn't hear her. "Everyone comes to my act," she says. "Sammy. Joey Bishop. Johnny Carson."

"Wow," Aida says, but she doesn't feel impressed. She isn't even sure she believes her. She studies her cousin's face, searching for signs of a lie. Cammie's makeup is practically sliding off, and everything except her hair and her breasts appears to be drooping.

"What exactly is your act?" Aida asks her.

"Oh, it's something," Cammie says. "Everybody who's anybody comes to see it."

"I know," Aida says. "But what is it?" As a child, Cammie was the star of the Al Angelone School of Dance, tapping and shuffling her way across the stage in glittery top hats and sequined costumes. "Is it tap dancing?"

"Kind of," Cammie says.

Aida sighs, frustrated.

"You want to see it?" Cammie says. She says it like a challenge.

"Yes," Aida says. "I do."

Cammie stands up. "I'll go get set up and then I'll talk to the band. See if they know my music."

"Okay," Aida says.

Nothing feels right. Surely weddings were the saddest things ever. Celeste has Terry propped against a wall, and Eddie is laughing like it's the funniest thing he's ever seen. They've wheeled the cake over to them for the cutting ceremony, and Terry is wedged between it and the wall.

The cake has six layers and lots of fake yellow flowers with a plastic bride and groom on the very top. Aida worries that her sister will fall over, onto the cake. But no. Terry cuts a piece, her hands shaking like crazy while the band plays "The Farmer in the Dell" and everyone sings, *"The bride cuts the cake . . . "* Then Eddie cuts his piece and the singing changes to *"The groom cuts the cake . . . "* Terry picks up the piece she cut and looks at it, confused. But Eddie takes his piece and shoves it right in Terry's face, smearing frosting and yellow wedding cake all over her mouth and nose and cheeks.

Everyone laughs, except Aida. Eddie keeps pushing the cake into Terry's face, long after the point is made. But Terry doesn't even seem to notice. Finally, Celeste leads her away, frosting clinging to her hair and crumbs falling onto her chiana wedding gown.

"Good job, Eddie!" the bandleader says. "Now we've got a real treat. The bride's cousin, Cammie Campo, is going to perform her act, straight from Las Vegas."

Applause fills the room, and Aunt Gloria gets to her feet, pride all over her face.

"Her show is a favorite with Joey Bishop and Dean Martin," the bandleader says, grinning in his shiny black tuxedo and bright-yellow ruffled shirt. "And I have a feeling it will be a favorite of yours, too! Ladies and gentlemen, I give you, Cammie Campo!"

Aida frowns as the band begins the song. She's sat through enough Sunday nights with Mama Jo to recognize the *Bonanza* theme song, the four men bursting through a flaming map of the Ponderosa.

Cammie has changed into white hot pants and a pink sheer blouse tied under her breasts and a pink cowboy hat and matching pink cowboy boots. As she sings, she moves her hips in perfect time to the beat. A man whistles.

Cammie sings, wagging her finger, *"He's gonna fight with me . . . "*

When she points her finger right at those big breasts, men start calling out to her: "I'll fight you, baby!"

Cammie keeps on singing, about Hoss and Joe, but the way she's gyrating and shaking her breasts, no one is really listening anymore. In one swift motion her hot pants are off and her shirt is off and she's standing on the stage in the Stardust Room in a G string and little tassels on her oversize thousand-dollar breasts.

Aunt Gloria's face has changed from proud to horrified and Mama Jo is shouting something that cannot be heard over the sound of men running to the stage to get closer, men calling to Cammie.

Hands on her hips, Cammie sings her finale: *"Bonanza! Bonanza! Bonanza!"* With each "Bonanza" she swirls her breasts in such a way that the tassels spin in perfect synchronization. Aida watches them as if she has been hypnotized, as they spin so fast they become nothing but a blur, like the cheap foil pinwheels children run with in the wind.

AIDA CANNOT EXPLAIN what happens next. How Mama Jo got home or who gave her the heart medicine she only took in extreme situations, a small pill placed under her tongue. Where Cammie disappeared to after she scooped up the dollar bills men threw at her feet and left the stage, wiggling her fingers over her shoulder in farewell. How the bandleader finally brought order back to the Stardust Room and managed to get Terry on the stage to throw her bouquet into the crowd below of eager girls, their fingers reaching greedily upward to grab the daisies tied with yellow ribbon.

But it all happens. Boxed wedding cake is handed out as guests leave. This was supposed to be Aida's one job, to hand out the cake and instruct women to sleep with it under their pillow so they can dream about the man they will marry. But she refuses to do it and lets Celeste perform even this task.

Terry appears in her going-away outfit, a yellow pantsuit. She smells like she has thrown up. Still she thanks everyone and takes Eddie's hand as they leave for their honeymoon. The next day the paper says, "The couple is touring the New England States." But really they check into a motel in Narragansett and drop acid and eat mushrooms for three days.

Aida is the last to leave the Stardust Room. She walks around, touching the stained tablecloths, the lipstick-rimmed glasses, the fountain gurgling with foam. There, on the floor near the stage, is a hot-pink tassel. She picks it up and crushes it to her face.

Anything can happen, she thinks. She can step outside and everything can change. Aida lets the tassel drop to the floor, and then she does just that. She steps outside. The parking lot is nearly empty. The air is different; she smells rain in it and hears the distant rumble of thunder.

"Aida!" her mother yells.

Fat raindrops begin to fall, splattering her face.

"Aida!"

The rain comes, hard and fast, shining in the headlights and streetlights, streaming down Aida's hair and bare shoulders. Aida leans her head back, opens her mouth, and drinks.

Captain Macaroni

WHAT ROGER KNOWS, WHAT HE HAS ALWAYS KNOWN, is that his brother Davy is the best. The best student, the best athlete, the best loved. When his mother makes roast beef for dinner, she gives Davy the extra pieces, trimmed of fat and sliced just right. When Davy practices the trumpet, everyone has to be quiet so as not to disturb him. Davy can sing like a bird, run like a cheetah, do science like Einstein, and write poems like Robert Frost. Davy is bigger than life.

That is why when he got drafted and sent to Vietnam, Roger's mother started lying on the couch in the afternoons with a damp cloth on her forehead and the curtains drawn.

"Entertain yourself," she tells Roger.

Roger knows how to do that. He has been entertaining himself for his whole life. He goes into Davy's empty room and touches everything on the desk. The typewriter. The trophy for football and the other one for baseball. He picks up the books lined up there. *The Making of the President* and *In Cold Blood*. Roger picks up *In Cold Blood* and reads: *On November 15, 1959, in the small town of Holcomb, Kansas, four members of the Clutter family were savagely murdered by blasts from a shotgun held a few inches from their faces. There was no apparent motive for the crime, and there were almost no clues.*

Creeped-out, he puts the book back on the desk. Why would Davy read a book like that? He stretches out on Davy's bed with its brown-and-gold plaid blanket and stares up at the ceiling, pretending he's Davy. What would it feel like to be his brother? To be so special? Did he lie here at night and fantasize about going into space? Or playing his trumpet in a jazz band? Or kissing his girlfriend, Diane? Ever since Davy left for Vietnam, Diane comes over for dinner every Tuesday night. She brings dessert from one of the Italian bakeries. His mother pretends to be grateful for the pastries, but later she will say, *I didn't leave Rhode Island and a bunch of wops to eat cannolis in Connecticut.*

Diane's hair is short in the back and teased on top, with little bangs. She outlines her eyes in thick black eyeliner and sometimes she wears false eyelashes and short white go-go boots. At some point during the evening she breaks into tears and tells them how much she misses Davy. Before he left for Vietnam he gave her a tiny diamond ring. They are not engaged; they are pre-engaged. Even though Roger's mother spends a good part of her days and nights crying, whenever Diane cries his mother stays dry-eyed. She lights a cigarette and sits back in her chair and watches Diane through narrowed eyes.

"I love Diane," Roger always says after Diane leaves. "Don't you love Diane?"

"You're twelve years old," his mother tells him. "What do you know about it?"

From Davy's bed, Roger sees Davy's old ventriloquist's

dummy sitting on the top shelf of the bookcase. For a while, Davy used to sit in the living room and practice ventriloquism, holding the dummy on his lap and talking without moving his lips. Except he did move them. Roger always saw them wiggling. He never pointed that out, though, because everybody always said what a good ventriloquist Davy was, how they couldn't even tell that was his voice coming from the dummy.

Their sister, Debbie, used to be afraid of the dummy and she cried whenever Davy practiced his ventriloquism. *Use your voice*, she used to beg. But Davy just kept wiggling his lips and moving the dummy's mouth, swiveling its head and flapping its arms. Davy was the oldest. Then came Debbie, five years younger. She used to have pretty soft blond hair and a soft belly. But now she is all hard sharp angles in hip-hugger jeans and a ratty Army jacket. Her hair turned a muddy brown and hangs down to her butt. She stays in her room mostly and plays Bob Dylan records. She is only three years older than Roger, but she seems much, much further away from him than that.

Roger takes the dummy down from the shelf and stares at his creepy face. His cheeks are round, like he's hiding food in them, and his nose is like Bob Hope's. Roger can't remember the name Davy gave the dummy, so he renames it Mike Nesmith after his favorite Monkee. He wishes he had a knit cap like the real Mike Nesmith wears for his Mike Nesmith. Maybe his Mama Jo will knit one for him. Even though Mama Jo smells like onions frying and maybe vaguely fishy, he loves her more than anything. Roger likes to sit on her lap and pinch the wrinkly skin on the top of her hand together, then watch how it stays that way for a long time before slowly settling back into place. Mama Jo is ancient.

Roger sticks his hand in Mike Nesmith's back and makes his arms and legs flop around. He swivels the head and opens and closes the mouth.

"Roger?" his mother calls wearily. "What are you doing?"

"Entertaining myself," he answers.

"You're not in Davy's room, are you?"

"No," he says, lifting Mike Nesmith's right leg and crossing it over his left one.

ROGER TRIES IT. He tries to talk without moving his lips.

"I hope Davy gets killed in Vietnam," he says, pushing the words through his closed mouth.

"Don't say things like that," Roger says in his regular voice. He gives Mike Nesmith a hard shake. "Don't ever say that again."

Mike Nesmith stares back at him with his heavy-lidded eyes.

ONE OF THE THINGS that his mother always reminds him of is that even though his ancestors are Italian, he is American. "We all are," she says. "You and me and Daddy and Davy and Debbie. We're American." Even when he had to do a report in school last year called "My Heritage," his mother wanted him to write about living in Connecticut and the big Fourth of July party she threw every year.

"But I want to write about Mama Jo," Roger said. He stared down at the yellow paper with blue lines, his pencil poised over it. "I want to write about being Italian."

His mother had looked at him with a hard, even gaze. "But we're American, sweetie," she'd said. "Doesn't Davy play football and baseball? Don't I make the yummiest pies?"

"Yes," he said, wondering what pie and football had to do with anything.

He wanted his mother to praise him, like she praised Davy. So he wrote about living in Connecticut and the Fourth of July party and all the things she told him made them American. For his last line, Roger wrote: *I am American through and through and proud.* His mother smiled when she read it and told him it was the best paper he'd ever handed in. But the day they read their papers out loud, it was Gilda DiCaprio who had the best paper, and Gilda wrote about her Italian grandmother and helping her make meatballs. Gilda's last line was: *Even though I live in America, I will always be Italian in my heart.* The teacher actually got teary-eyed when Gilda read that, and the whole class applauded. Except Roger. He stared at his own stupid paper and tried very hard not to rip it up.

THE DAY THE TWO SOLDIERS in their neat, crisp uniforms ring the doorbell with the news, Roger is home from school sick with tonsillitis. *Golf balls,* Dr. DiMarco said when he came to the house the night before, swinging his black bag. *Tonsils as big as golf balls.* Roger's mother made the doctor coffee and waited outside the bedroom door holding a cup of it for him while he examined Roger's throat. She put on perfume, too, which made Roger's throat hurt even more.

After Dr. DiMarco gave him a shot of penicillin, he patted Roger's head and told him to sleep. Then he went and sat with his mother in the kitchen, the sound of their voices rising and falling lulling Roger to sleep. In the morning, he tried to get his mother to play Crazy Eights with him, but she said she wasn't in the mood.

That is why Roger is on the couch under one of the afghans Mama Jo crocheted watching *Jeopardy!* when the doorbell rings. Art Fleming is one of his heroes. Roger believes Art Fleming knows all of the answers that the contestants say in the form of a question. He believes that Art Fleming is maybe the smartest man in the world.

The category is "Fairy-tale Heroes."

"In this fairy tale," Art Fleming says, "she restores Ariel's voice."

"Roger," his mother calls from somewhere in the house. "Are you too sick to get the door?"

Roger wants Paul Marx from Phoenix, Arizona, to win, mostly because he has two *x*'s in his biographical information but also because he is an amateur ventriloquist. During the interview portion of the program, Art Fleming asked Paul Marx to talk without moving his lips, and Paul Marx said: *What is the art of ventriloquism, Art?* His lips really didn't move, unlike Davy's.

Paul Marx doesn't buzz in fast enough and the three-day winner answers correctly.

The doorbell rings again.

"Roger?" his mother says. "Tell whoever it is that I'm busy."

She is vacuuming. She vacuums all the time, rolling the baby-blue Electrolux around the house with a vengeance.

"I'll take 'Fairytale Heroes' for three hundred," the three-day winner is saying.

Roger sighs and gets up from the couch. He has on his old fuzzy footy pajamas, red ones with cowboys and Indians on them. They don't really fit anymore; there is a hole in the feet part and his big toes poke out. He will always remember that he was wearing those pajamas that day, and that as soon as the men left he went into Davy's bedroom, took them off, and cut them into pieces with the scissors in the desk drawer.

Just as he opens the door, he hears the vacuum turning on.

Surprised to see Army men there, he thinks maybe the Russians have attacked Connecticut and the Army is here to evacuate them.

"Should I pack my stuff?" Roger asks them. He tries to think what he should take and what he should leave behind. Mike Nesmith he will take. Underwear. Socks. His toothbrush.

"Is your mother or father at home?" one of them says, looking straight ahead at a spot somewhere above Roger's head.

Both men are tall and lean and clean-shaven. Their hats sit low on their foreheads and their jackets have all sorts of medals and stripes and patches, not unlike Davy's Boy Scout uniform.

"Um," Roger says, "my mother's busy." His father is never home anymore. He is on the road, selling copy machines.

"Please get your mother, son," the same man says.

Roger hesitates. She is going to be mad at him for sure. When she says she doesn't feel like talking or seeing people, she means it. Ever since Davy left for Vietnam, his mother avoided everybody. Iris from next door, who always brought tomatoes or zinnias or whatever was in her garden—*Just tell her to leave it on the table*, she'd instruct Roger; the milkman, who showed up whistling every Saturday morning with two bottles of regular milk, one bottle of chocolate milk, and a small bottle of cream—*Just give him the order for next week, Roger*; the paperboy, Bobby Anderson, who came around suppertime on Tuesday nights to collect payment—*Roger, get the money out of my purse and make sure to give him an extra dollar.* She didn't want to be bothered and Roger's job was to make sure she wasn't.

"I can't," he tells the Army men. "She's super-busy."

The same one kneels down so that he is eye to eye with Roger. "The United States of America requires your mother to come here, son." His breath smells like the Black Jack gum that Mama Jo chews.

Roger swallows hard. "Like the president?"

"Right," the man says.

Slowly, Roger follows the sound of the vacuum. At school they did a drill. *Let's say the Russians have dropped the atom bomb*, his teacher Miss Sullivan would say. *What are you going to do? Duck and cover!* the class shouted, and they all hid under their desks. Is that why the Army men are here?

"Mom?" he says.

She is pushing the vacuum across the mauve wall-to-wall carpeting on her bedroom floor.

She doesn't turn around. She doesn't turn off the vacuum.

"I think the Russians," Roger says, and then he begins to cry. "I think they dropped the atom bomb in Connecticut."

"Uh-huh," she says.

He watches how hard she pushes the hose, like she is at battle with dust bunnies.

"I think we have to evacuate." Crying makes his throat hurt more, but he can't help it.

"And why do you think this?"

Her back is bent over the Electrolux. She has on orange pants and a flowered top that doesn't quite match. It must be laundry day.

"Because the Army is here and President Johnson said so."

Without turning off the vacuum, his mother slowly swivels around to face him. There is a look on her face that he's never seen on anyone before.

"Tell them I'm busy," she says.

Roger shakes his head. "They said—"

His mother opens her mouth and screams, "Tell them I'm busy!"

The way she sounds scares him and he runs out of the room, all the way back to the door where the two men still wait, standing at attention, staring at something Roger can not see. From behind him, he hears his mother wailing. For an instant, one of the Army men's jaw tightens and he swallows in a way that makes his Adam's apple bob up and down, like someone trying not to cry.

EVERY SUMMER MAMA JO goes to Vermont to visit Auntie Chiara, the nun. Her nun name is Sister Sebastian. Roger believes that she doesn't have any hair—just a high, smooth forehead that ends in her stiff, white wimple. The wimple is topped by a long black veil that makes a sound like someone saying *shush* when she moves. This summer, Mama Jo is taking Roger to Vermont with her so that his mother can recover. She is mourning Davy and as far as Roger can tell, mourning is a full-time job. Ever since the Army men came to tell them that Davy was MIA and presumed dead, Roger has not been able to look his mother in the eye. He had wished his brother dead, and now he was.

His father packs the medium-sized piece of American Tourister luggage for him, keeping up a cheerful banter the whole while.

"Covered bridges, Roger," his father says. "And little candy shaped like maple leaves. And good cheese. Boy, are you in for a treat."

When his father sold Royal typewriters, Vermont was part of his territory. He knows these things.

"What are the bridges covered with?" Roger asks him.

His father frowns. "Wood," he says.

"Oh," Roger says, disappointed.

"THAT THING NOT COMING," Mama Jo says, pointing to Mike Nesmith. Then she says something in Italian.

"She thinks he's sacrilegious," Mama G says.

Mama G is driving them to Vermont. They will sleep in motels with beds that shake if you put a coin in them. There will be swimming pools too, and real maple syrup for their pancakes. *Aunt Jemima*, Roger's father told him, *she's nothing but a fake.*

Everyone stands around Mama G's dark-green Valiant, waiting for Roger's mother to come out and say good-bye.

But Roger knows she won't. She isn't speaking to Mama Jo. Right after the Army men came, Mama Jo arrived. *I know what it's like to lose a child, figlia mia,* she'd said, wrapping her arms around his mother. But his mother pulled away. *How dare you?* she'd said. *You have no idea. None.* Then his mother slapped Mama Jo across the face and went back into her bedroom. All the aunts screamed and yelled, but Mama Jo just said, *Let her go. I understand.* For days afterward his mother would blurt, *How could she say such a thing?*

When it becomes clear that Roger's mother isn't coming out, Roger and Mama Jo climb into the backseat and Mama G takes her place behind the wheel and they back out of the driveway. The car smells like Christmas trees from the tree-shaped air freshener that hangs off the rearview mirror. The front seats have strange beaded covers over them, adding to Roger's feeling that he has entered an exotic magical world. He doesn't even wave good-bye or look at his father standing there. He is so filled with relief that he is leaving that all he can do is pinch the skin on Mama Jo's hand and watch it stay there a moment before settling back down.

EVEN THOUGH MAMA JO can't speak very good English, somehow Roger understands her. He knows when she is tired or hungry or when something strikes her as funny. It has always been this way. Most of the family ignores her, or treats her like she is a nuisance, when all she does really is cook for them and crochet afghans that everyone thinks are hideous. Except Roger. He loves them, loves the clashing colors and wavy pattern. Mama Jo gives him coffee with lots of milk and sugar in a chipped bowl. *He's too young for coffee!* his mother scolds her, but Mama Jo pretends she doesn't hear her.

Sometimes Roger wishes he could crawl inside Mama Jo's head and see the world through her eyes. Once he told his mother this and she looked at him horrified. His mother doesn't like most of the things Mama Jo cooks, like veal and peas or polenta with kale. But Roger does. On the rare visits they make from Connecticut to Rhode Island, to see Mama Jo and the rest of the family, he eats so much that he has to take an Alka-Seltzer before bed. *Too much oil*, his mother says, grimacing in disgust. Mama Jo gives him a tiny glass of apricot brandy for his stomachache. During the night, she comes in to check him. He can smell Black Jack gum and Milk of Magnesia on her breath as she leans over to touch his forehead. Her hands are not soft like his mother's, They're calloused and rough and smell like garlic. Mama Jo whispers something in Italian, and even though Roger doesn't know what it means, he understands that she is telling him she loves him.

On the ride to Vermont, Mama Jo keeps surprising him with treats that she pulls from her big black bag.

"Mama Jo," Roger says in the car as he leans his head against her arm, "will you teach me how to cook someday?"

Mama Jo pats his head.

"Do you think Davy's dead?" Roger asks her.

"Morto," Mama Jo says.

MIA is better, Roger knows that. MIA means living with buffoonish officers like on *Hogan's Heroes.* Even though his father explained that Hogan isn't MIA, he's a POW, a prisoner of war, Roger still pictures Davy performing zany antics at a camp.

But when Mama Jo says *"morto"* with such decisiveness, Roger sits up straight.

"He's dead?" he asks her.

"Eh," she says, raising her hands in defeat.

IT IS ALREADY DARK when they get to Vermont. Mama G puts a quarter in the coin slot on his bed and Roger lies there as the bed rocks back and forth. In the morning they will let him swim in the pool before they continue north to Sister Sebastian's convent. For now, Mama Jo and Mama G are tired. They climb into the bed across from his, both of them in long white nightgowns. Mama G has three pink curlers on the top of her head, and Mama Jo has taken all of the bobby pins out of her hair to reveal a long white braid. In no time, they are both asleep.

But Roger can't sleep. The room is too dark and it smells strange. He wishes he had Mike Nesmith with him. The dummy is not cuddly, but it would be nice to feel its weight beside him on the bed, to maybe see its white teeth in the dark. Every time Roger closes his eyes, he thinks about Davy being dead instead of playing tricks on a group of Ho Chi Minhs. That thought makes him so scared he calls Mama Jo's name out loud.

"Basta," she says in a tone that lets him know he should be quiet.

Roger squeezes his eyes shut. He tries not to miss Mike Nesmith. He tries not to think about being dead. Or how his most secret wish has maybe come true. He tries not to think about what will become of his mother now that she doesn't have Davy to love. To calm himself, he thinks about Mama Jo. Once he saw a picture of her as a young woman, before most of her teeth fell out and before she got so many wrinkles, and she looked almost pretty. In school he had to make a family tree and his mother said, *Be sure to put everyone's American names, sweetie. Okay,* Roger said. *But what's Mama Jo's American name?* His mother had to think hard before she answered, *Joanne.*

But lying here in the dark with Mama Jo snoring softly and the room a heady mix of the cheese in her purse and the mildewed carpet and Black Jack gum, Roger doesn't care what his mother says. He isn't American. He's Italian. He can feel it seep inside him. Someday he will be able to stir the polenta with that big wooden spoon until it is done. No lumps. He will be able to speak fluent Italian so he can talk to Mama Jo about her long life, and he will carry pepper biscuits in his pockets to nibble during the day. He will change his name so that everyone knows he is Italian. Roger is a terrible American name. So is Debra, his sister's name. *So is Davy,* Roger whispers to himself.

He will become an Italian superhero. He will become Captain Macaroni, the bravest Italian ever. Captain Macaroni can fly and cook and be invisible. But his biggest superpower is that Captain Macaroni will never die.

Maybe he fell asleep. Or maybe time just went by. But as Roger lies there, he feels something changing. His arms and legs grow hard and rigid. Daylight peeks in through the heavy curtains, and in its soft silver light Roger can see his transformation. His legs are lasagna noodles, his arms long strands of spaghetti. His torso is rigatoni, his ears two perfect orecchiette.

From the other bed, Mama Jo lets out a long, low fart and begins to stir awake.

"Roger?" she says.

But he cannot answer her. He cannot move his penne fingers or his small shell toes. He is ziti and ravioli and gnocchi. He is Captain Macaroni.

"Roger?" Mama Jo says again, and her voice is anxious.

Roger wishes he could answer her. He wishes she would just look over at him, silent and happy in his hard, empty shell. She wishes she could see that he is Captain Macaroni, protected, loved, invincible.

The Boy on the Bus

"I'M RUNNING AWAY," AIDA WHISPERS INTO THE DARKness of the Greyhound bus as it hurtles west.

It is her nightly ritual. This is her third night on the bus. A week ago, she bought a Greyhound "See the USA" pass for ninety-nine dollars. She stole the money from her sister, Terry, who got it from selling pot. Terry kept her earnings in her underwear drawer and the night before Aida bought the pass, when she was babysitting for Terry's baby, Dylan, she went into the bedroom, opened the cigar box, and pulled out three hundred dollars: one hundred for the "See the USA" pass, two hundred for expenses.

She has only gotten as far as Pittsburgh, but that is farther than Aida has ever been in her life. Once, her aunt Francie and Mama Jo took her along on a car trip to see fall foliage in Vermont. Aida got carsick on the winding back roads and Aunt Francie worried about the upholstery. They came home three days later, exhausted from each other. In seventh grade she took a class trip to Mystic, Connecticut, where they climbed aboard old schooners and fishing boats, ate lunch at Burger Chef, then toured historic homes. Aida bought a white bracelet made from rope that she hasn't taken off in four years. Last year Terry took her to Boston. She made Aida drive even though she only had a learner's permit because, as Terry said, "I'm too wasted." Aida hadn't even learned to merge yet, but she drove Terry's baby-blue Bug all the way into the city, Terry red-eyed and stoned the whole way, her head lolling all funny and her fingers twitching in time to the eight-track Aztec Two Step tape stuck inside. That stupid tape played over and over because no one could get it out and the radio was busted.

That was it: puking in Vermont, a school trip to Mystic, and a drug deal in the Combat Zone in Boston, Aida looking the other way the whole time, keeping busy by deciding what she would order at the Chinese restaurant, Terry's way of thanking her for driving. But now, here she was, alone, on a Greyhound bus leaving Pittsburgh. The city had a funny green tone and smelled like chemistry class.

The woman beside Aida also smelled sour. She kept muttering, "I'll show him. Yes, I will. I will show that man. Hmmph." In front of her sat two women wearing large hats. One hat was red and decorated with plastic cherries; the other one was yellow and covered with silk flowers. Even in the dark, Aida could see those cherries and flowers dipping and bobbing as the women wearing them bent their heads together, talking conspiratorially.

"I'm running away," Aida whispered again, loving the way it sounded in the still bus.

"So am I," came a voice from across the aisle.

Aida's breath caught. She squinted to see who had said it. A boy, maybe nineteen years old, grinned back at her. He was smoking a cigarette. He had a dimple in his chin, like Kirk Douglas, and a good suntan.

"You weren't supposed to hear that," Aida said. If anyone knew she was only seventeen years old and running away from home, she would be hauled off this bus and sent back to Rhode Island.

"Then you shouldn't keep saying it," he said, smiling his white teeth at her.

"Hmmph," Aida said, just like her seatmate. She folded her arms across her chest and focused straight ahead at the hats.

The boy leaned toward her. "I'm supposed to get *married*," he whispered. "On Saturday."

He smelled good. Like cigarettes and aftershave. Now that his head was in the aisle like that, she saw that he was as cleanshaven as a person could be and had short hair and no sideburns. She frowned. She hadn't seen a guy with so little hair since her cousin Davy shipped off to Vietnam. She thought of Davy and made a quick sign of the cross, hoping the boy didn't see her doing something so uncool. May he rest in peace, she thought, then dropped her hands.

"What are you?" Aida said, not bothering to whisper. "In the Army or something?"

"Not anymore," the boy said, and sat back in his seat.

The *Army*? Aida thought. Ugh. She opened her book, *The Tin Drum*, by Günter Grass, and pretended to read. It was about a dwarf during World War II, and sad. Aida didn't really like the book; she'd preferred *To Kill a Mockingbird*, which they'd read in tenth grade. And *Lord of the Flies*. Also from tenth grade. But books like that looked young, school-girlish, not the kind of books a person took with them to run away. In her overnight bag she had *Siddhartha*, *The Electric Kool-Aid Acid Test*, and Rod McKuen's book of poetry, *Stanyan Street and Other Sorrows*. Stanyan Street was in San Francisco, and that was where she was headed.

"You ever read *Lord of the Flies?*" the boy asked. He was leaning toward her again, his head jutting out into the aisle, bouncing along with the movement of the bus.

"In high school," Aida said, not taking her eyes from her book.

"That's what Vietnam was like," he said. "No shit."

Aida swallowed hard. All spring, when she imagined this bus trip across the country, she always imagined meeting a boy. A boy with a guitar who sang Simon and Garfunkel songs as the bus rolled toward California. She and the boy would fall in love, and walk in meadows filled with wildflowers like in the Herbal Essences commercial. He would wear a flowing shirt, Guatemalan, or Mexican, kind of like Donovan. They would have their first kiss in a rainstorm. Aida sighed. Never, in any of her fantasies, was the boy she would fall in love with on a bus a Vietnam vet. Every day last year she had worn a black armband to school to protest the war. Baby killer, she thought, turning the page she had not read. Hawk.

"What are you running away from?" the boy asked her.

She glanced at him. His eyes were light, blue or maybe green; it was hard to tell in the dark. He had small ears. Usually, you didn't see a boy's ears because his hair covered them. This boy's ears looked like seashells.

"Like I said," he continued, "I'm running away from my wedding. How about you?"

"I'm moving to San Francisco," she said matter-of-factly.

"No shit!" he said. "Me too. Guess we're together for the long haul."

He lit another cigarette. "Smoke?" he said.

Aida shook her head. "I only smoke clove cigarettes," she said. This wasn't true, but she had seen them in a head shop in Providence, where her sister, Terry, sold her homemade hash pipes. Terry and her husband carved the pipes themselves out of soapstone. One day, while Terry was dropping off a load of new ones, Aida had seen the small square packages of clove cigarettes, red and covered with Hindu signs and letters. Aida knew that if she ever smoked anything, it would be clove cigarettes. She had considered asking Terry to buy her a pack. Terry would have; she didn't care what Aida did. Terry only cared about getting stoned. Her whole life revolved around scoring good pot, windowpane LSD, and magic mushrooms. She and her husband spent all their time at the pay phone in the gas station down the street from their apartment making drug deals. For this reason, Aida did not feel guilty for stealing their money.

"Clove cigarettes?" the boy said, sucking on his Winston. "Interesting." Then he sat back in his seat and didn't say anything else until the bus stopped somewhere in Ohio.

AIDA LOVED THE BUS STATIONS. They were dirty and gray and smelled like pee, every one of them so far. Usually a janitor was mopping the floor. Usually people were sleeping on the benches. Usually, the ladies' rooms were out of toilet paper, or a toilet had flooded, or someone had left poop without flushing. Aida loved getting food from the vending machines: cheese sandwiches cut into perfect triangles, slightly stale and tasting of cardboard; watery hot chocolate that was tepid at best; M&M's; Fritos.

Aida stood in front of the row of vending machines, making her choices. Across the room, a fat man with a wandering eye mopped the floor and sang, "Hit the Road, Jack," in a booming baritone. She spotted a cheese sandwich and carefully counted out three quarters. Just as she reached to put in the first coin, a hand stopped her.

The Vietnam vet.

He was tall and broad-shouldered, like someone on a football team.

"Let me buy you some real food," he said. He jerked his thumb toward a diner attached to the bus station. Through a plate-glass window, Aida could see uniformed waitresses, slouched and weary, pouring coffee for the passengers from her bus.

"I like these sandwiches," she said.

"Ah, get one next time. We're here for an hour anyway." He tugged on her arm and she followed him, lagging behind so he didn't get the wrong idea. He wore khaki pants and a blue button-down shirt. She could see the white of a T-shirt poking out behind the collar. She wondered how he could wear long pants and long sleeves in July. Wasn't he sweating to death? Maybe he was wounded, she thought. Maybe he had scars. This made her like him more, and she quickened her pace to catch up.

He slid into a booth, red ripped vinyl with big strips of green masking tape over some of the rips and puffs of white filling popping out. The table was sticky, and the ashtray was dirty. The vet lit another cigarette.

"Those clove things you smoke," he said, "do you get high from them?"

Aida rolled her eyes. "They're *cigarettes*," she said.

The waitress came over. She only had about five teeth in her whole mouth. Except for her great-grandmother, Aida had never seen a person walking around without teeth like that. She couldn't stop staring.

"You gonna kiss me or order some food?" the woman said.

"Oh, uh, pancakes? And chocolate milk?"

The vet ordered three eggs and home fries and bacon and ham and a short stack of pancakes. "And chocolate milk," he added, winking at Aida.

Winking was smarmy. She hated winking. She pretended not to notice.

"So," he said, after the waitress walked away, "you going to college or something out there?"

Aida brightened. "Yes," she said with too much enthusiasm.

"You have friends or something there?"

"An uncle," she said. This was maybe true. Five years ago, her uncle Carmine had walked into the house and announced he was moving to San Francisco. He had seen on television that people there believed in free love. "I'm going to get me some," Uncle Carmine said. He tied a plastic daisy to the radio antenna on his Dodge and drove off. No one had heard from him since. Mama Jo said novenas to pray for his safety, and once asked Aida to call Information to see if he was listed. But he wasn't.

"He's, like, seventy years old," Aida said. "But he's cool."

Their food arrived and the vet started eating like he hadn't had anything in a million years.

"Aren't you hot?" Aida said as she carefully cut her pancakes into triangles.

"Yes, I am," he said. "But I walked out of our double shower and this is what I was wearing. Walked out, bought a ticket to San Francisco, and here I am." He shook his head as if he couldn't believe it himself.

"You left the bride? At her shower?" Aida said. The maple syrup tasted funny, like kerosene. She scraped it off her pancakes.

"I'm terrible," he said. "I know. But I just couldn't stay."

Aida understood this. That's why she was running away. She couldn't stay in that house, in that town, for even one more minute.

"Beth," he said. "She'll do fine. She's real pretty and nice. Studying to be a nurse." He shook his head again. "She'll be fine." He motioned the waitress for more chocolate milk, holding up two fingers like a peace sign. "We dated in high school, and then I got unlucky in the lottery. Number three, if you can believe it, and got sent to Vietnam instead of Carnegie Mellon, where I was supposed to go. And you know, when you think you might die, you do crazy things. Like say if you manage to live and come back, you'll marry somebody. Then you come back and you've changed a lot and the girl doesn't even seem like someone you know. She's talking about getting shoes dyed lavender to match bridesmaids' dresses and seating arrangements and whiskey-sour fountains and all you can think about is the way you were walking along this gorgeous mountain pass and the South China Sea is glittering in the sunlight and all of a fucking sudden you're getting shot at and people are dying all around you and you don't even know what the fuck you're doing halfway across the world anyway."

The waitress banged down two glasses of chocolate milk.

"You're saving democracy," she said to him, air whistling through the gaps where teeth were supposed to be. "That's what you're doing over there."

"Right," he mumbled.

Aida stared at him, hard.

"What?" he said.

"Do you play the guitar?" she asked him. But she didn't really want to hear the answer, so she got up, banging her knee on the booth, and walked back to the bus.

DURING THE STOP, passengers got off and other passengers got on and everything rearranged itself. Aida grabbed an open window seat. She had not had a window seat in three days, and wasn't part of running away seeing things? Wasn't the bus pass called the "See the USA" pass? Here was Ohio, Aida thought happily. I am watching Ohio go by. The vet took the seat next to her.

"This is lucky," he says as he stretches his legs. "Isn't it?"

The bus pulls away and Aida stares with determination out the window.

"Ohio," the vet says. "I think it produced more presidents than any other state."

Aida finds this hard to believe. "What about Massachusetts?" she says, watching the rolling hills. "What about Virginia?"

"Can you name the presidents for those states? Let's try, okay?"

She looks at his open, hopeful face. Does he really expect her to play car games with him the entire way to San Francisco? She remembers how on that car trip with Aunt Francie, she had to play Travel Bingo, keeping her eye out for cows and stop signs and other ridiculous things. The Bingo cards had little red see-through shades that you pulled down when you found an item. But reading the cards and scanning the back roads for mailboxes and silos had only made Aida more queasy.

"I hate games," Aida tells him.

"This isn't a game," he says. "It's more of a challenge."

Aida sighs. "Look," she says, "you need to know that I'm against the war. I hate Richard Nixon, and I've been very active in the antiwar movement." She thinks of that black armband, how much she loved tying it on every morning.

"I'm glad to know that," he tells her. "I'm also against the war. You have no idea."

Aida tries to figure out the ethics of falling in love with a vet. It seems wrong, even if he is also against the war.

"I'm Bill," he says. "Bill Henderson."

Aida blurts her own name before remembering that she was going to change it to something like Heather or Juliet. Aida is old-fashioned and ugly. She adds, "Aida with an A," to make it special somehow.

Bill nods at her. "Like the opera," he says. "I-ee-da."

He has given her a gift and he doesn't even know it. I-ee-da, she thinks. An opera. She would have to look that up in the library when she got to San Francisco.

"Well," she says finally. "There's Jefferson and Monroe and Washington. They're all from Virginia."

She can feel his knee against hers. He has rolled up the sleeves on his shirt, and she can see the light blond hair on his arms, the beginning of a five o'clock shadow on his fine angled cheeks.

"The two Adamses," he says, "John and John Quincy. They're Massachusetts. And Kennedy, of course."

Ohio rolls by, but Aida isn't watching.

THEY NAME ALL the state capitals. The states themselves, alphabetically. The Seven Dwarves. The Seven Deadly Sins. Aida wonders if he will kiss her. Or even hold her hand. Bill Henderson is a tragic hero. She knows that loving a tragic hero is morally right. He tells her his middle name is Warren. In her mind she says his name over and over: William Warren Henderson.

At night, he lets her put her head on his shoulder, his own windbreaker rolled up beneath it as a pillow. Aida whispers, "I'm running away." She expects him to say it too. This can be their private ritual. But he is already asleep.

Sometime in the middle of the night, the bus pulls into St. Louis. She is too tired to get up and walk around and he promises to bring her one of the vending machine cheese sandwiches if they have them. Aida watches through half-open eyes as he goes into the bus station and walks directly to a bank of pay phones. She sits up straight. Is he calling Beth? An image of the cover of *Cherry Ames: Student Nurse* comes to her. Does Beth look like that? Does she have adventures? Bill feeds change into the phone and wraps the cord around his hand as he talks. He looks pained, she thinks. Maybe he's telling Beth that he has already met someone new.

After he hangs up, he disappears into the station. Aida holds her breath. What if he is getting on a bus back? But soon enough he appears again, and walks outside, straight to the bus. When he sees her watching him, he holds a cheese sandwich up for her to see. Aida exhales. This is what it is like to have a boyfriend, she thinks, wondering when they will kiss and what it will feel like.

THEY ARE DRIVING through Kansas, which is flat and long. This is the west, Aida tells herself. She is out west now.

"Middle name," he says.

"Don't have one," Aida tells him. "My sister is Teresa Josephine. The Josephine is after our great-grandmother. But I'm just Aida. Like the opera," she adds.

"Date of birth," he says.

"I'm a Cancer," she tells him.

"Whatever that means." He laughs.

"I have the same birthday as Ringo Starr."

He elbows her lightly in the ribs. "Come on," he says.

Is she imagining it, or is his arm pressed closer to her than it was? Maybe she should hold *his* hand.

"July seventh," Aida says, and wiggles a bit so that everything of hers is just a little closer to all of him. He doesn't move away.

"I'm October ninth," he says.

"What? That's John Lennon's birthday!" Aida says. They are like half the Beatles, she and Bill Henderson. Surely this is a sign.

"That makes me a . . ."

"Libra," she says. She wishes she had brought her copy of Linda Goodman's *Sun Signs* with her. Then she could read it out loud to him, read all about Libras and how well Cancer and Libra got along together.

"That's right," he says. "The Scales. Indecisive, right?" He laughs sarcastically. "Beth would agree with that, I guess."

At the sound of Beth's name, Aida's stomach hurts.

"All she did was yell at me last night when I called. Yelled that I woke her up. Yelled that I walked out. Yelled about all the electric can openers and fondue pots and yogurt makers she has to return if I don't get my ass back to Pittsburgh."

"Well," Aida says, her mouth suddenly so dry she can hear her tongue smacking as she talks, "did you tell her you're not going back to Pittsburgh? That you're on your way to San Francisco?"

Bill shakes his head. "Boy, can she yell," he says. He says it like it's not a bad thing, but something marvelous.

THE ROCKY MOUNTAINS are snowcapped and purple in the distance. Aida can't stop looking at them. She slept the night with her head on his windbreaker again, the windbreaker rolled up against his shoulder. Sometime during the night Bill had reached for her hand and held it lightly. Now, as the bus pulls into Denver, where they would have to change to a new bus, he is still holding on. Aida turns from the mountains and looks right into his eyes. She puts a spell on him; the spell will make him kiss her in Denver. If they see three particular things, the spell will work. She chooses the things: a man in a cowboy hat, a pregnant woman, and someone asking for change. Satisfied, she lets Bill tug her to her feet. He doesn't let go of her hand as he guides her down the aisle and off the bus.

She expects Denver to be cold with those mountains so close. But instead it is hot and humid. Aida worries that her hand will start to sweat and Bill will get grossed out and get on a bus going east. But he drops her hand altogether in order to open the door for her to step inside. The bus station is bustling, and crowded. To her delight, there are lots of men in cowboy hats. Lots of them. She is one-third on her way to her first kiss.

As she stands beneath the departure board, peering up, Bill comes behind her and casually puts his hands on her shoulders and massages her sore muscles. Aida thinks that she can stand there like that forever. She doesn't ever want him to stop.

But he does. He points to the board and says, "Gate Eleven."

Aida turns to follow him and almost walks into a hugely pregnant woman.

"Excuse me," Aida says so happily the woman shakes her head at her. Two-thirds there. Her eyes scan the station. There must be at least one panhandler here.

Their bus pulls into Gate Eleven as soon as they arrive. From somewhere nearby, Aida can hear a guitar and the soft voices of a man and woman singing in harmony.

"Be right back," Bill whispers right into her ear, his breath warm.

Aida is tingly with excitement. A kiss on a bus leaving Denver with a tragic hero is even more thrilling than one in a meadow, even in the rain. She sees Bill push his way through the crowd and walk directly to a pay phone.

The couple is singing, "I'll taste your strawberries . . . I'll drink your sweet wine . . . "

He is talking, agitated, his face scrunched up in frustration.

The line starts moving forward. People are getting on the bus, and Aida worries that Bill will not even notice.

A scratchy announcement calls passengers for the bus to San Francisco, and Aida starts waving like crazy. But Bill has his back turned and can't see her.

The bus is right there, waiting, the front like a grinning cartoon bus. Above the window, Aida watches the sign shift from DENVER to SAN FRANCISCO. Behind her, she hears thundering footsteps, Bill's voice calling for her to wait up. Is there a kiss coming? Or is he going to simply wave good-bye as the bus pulls away? She keeps moving forward; she has to.

Someone tugs at her arm and she turns, expecting to see Bill. Instead, it is a dirty girl, not much older than Aida herself. Dirty bare feet, tangled blond hair, a peasant blouse with unraveling embroidery. Beside her is a bearded boy, also dirty, also barefoot, a guitar slung over his shoulder.

"Did you like our singing?" the girl is asking, but all Aida hears is Bill trying to get through the crowd, calling her name.

"My name is Melody," the girl says. She holds a wilted daisy out for Aida, her hand trembling.

"Melody," she says again, smiling in a way that makes Aida think of her sister Teresa, stoned and foggy.

Aida takes the flower and, unsure what to do with it, tucks it behind her ear.

"Pretty," the girl says, forcing a smile. "Maybe a couple quarters for the flower? Your boyfriend will like it there."

Aida is at the bus door now, the girl pressing against her.

"Get that fucking hippie out of the way," someone in the line says.

"It's worth a dollar," the girl is saying.

Aida grins at her. The girl, Melody, is a panhandler. She is asking Aida for change. Out of breath, Bill reaches her finally. "Shit," he says. "Thought I was going to miss the bus." He takes Aida's elbow in his hand and hoists her up the steps of the bus.

Aida pulls her loose change from her pocket and manages to drop it in Melody's grimy outstretched hand.

"Peace," Melody says.

"Get the fuck out of my way," Aida hears someone say. But she is on the bus, and Bill is right behind her, a sheen of sweat on his forehead.

"You were just going to go," he says. "Without me."

Aida shrugs.

There are people ahead of her putting bags in the overhead racks, and people behind her, urging them on.

Bill takes her face in both of his hands and kisses her hard and quick on the lips.

"Wait for me next time, okay?" he says.

"You can make out when you sit down," that same guy shouts, and some of the passengers giggle.

But Bill doesn't move. "Okay?" he says again.

There's a window seat still available, and Aida slides into it. Bill is still standing there, waiting.

"Okay," she says.

He slides into the seat beside her, stretches his long legs. Aida places her hand in his sweaty one, and looks out the window. The sun is up, full and white, over the mountains. The bus backs up slowly, then lurches forward.

IT IS NIGHT and they are somewhere, but Aida has lost track. What is after Colorado? She tries to remember but can't. Her lips still vibrate from that one fast kiss, like a beesting. If he doesn't kiss her again soon she might die from anticipation. But he doesn't seem at all in a kissing mood. Instead, he is telling her an unbelievable story about a group of pioneers who got caught in a freak spring snowstorm in the mountains and ended up having to eat each other.

"They did it for survival," he says. "People will do anything to survive."

"You got that right," a woman behind them says, and Bill laughs softly.

Another woman says, "I heard about this sports team somewhere, in Argentina or Australia or somewhere who ate each other. They were in a plane crash, and they were up in the mountains, and those dead ones just got eaten."

She is certainly not going to be kissed when the whole bus is in on her conversation.

"See?" Bill says softly. He tucks a strand of her hair behind her ear and she gets a surge of excitement again. "Cannibals are everywhere," he whispers.

Aida smiles despite herself.

He laces his fingers in hers. He leans close to her, bends his head, and nibbles her neck playfully. "Yum," he murmurs. "Delicious."

Aida stiffens. As much as she wants to kiss him, she doesn't know really what it all involves. The bus is dark and safe, but what if he wants to make out? What exactly does that entail? This, she supposes as his lips move from her neck, slowly, kissing her chin and then finding her mouth. This time, when he kisses her, it is soft and slow. I am a person kissing a boy on a bus, Aida thinks with awe.

Bill's tongue slips inside her mouth and she tries to remember what she should do. Her friend Linda Martino made out with a boy at the Portuguese carnival last summer. She told Aida how their tongues poked at each other like two snakes. Relieved for this tidbit of guidance, Aida lets her own tongue meet his.

But he doesn't kiss her again, and Aida wonders if perhaps she is a bad kisser. Maybe she should have held her tongue flat in her mouth. Maybe Linda Martino lied to her. Linda had also said that the boy felt her up over her shirt. That part, Linda said, was stupid. He just rubbed at her purple poorboy shirt and it was incredibly boring.

Bill puts his hand on Aida's knee. She feels it there, heavy and warm, convinced that he had called Beth from Denver and told her good-bye once and for all.

———

FOR THE NEXT TWO NIGHTS, Aida sat waiting for more kissing, her body both rigid and melting, afraid and ready. But Bill did not kiss her again, and on the night before the morning they are going to arrive in San Francisco, she is certain she is the worst kisser in the world. Hadn't Linda Martino said their tongues had poked like two snakes? And Aida had arched her tongue and met his, imitating the way she'd seen snakes on *Wild Kingdom.*

They are somewhere in California, driving down a deserted highway, when the bus driver slows.

"Uh," he says into the microphone, "we got a problem."

There is a clunk and a grinding, and the bus swerves into the breakdown lane.

"Uh-oh," Bill says, "I hope we don't have to eat each other to survive."

Aida rolls her eyes. She thinks she might hate him.

The bus driver is on some kind of radio, describing the noises the bus made, his voice urgent. Then he says, "We ain't going nowhere."

Speaking into the microphone again, he says, "Uh, people, we're stuck here for a while. You can get off the bus if you want. These here are lettuce fields. Just watch out for trucks and things coming down the highway."

Passengers moan and complain. Some get off the bus right away, but they stand close to it, staring out over the lettuce fields. A man starts yelling at the bus driver, telling him he needs to be in San Francisco, he needs to!

"Do you want to stay on the bus?' Bill asks Aida.

She wants him to kiss her again, that's all she wants, so she says nothing.

"Let's walk a little bit," he says.

They leave the bus. It is so dark that Aida feels disoriented, off-balance. Bill takes her hand, whispers, "Careful."

The dirt in the lettuce field is dry and cracks under their weight. Her eyes start to adjust and she can make out neat rows of lettuce on either side of the path they walk down. They don't wander too far from the bus, which sits in the distance looking lopsided and broken.

"Feels good to be away from buses," Bill says.

Aida believes that she could ride these buses without ever stopping, Bill sitting beside her, America whizzing past.

"Rice paddies," Bill says. "Rice paddies are beautiful. Like works of art."

He is quiet a moment. Aida wonders if Beth wouldn't listen to him when he strayed like this, his voice dreamy and distant. Maybe Beth was afraid of what he had seen. But Aida isn't.

"I don't know anything about it," she whispers. "Tell me."

Bill tucks her hair behind her ears again and says her name the way you say it in the opera. Then he finally kisses her again, not slow this time but right away opening his mouth, his tongue finding hers. He is kissing her with an urgency that almost frightens her. His breathing is sharp, his hands clutch her back, pulling her close enough to him that she feels the buttons on his shirt digging into her and the hardness in his khakis against her.

Bill tugs her down to the dirt with him. It doesn't smell like Mama Jo's garden back home, but more like dust.

They kiss for a long time. This, Aida realizes, is making

out. She believes there must be an order to things, and that Bill will start to rub her shirt the way the boy at the Portuguese carnival did to Linda Martino. She tries to decide at which point she should say no. Linda Martino said that you should never kiss a boy lying down; it leads to things, the way smoking pot can make you a heroin addict. But here she was, lying in a lettuce field kissing a boy. Did that mean they had skipped over the rubbing part?

Bill pauses. He looks right at her, like he is trying to figure something out.

"We'd better stop," he whispers, "before I can't stop."

Aida swallows hard before she says, "You don't have to stop." She doesn't recognize the girl who says this. But she understands that she is that girl. Aida Caruso is lying down kissing a boy in a lettuce field in California. She will give herself to him. It is so romantic she thinks she might cry.

He kisses her lightly on the lips. "Not here," he says. "Not now."

She turns away from him because she thinks she really is going to cry. She wants him to keep going, even though she is unsure exactly what that means. She and Linda Martino read all of the dirty parts in *The Harrad Experiment*, so she understands basically what would happen. But she cannot imagine how it would actually feel, any of it.

"Hey," he says.

"It's romantic," she manages to say. "Out here in a lettuce field."

He gets up and pulls her to her feet. He drapes his arm around her shoulder as they walk back to the bus, and holds on to her, tight.

—

SIX HOURS LATER, the bus rolls into San Francisco. Aida had expected sunshine and soaring skyscrapers; she expected to see flowers everywhere, like in that song. But it is cloudy and cold, the buildings squat and dingy.

Stiff and aching, she steps off the bus, trying to hide her disappointment.

Bill stands awkwardly beside her, like a stranger.

"So," he says, "is your uncle here or do you have to call him?"

"Oh," Aida says, caught off-guard. "He doesn't even know when I was coming for sure."

Bill nods and lights a cigarette.

They stand like that, like they hadn't made out in a lettuce field last night. His words had held a promise. Not here, he'd said. Didn't that mean, *but somewhere else?* The air stinks of diesel and urine.

Aida says, "I know your face by touch when it's dark, I know the profile of your sleeping face, the sound of you sleeping."

He raises his eyebrows, confused.

"'Stanyan Street,'" she says, embarrassed. "It's a poem. By Rod McKuen."

He takes a drag on his cigarette.

"Maybe we could hang out together for a few days," she says bravely. "Before I call my uncle."

He focuses on the arrival of another bus. Its doors creak open, and schoolchildren spill from it.

"About that," Bill says. "I was thinking I'd maybe go back."

Her poem hangs stupidly between them. "Back?" she says.

"Beth finally stopped yelling at me," he says. His eyes flit over her face, then back to the bus.

"Oh," Aida says.

"She finally gets it. That stupid war changed me. How could it not? I don't want an electric can opener or an ice crusher or any of it. I want to come back out here and breathe, you know?"

Aida nods. "That's what I want too," she says, wondering if he can hear her pleading with him.

"Outside the city there's all these great towns along the coast. A buddy of mine told me about them in Nam. Point Reyes and Bolinas and Bodega Bay. We could get a shack there, right on the beach, you know? We could light bonfires and stay up all night."

Aida keeps nodding until she understands that he isn't talking about her. The "we" is him and Beth.

Finally he looks at her. "You'll be in college in no time," he says. "Maybe someday you'll think about me, the guy on the bus."

"Maybe," she says, her voice as light as air.

"Can I have a kiss good-bye?" he says.

You fool, she thinks as she stands on tiptoe and offers herself to him, you could have had everything.

She doesn't look back, not once, as she walks away from him, her lips buzzing with that bee-stung feeling. Aida thinks of that poem, "Stanyan Street." She thinks of having read it and cried over it in her small bedroom back home. Downstairs, her aunts had yelled at each other; they rolled ground hamburger and breadcrumbs and eggs and parsley from the garden into meatballs; they drank strong black coffee and smoked Pall Malls; they called her name, "Aida!" Aida!" in a way that was not at all operatic.

Aida recites the poem out loud as she walks past hippies asleep on the bus station floor, past creepy men with ragged beards offering her baggies of pot, past one lone antiwar protester sitting quietly with a big sign: MAKE LOVE NOT WAR.

Finally, she is outside. It looks like the Combat Zone in Boston, not like the San Francisco where Karl Malden and Michael Douglas chase criminals up sky-high hills. Aida raps her knuckles on a taxi's window. The driver is Indian. He has nervous eyes and a turban. She has never seen anyone wearing a turban before. She hopes Bill is watching her.

"Stanyan Street?" she says.

"Get in!" he barks.

Aida opens the door of the cab and steps inside.

The Importance of Similes

PENELOPE'S BOARDING SCHOOL WAS ALL GIRLS, SO THEY had to sneak out of the resident halls, down the beautiful sloping, manicured hills, under the back fence, to the river. That was where they met the boys. They ran, Penelope and the others, sometimes wearing their pajamas, sometimes barefoot, sometimes their hair wet and smelling of Prell shampoo; they ran to the river, across the rocky bank, across the mud, in the dark—no lights here, although the distant lights of the school could still be seen; they ran, long hair flying, arms open wide, breathing hard; they ran until they reached them, the boys, waiting.

This was 1972. The world was shifting. Even as Penelope's world stayed the same—no-show dad, mother obsessed with finding the woman who birthed her and gave her away—the world around her kept tilting, changing, keeping her off balance. It used to be, before Penelope or the others arrived at St. Lucy's, that the girls dressed for dinner, wore skirts to class, kept their hair tied back with ribbons or headbands; it used to be that the boys from Maxwell Academy were kept hidden except for once-a-month Friday-night mixers, or an occasional combined field trip to the Museum of Fine Arts or the Isabel Gardner Museum in Boston. There used to be rules. There still were rules, but no one followed them.

Everything was changing, faster than Mrs. Landon, the headmistress, could keep up with. Faster than even the girls themselves could. Mrs. Landon still wore knee-length wool skirts with pencil pleats. She still wore pearls, cashmere sweaters, nylon stockings. But the girls dressed in camouflage, ripped jeans, gypsy skirts. They snuck cigarettes, beer, Mrs. Landon was afraid to imagine what else. Boys were always discovered, jumping out of resident-hall windows, sneaking into the library basement, lurking around the perimeter of the grounds. Maxwell Academy boys still had to wear gray trousers, white or blue dress shirts, ties. They still wore the navy blazers with the school crest on the left-hand pocket. Their hair could not hang over their collars.

Julie Matthews, the house mother at Figg, made Mrs. Landon nervous. Julie wasn't a St. Lucy's girl; she'd graduated from Rosemary Hall. She had different ideas. Her cat eyes, green and almond-shaped, seemed mysterious, mocking, up to something. Keep an eye on your girls, Mrs. Landon told her every evening. Oh, Julie Matthews said, I do.

The girls waited until ten, lights-out, and then they went down to the river, where the boys waited. Penelope's leg jumped and tapped until ten, a habit she had that drove her mother crazy. In movies and restaurants, her mother would grab Penelope's knee hard, to hold it still. But it wasn't something she did deliberately. Her leg had a mind of its own. At ten, lights-out, she jumped up, slipped out, ran down to the

river. Racing along the rocky bank, the mud making thwack-
ing noises against her feet, she would always pause when the
boys came into sight. There they sat, smoking joints, waiting.
Penelope paused, as if making them wait these few seconds
more mattered.

Then she joined the others who had charged ahead. They
gave a war cry, a whoop that St. Lucy's girls had perfected for
their field hockey games. It was a call to victory. They raised
their arms over their heads, and shouted: Here we are!

The girls had rules. No falling in love with any particular boy. No asking the boys about any of the other girls. No
telling secrets to the boys. When they arrived, they picked
out the boy they would be with that night—never the same
one three times in a row. They went and sat by him, to claim
him. Then they got stoned. Penelope loved getting stoned,
loved the way her body kind of lifted out of itself, her mind
hummed, strange shivers of something shot through her. The
boys brought the pot. The boys brought the potato chips, the
Chips Ahoy!, the M&M's. The girls just brought themselves.

And after they were good and stoned, clumsy with it,
thick and cloudy, the girls and boys had sex. Sort of. The rule
was: try anything but. Stoned, and lying on the riverbank,
the rocks hard beneath her back or legs or knees, looking
into the stupidly grinning face of a boy, was the only time
Penelope was happy.

Later, the girls told one another about the boys. They
compared penis sizes and widths, techniques and lack of techniques, stupid things the boys said when they came. They
imitated the sounds the boys made. Use similes! That was

another rule: He sounded like a train slowing down, like a tea-
kettle at full boil, like someone trying to go to the bathroom.
His penis was like a Slim Jim, a bratwurst, a knitting needle.

They did this because everything was changing. Their
parents were fucked-up—divorced, unhappy, even dead. There
was a war that was never going to end. The government of
the United States of America had betrayed them. They were
lost. They were confused. They were searching for something
that none of them could name. So they ran down to the river
and gave boys blow jobs and got stoned and acted like nothing else mattered.

PENELOPE WATCHED HER mother step out of her ridiculous car—a pea-green Citroën. Her mother was, of course,
an embarrassment with her fake British accent and Katherine
Hepburn pants and that car. Not as bad as Rainier's mother;
she wore jeans and Army jackets, said *fuck* all the time, got
stoned. Every spring, they showed up, all the mothers, for St.
Lucy's Mother's Day Tea. It was a misnomer, this tea. There
was a full bar where Penelope's mother got an endless supply
of gin and tonics. Mrs. Landon gave a slide show of the girls
looking studious, waving field hockey sticks, performing in
plays, or making pottery. The freshmen had to serve everyone else, a lavish five-course dinner on china and linens, with
crystal and silver.

Rainier showed up in Penelope's doorway. She opened her
palm to reveal a joint.

"I need it to get through this," she said. "What do you say?"

Penelope's mother had paused to talk with Samantha's mother. Samantha's mother was an artist, with unruly curls and flowing dresses.

Quickly, Penelope pulled Rainier inside, closed the door, rolled up her still-damp bath towel, and stuck it under the door. Rainier had already lit up, and that sweet, sharp, beautiful smell filled the room. While Rainier took a hit, Penelope closed her eyes and took a deep breath.

"Not the best," Rainier said, "but it'll take the edge off."

The girls passed the joint back and forth until they heard high heels in the hallway. Mothers were arriving. Penelope had a nice buzz going.

"Thanks," she told her friend.

Rainier hesitated at the door.

"What?" Penelope said.

"My mother said she's going to bring me some acid. She's been doing a lot of it out at her house in Nantucket. She says she thinks it'll do me good."

Penelope shook her head as if it would help her understand better. "LSD?" she managed finally.

Now voices, high and shrill, filled the corridor outside the room.

"Maybe next time we go down to the river we can all do it?" Rainier said, uncertainly.

Penelope didn't want to seem afraid, although she was. A boy from Maxwell Academy had taken LSD in the fall and jumped off the chapel roof, believing he could fly.

"That boy who died was stupid," Rainier said. "You never drop acid alone."

"I even forgot about him," Penelope lied.

There was a loud knock on the door, and her mother's stupid voice: "Penny?"

Penelope rolled her eyes. "She knows I hate that name," she said, and yanked the door opened.

Her mother and Mrs. Woodson were standing there. Penelope saw her mother's nose twitch and cursed herself for not opening the window.

"Smells sour in here," Mrs. Woodson said, walking right in and cranking the bank of windows open. "Don't you girls ever clean?" She had stiff beauty-parlor hair and orange ovals for fingernails.

"Deborah stepped out for a minute," Penelope said.

Then she giggled. Deborah Woodson had gone into town to a doctor; she thought she might be pregnant. Deborah had not followed the rules. She had done everything, including. She had done it with Jeremy Jackson, whose father was a mucky-muck in the Army, West Point, this and that, now dead.

Her mother looked at her sharply.

"I thought she'd be back by now," Penelope said, strangling another giggle.

"I saw your mother in the parking lot, Rainier," Mrs. Woodson said. "Isn't she exotic? What do you call those shoes she has on?"

"Dr. Scholl's," Rainier said.

"I told Deborah I would escort you to the dining hall if she wasn't back when you came," Penelope said. It was all so stupid and funny, this tea and Mrs. Woodson in her Chanel suit and her own mother frowning at her. Penelope sat on her bed with its pale-yellow duvet and Marimekko sheets, and hid her face in her hands, laughing.

"Well, I don't understand," Mrs. Woodson said.

Rainier started to laugh too.

"Honestly," Penelope's mother said. She took her by the arm, roughly, and yanked on her.

Penelope used to dismember her dolls. She loved the way the arms and legs pulled out of the sockets, the way the heads came off with a pop. It seemed her mother was trying to take her apart, the way she pulled on her. Or was that just the pot making her feel all loose and liquidy?

She looked up at her mother, and for an instant Penelope felt bad for her, for all the mothers who paid so much money to send their daughters to a fancy school to learn about sex and drugs.

"I'm sorry," she managed to say.

She got to her feet clumsily. She straightened her shoulders, her head feeling slightly disconnected from the rest of her body.

"Shall we?" she said.

Her mother, that Anglophile, would like that. Penelope glanced over at her, and yes, she was smiling.

AFTER THE DINNER, bloody roast beef although half the girls and even some of the mothers were vegetarians, Penelope leaned against her mother's car. The sky was purple and black. Her head hurt a little and the taste of the coconut layer cake was making her queasy.

"Well," her mother said, not looking at Penelope, "I have a good lead. I'm driving to Rhode Island tomorrow."

"Three hours and seventeen minutes," Penelope muttered. She had timed how long it would take her mother to bring up yet another lead on the Holy Grail of finding her birth mother.

"What?" her mother said. Her face had gone blank, the way it did when she drank too much. Her eyelids drooped in a way that half an hour ago might have been sexy but now looked kind of sad.

She had been adopted by a rich family in Vermont as a baby, but all of a sudden all she could think of was who her real parents were. Every few weeks, she went off somewhere, chasing some wrong information. At Easter, she'd flown to Colorado, only to learn that the couple who might be her parents had had a boy. It was all so stupid, so long ago. If Penelope's mother had given *her* away at birth, Penelope doubted she'd be wasting her middle age looking for her. She'd say, *Fuck you very much for abandoning me* and move on with her life.

Her mother was telling her about Rhode Island, a Catholic hospital.

"This time I think I've found her for real, Pen, Penny, my Penelope," she said drunkenly. Her mother had lived in England for a year or something a long time ago, and she used this fake accent that drove Penelope crazy. When she drank too much, her fake English accent got even stronger.

Penelope's leg jumped, up and down, up and down. She wished she'd taken the end of that joint with her so she could sneak into the ladies' room and have a hit or two, just to calm her down. Just to blot out her mother's voice.

Across the parking lot, Penelope watched Rainier and her mother bent together at their Volvo. Her stomach flipped over. Rainier was probably getting the LSD right now, and tonight or tomorrow night Penelope was going to have to take it. She sighed. Why did everything have to get complicated?

"I was thinking you could come with me," her mother was saying. "We could have a nice drive in the morning after breakfast and check out this lead."

Penelope chewed her lip. Rainier came skipping across the parking lot. As she passed them, she flashed a peace sign. Or maybe a *V* for Victory?

"I don't like that girl," her mother said in a low voice. "She always looks like she's up to no good."

"She's all right," Penelope said.

She was thinking of that boy again, the one who jumped out that window, and her stomach cramped. She remembered how Rainier had said after they heard, "God! I wonder if I blew him? I hope so. You know, it would be a pity to die without ever doing anything like that." Penelope had had the same thought, but it had made her sick to think it. Not Rainier. Rainier had laughed.

"So," her mother said, jingling her keys, impatient to leave, "what do you say?"

Maybe Rainier would wait until tomorrow and if Penelope wasn't here, or got back super late, she could avoid this whole LSD thing. But a whole day, in the car, with her mother. Which was worse?

"Stop jiggling your leg, Penelope," her mother said, grabbing Penelope's knee and holding on tight. Beneath her mother's hand, Penelope's leg trembled, wanting to move.

"Stop," her mother said again. Penelope saw that she had a faint smear of lipstick across her two front teeth. Had it been there this whole time?

Rainier had gone inside now and was miming something to Penelope, something too complicated to mime. It could be: *Let's go smoke a joint.* It could be: *Let's go give some lucky boys a blow job they'll never forget.* It could be: *Let's drop this acid now!* Penelope turned her gaze away from Rainier. She felt suddenly very tired.

"Sure," Penelope told her mother.

"Really?" her mother said, so pathetically pleased that Penelope wished she had said no. "That's great, darling. Shall we have breakfast first?"

Penelope shrugged. "I guess," she said.

Her mother kissed her on the cheek, her breath all coconutty and sour gin. "All right then," she said. "Cheeri-o until morning."

Penelope slipped away from the hug her mother was drunkenly trying to execute. "Cheeri-o!" she muttered heading up the hill toward Figg. "Ta-ta and all that bloody rubbish!"

JULIE WAS STANDING in the hallway outside the common room when Penelope walked in. Last year, Julie had been Ms. Matthews; this year she said to call her Julie. She taught English and coached the debate team, a dismal group that always came in last place. But Penelope liked the way Julie wore her hair cut short and shirts she embroidered herself, and an old pair of jeans with a red felt heart sewn on the butt.

"You okay?" Julie asked, frowning. Her hair was rust-colored, and so were her eyebrows and her freckles, which made her look a bit disconcerting.

"You know." Penelope shrugged. "Mothers."

And LSD trips, she added to herself. And flying out windows. And death. She forced a grin but it came out more like a grimace.

"Ah!" Julie said. She cocked her head toward the door to her suite. "Want to sit and talk a bit?"

Relieved, Penelope nodded and followed her inside. The red heart on the back of her jeans seemed to smile at her. Penelope loved Julie's suite, even though she wasn't one of the girls who visited here often. Last year, Pamela Grundy had practically lived in here. This year, August Frank could almost always be found here. There were rumors about them, Pamela and now August, that they were lesbians. And so was Julie. But Penelope thought it was dumb to think every woman with short hair was a dyke.

The suite was small, just two rooms. The bedroom lay behind a closed door; the sitting room and kitchen were separated by a counter with two stools at it. According to August, Julie had salvaged those stools from an old diner in Worcester. The seats were aqua vinyl. And Julie's plates and bowls were all pink and orange and baby-blue, also rescued from somewhere. That's what she does, August said. She rescues things. August never went down to the river, giving more evidence to her rumored lesbianism.

"So," Julie said, "mothers."

She took out two metal cups, one green and one gold,

opened a jug of red wine, and poured some in each glass. "Don't tell," Julie said, winking. "At Rosemary we relied on our house mother to buy all of our alcohol."

Penelope pretended not to be surprised. The wine tasted like grape juice.

"Of course," Julie said, "we liked vodka and orange juice. What is that called? A screwdriver, I think? We carried it around and no one knew the difference." She smiled to herself.

"My mother's on a quest," Penelope said. "She wants to find her real mother. Like, what's a *real* mother anyway? She was adopted," she added.

"So was I," Julie said. "But I don't want to meet the woman who gave me away. I mean, honestly. Fuck her. Right?"

Penelope sipped her wine. It was like Julie wanted to shock her. Suddenly, Penelope wanted to be in her own room listening to her new Cat Stevens album. But Julie was pouring them each more wine.

"Tell me," Julie said, "what do you girls do down at the river?"

When Penelope choked on the wine, Julie laughed. "Don't worry. I won't tell. Is it drinking?"

Penelope shook her head. She loved that song, "Wild World," and she wanted to play it over and over until it became part of her. That's what she did when she liked a song.

"Pot, then?" Julie asked.

"I . . . I don't know," Penelope said, and Julie laughed again.

"I never liked it myself, but hey," Julie said. "And I suppose Maxwell boys are there too."

The album was called *Tea for the Tillerman*. Penelope wondered what a tillerman was. Julie probably knew. Julie had been the one to tell her who Penelope was in Greek mythology, a woman who waited for, like, twenty years for a man to return for her. She just sat there knitting or something. Leave it to her mother to give her such a stupid name.

"Just be careful," Julie was saying.

Penelope stood up, lightheaded from the two glasses of wine.

"Don't want anyone coming down to tell me they're preggers," Julie said.

Deborah's face came to Penelope's mind. At the tea, she had looked over at Penelope solemnly and ran her finger across her throat. Preggers.

"Well," Penelope said, "thanks for the talk and stuff."

Julie touched her arm so lightly it felt like a feather had landed there. "Do you like the boys?" she asked. "Do you like kissing them?"

Her fingers stayed there, hardly touching. Penelope thought of butterflies, light things. "I guess so," she said.

"At Rosemary we kissed each other," Julie said. "To practice, you know. We didn't mean anything by it. We weren't dykes or anything. No, it was more like the Native Americans. When a boy came of age, his mother taught him what to do. How to please a woman."

"Really?" Penelope said. She felt confused, and a little drunk. Julie's fingertips seemed suddenly burning hot.

Penelope was tall, one of the tallest girls at St. Lucy's. And Julie was small. *A slip of a thing*, Penelope's mother had said when she'd met her last fall. Julie stood now on tiptoe, and tilted her face upward, like a girl waiting to be kissed. Without hesitating—and that was what confused Penelope even more later—Penelope leaned down and kissed her, full on the mouth. She had never been anywhere so soft. She thought she might crawl into those lips forever. Use similes! She told herself. Like clouds. Like marshmallows. She heard herself gasp a little, at the softness. She couldn't stop pressing her lips against Julie's. All those Maxwell boys with their rough faces, their chapped lips, their boy tastes. Julie tasted like grapes. Like cotton candy. Now their lips parted and their tongues were touching, Julie's soft like . . . like what? Penelope couldn't think. She felt herself getting wet down there where Maxwell boys jammed their fingers in.

Then like an interrupted dream, Julie pulled away. "Remember that," she said, her mouth wet with their spit, "when you're kissing that Maxwell boy tonight. See?"

Penelope nodded stupidly and stumbled out of Julie's suite. Some girls were sitting cross-legged in the common room and looked at her all funny.

"Did you hear?" one of them said. "Deborah Woodson slit her wrists. They've taken her to the hospital."

"What?" Penelope said. She thought of Deborah dragging her finger across her throat.

"Don't worry," that little tight-ass Yvonne Mack said. "She did it in the library. Not in your room."

Just then Julie's door flew open. She had on the faded corduroy jacket she always wore, and a panicked look. Penelope ran to her. Julie grabbed her by the wrist, dragging her along.

THE GIRLS STILL RAN down the hill to meet the boys, even with Deborah in the ER and then up in the psych ward. They went down there and got stoned and took off their panties and let the boys finger them. They opened their mouths and the boys stuck their dicks in, pushing against their teeth, yanking on their hair. Don't swallow! That was one of the rules. But Penelope always did. She'd read somewhere, maybe in *Cosmopolitan* magazine, that semen was a good source of protein. But that wasn't why she did it. She did it because she earned it. All that work, her jaw sore for hours afterward. It didn't taste bad either. Like saltwater. Like asparagus. Like the smell in chemistry lab.

But tonight, after Penelope and Julie got back to St. Lucy's from the hospital, the calls made to Deborah's parents to come first thing in the morning, Deborah locked up in the psych ward, Julie unlocked the door to Figg and said, "Boy, do I need a drink. You?"

And Penelope, knowing where all the girls were, knowing she would have to face her room alone, and see all of Deborah's stuff there like nothing had happened, said yes.

"I just have to check something," she told Julie. "I'll be back in a flash." She had never said *I'll be back in a flash* before, and it sounded stupid.

Penelope went into her room and without turning on the overhead light because she did not want to see Deborah's jean jacket tossed casually on the bed, or her Simon and Garfunkel album covers or anything Deborah, she retrieved the end of the joint and smoked it, every bit.

"I'm high as a kite," she said out loud to the room. She was thinking and speaking in clichés. This had to stop.

Julie had left her door ajar and Penelope hesitated before pushing it open. The apartment looked different. An Indian blanket thrown over the lamp made the light diffused and tinted red. Julie was standing in the dark, drinking from a water glass full of wine.

"I didn't think you were coming back," she said.

Penelope shrugged. "My room is kind of creepy."

Julie walked over to her and stroked her hair. "You poor baby," she said softly.

Penelope stood still, stiff.

"I don't need to practice kissing, you know," she said. "I kiss boys all the time."

"Do you fuck them?" Julie asked, her voice so soft that Penelope wasn't sure she was hearing right.

"Sure," she said. She was perfectly high, the way she liked most, when her body felt like it was being lifted up even though she wasn't moving at all. A light breeze moved through her hair, tickled her neck, touched her collarbone. Penelope closed her eyes and enjoyed it.

"You went and got high, didn't you?" Julie said. "I can smell pot in your hair."

That's when Penelope realized that it wasn't a breeze; Julie was touching her with her fingertips. Goosebumps rose on her arms as Julie's fingers moved, light, light, to her shirt, right at her nipples.

"Do you like having sex with those Maxwell Academy boys?" Julie asked.

"I do," Penelope said. This wasn't a lie, though technically what they did was not sex. There was a rumor that Amy Brear let boys put it in her butt because that way she was still a virgin. Penelope considered asking Julie about this technicality, but her brain was too fuzzy. All of her energy and power seemed to be in her nipples. Amazing. Amazing that so much could be centered in such a small part of her body. She remembered when she broke her baby toe, back in junior high, how she couldn't believe how much a tiny thing like that could hurt. For days, all she could think about was that toe, as if all of her blood and nerves were in that one place.

"Your toe?" Julie asked.

Penelope laughed. Had she said it out loud?

"I broke it," Penelope said, trying to stop laughing. "And all I could feel was my toe."

"That's why I hate pot," Julie said. "It makes you stupid."

Julie pressed the glass of wine, now half-empty, to Penelope's lips. "Have some," she said. And when Penelope gulped some wine, Julie whispered, "Good girl. Good girl. Does anyone ever call you Penny? Hmmm?"

Penelope wanted to explain that she hated that name, that her mother called her that. The one time she could remember seeing her father, he'd called her Penny.

"I want to call you Penny," Julie was saying. "Penny. Penny. My Penny."

Penelope's head was spinning ever so slightly. She liked having the spins, liked lying on her back and watching the lights and walls and faces spin past her.

"Not here," Julie said, laughing softly.

She was tugging Penelope to her feet when she had not even realized she'd lain down. Walking into the bedroom, Penelope bumped into the walls. Like a pinball machine, she thought, which made her laugh again. Hard.

"Use similes," she said.

"Okay," Julie said, nodding her pretty head. She had curly hair, like Slinkys. Penelope reached up and touched it, and told her that.

"Your hair is like Slinkys," she said.

When Julie pulled off Penelope's shirt, her small breasts pointing into the air because no one wore bras anymore, Penelope said, "I like boys, you know."

"Absolutely," Julie said. "There are no lesbians on this bed."

"None," Penelope said, yanking her jeans off, and her little yellow panties, too.

Julie's tongue began to trace the same path her fingernails had. Hair, neck, collarbone, nipples. She hummed "Penny Lane."

"Because," Penelope said, "I don't know how they do it, you know?" It was something the girls discussed. How did lesbians even have sex? There were theories, but none of them made any real sense.

"I don't know," Julie murmured, Penelope's left nipple in her mouth. "The only thing I know is that whatever one woman does to another, the other woman has to reciprocate."

"Uh-huh," Penelope said, not understanding. All she could really concentrate on was the electric buzz that seemed to emanate from her nipples to down there. She wished she could explain it to Julie, but her words were so blurry.

She watched Julie's Slinky hair bounce as her tongue moved down Penelope's ribs, and belly button, and then down there.

"Whoa," Penelope said, or thought she said. Her thoughts were getting even more jumbled. No boy had done this, and why not? she wondered, because surely this was the thing she'd been waiting for, maybe her whole life, this tongue making light circles, around and around, until Penelope's back was arched and she was pulling on those Slinkys and she was making noises like she was an animal.

"What?" she said when her body stopped shaking. "What?"

"I don't know," Julie was saying into her mouth, kissing Penelope with her mouth tasting of . . . tasting of Penelope. "Maybe they do that?"

Penelope couldn't make sense of what she meant. Until Julie said, "My turn, Penny Lane."

"PREGNANT?" PENELOPE'S MOTHER SAID. They were driving down Route 95, heading south toward Rhode Island.

It was the sunniest, bluest-sky day ever, Penelope thought. Her head pounded. Her body felt bruised and sore, but in a good way. She woke up this morning and decided that she would have sex with the next Maxwell Academy boy she was with. All of it. She would have sex with every boy who kissed her. She was not a lesbian. She would prove that.

"A girl gets pregnant," she said, looking out the window and enjoying shocking her mother, "and she has no choice. You think they want that baby? I mean, she's seventeen years old."

"And the boy?"

Penelope shrugged. "The same, I guess."

"Do you think that's what happened with my parents?" her mother said softly. "Too young. No options. Sure, they would have kept me if they could, but how could they?"

Penelope gave a big exaggerated sigh.

"She almost died, Mom, and all you can think about is you."
This actually wasn't true. Deborah didn't even come close to
dying. The razor hurt too much, and the few cuts she managed to inflict were not deep at all.

"Excuse me, love," her mother said, all fake British. "I'm on
my way to possibly meeting the woman who gave birth to me.
I think I'm allowed."

Penelope didn't answer. She and Julie had just been wondering how girls did it together, that's all. Hadn't they talked
about that? Hadn't they both said they didn't know?

"You don't do anything like that, do you?" her mother asked.

"Oh no," Penelope said. "I give blow jobs and have sex
with women."

"Honestly, Penny," her mother said, wrinkling her entire
face in disgust. "Can't you ever be honest?"

"I guess not," Penelope said.

The radio played "Bridge over Troubled Water" for the
millionth time.

"I hate that song," Penelope mumbled, spinning the dial to
change the channel. It reminded her of Deborah, poor Deborah locked in the psych ward, still pregnant, her parents
arriving from Chicago any minute.

She stopped. The Beatles were singing "Penny Lane."

"I thought you hated that song," her mother said.

Penelope didn't answer her. Instead, she sang along.

THE WOMAN AT THE DESK had on too much lipstick and
old-fashioned cat-eye glasses, rimmed with rhinestones.

"I'm sorry, but only family is allowed," she said, not looking at all sorry.

Penelope saw her mother twitch slightly at the word "family."

"But you see, I am family," she said.

The woman's eyes scanned the paper she'd retrieved.

"No Martha," she said finally.

"I wouldn't be on the list. It's complicated, but—"

"She's dying," the woman said. "The family's been called and they're all in there, waiting."

"All of them? Are there a lot of children?"

The woman nodded. "Italians," she said, rolling her eyes. "You know."

There seemed to be nothing more to say. Penelope waited to see what her mother would do next, but her mother didn't seem to have a plan. She wished she'd thought to get a joint from someone. Tonight, she would meet them down the hill and take acid with them. The acid was called Purple Haze, and it was in sugar cubes. All you had to do was let the sugar dissolve in your mouth, and before you knew it, you were tripping. Just yesterday that had frightened Penelope, but after everything that happened last night, she found herself wanting to do it.

Her mother walked across the small lobby. She sat on one of the faded couches. The place smelled like pee and strong disinfectant, the kind they used at school to cover the smell if someone puked. Penelope sat beside her.

"I have papers from the hospital. I was born on Valentine's Day, 1919. Josephine Rimaldi gave birth to a baby girl that day and gave her up for adoption to a family in Vermont."

She had repeated this information about a million times in the car. Penelope sighed. She thought about her own father, a real loser who had been married to her mother just long enough to get her preggers and then disappear. Whenever Penelope asked her mother why she'd married him in the first place, she said he reminded her of someone else. He'd shown up once, when Penelope was eleven. Her mother wouldn't let him in the house, so Penelope had stood at the door to talk to him. He'd smelled of booze, and swayed in the doorway, a big man with a nose like Barney Rubble and pale-blue eyes. He said, "You're a Collier. Don't you forget that." "Okay," she said. He handed her a blond doll with eyes that opened and shut in a creepy fluttering motion. She hadn't played with dolls since second grade. "Take care now," he told her.

Penelope had no desire to go looking for Jim Collier. Why was her mother so obsessed with finding this woman?

All of a sudden, her mother was on her feet, practically running across the lobby.

"Stop! Please!" she called.

A sad-looking woman was lighting a cigarette with trembling hands.

"Are you related to Josephine Rimaldi, by any chance?" her mother asked.

"She's my mother."

Penelope watched as her mother took in this stranger's face, as if she was trying to find some resemblance to her own.

"I think she's my mother too," she said finally.

The woman laughed. She inhaled her cigarette, then let the smoke out in a slow stream.

"I don't think so," she said.

Her mother repeated the facts again.

But the woman shook her head. "There's been some mistake," she said. She frowned. "I remember talk about a baby who died," she said, her frown deepening.

"I can understand changing the story. In those days—"

"She's dying," the woman said. "There's no point."

Before Penelope's mother could say anything else, the woman was snuffing out her cigarette and moving away.

Penelope rushed toward her, her heart suddenly full.

"We've come a long way," she said.

"This isn't the time," the woman said. Her dark eyes had gone icy.

"It's all right, Penny," her mother said.

Penelope watched the woman walk back down the hall. Her mother put her hands on Penelope's shoulders.

"It's all right," she said again softly.

BACK IN THE CAR, "Bridge over Troubled Water" played on the radio as Penelope watched Rhode Island pass by. She couldn't explain why, but she felt a tenderness toward her mother. It felt like the night, like a sky overflowing with stars, like love.

In a few hours, she would be back at St. Lucy's. She would sneak out with the other girls and run down the hill to the spot where the boys would be waiting. She would give herself over to one of them. She would put that sugar cube under her tongue and take her first trip on acid. At some point, maybe just as the sun was coming up, she would find herself back in Julie's apartment and Julie would scold her for taking drugs.

But she would lead Penelope into her bed and undress her and whisper to her. *Your turn,* she would say, as she began the journey down her body.

Even later, in a year or two, St. Lucy's would close and merge with Maxwell Academy. By then, Penelope would have taken dozens of acid trips. She would have tried speed and cocaine and snorted heroin once. She would have slept with more boys than she could name, on beaches and in cars and in the narrow beds in the dorms of Maxwell Academy. She would keep making love with Julie until St. Lucy's closed and Julie moved to San Francisco. That day, Penelope would go with her to Logan Airport to say good-bye. She would sit by the gate crying long after Julie looked over her shoulder one last time and blew her a kiss. By then her mother would have died, swiftly, from pancreatic cancer, not even knowing that Penelope had gotten into Brown.

"I don't understand," Penelope said.

"What, love?" her mother said. She didn't take her eyes from the road.

"Anything," Penelope said.

America

JOSEPHINE RIMALDI OPENED HER EYES, PULLING HER-self from that place that is neither sleep nor wakefulness. That place was where she spent most of her time now. Voices swirled around her, but who they belonged to she could not say for sure. Faces appeared in front of her own, and she struggled to identify them. Was that blond girl her own lost Valentina? Why was her Elisabetta dressed like a soldier in army-green fatigues? Who was this young girl dressed like a gypsy who kept visiting and begging Josephine for stories? She studied each of these faces with great seriousness, wishing they would speak to her in Italian.

After all this time, Josephine still could not grasp the complexities of English. Words here and there made sense to her. Water. Hungry. Cold. Sometimes she even managed to ask the nurse who she liked, the young one with all the dark curls, if she'd had a gentleman caller. "Tommy Petrocelli?" Josephine asked politely. "He come to see me today?" She had to practice the words before she said them and still she managed to forget the "today" or to mix up her verbs. "He see me?" she might say. Or, "He come to me?" But she never had to practice the name. "Tommy Petrocelli?" she said, and nothing more. And always the nurse—the one she liked with the dark curls, or the stern overweight one with the haircut like a man's, or the silly one with the blue eyes and wispy hair—always the nurse shook her head. "Sorry, Mrs. Rimaldi, Tommy didn't come today."

The blue-eyed one was staring at her now. "Mrs. Rimaldi?" she said in her little girl voice. "You awake?"

Josephine frowned. *"Si,"* she said, adding silently, *you stupid girl.* At least she hoped she said it to herself. Words slipped out of her sometimes like seeds from a watermelon: Pop! Pop! Other times she opened her mouth to send a torrent of words out into the world and nothing came at all.

The silly nurse wore a rose-colored uniform with pale-blue teddy bears all over it. Her hair, a froth of pale blond, was kept in a messy pile on top of her head with a fat silver barrette shaped like a butterfly. Once, when Josephine was staring at the thing, trying to figure out what it was sticking out of her hair like that, the girl had grinned at her and said, "Oh! You like my barrette, Mrs. Rimaldi?" She had taken it off, her hair falling around her like cotton candy, and opened and closed it right in Josephine's face. "It's a butterfly," the girl said in that loud voice people used when they spoke to someone who didn't understand English very well. "See?"

A butterfly? Josephine thought of the dusty wings of butterflies, blue spotted with black, or the sunset orange of a Monarch. If you touched their wings, they couldn't fly anymore, that dust the magic that lifted them up. This cheap thing looked nothing like a butterfly.

Josephine was wondering if she had conveyed any of this

to the nurse, or if it was all in her head, when the nurse leaned forward and put the ridiculous barrette in Josephine's own white hair.

"You look so pretty!" she said, grinning like the idiot that she was. "Here," she said, wheeling Josephine over to the mirror that hung on the door. "See for yourself."

Josephine squinted at the image in the mirror. But all she saw was a very old woman, hunchbacked and wizened, with thin white hair with an ugly thing jutting from the top of her head.

"You can keep it," the nurse said. "I have a million of them."

Now the girl was calling to her. "Mrs. Rimaldi? You know what today is, don't you? Remember, I told you yesterday?"

Every day when a nurse came in she said, "Good morning, Mrs. Rimaldi. It's Monday, the second of June." Or whatever day and month it was. Some nurses would quiz her later. "What day is it today, Mrs. Rimaldi?" As if it mattered whether it was June or February, Monday or Thursday.

The girl was looking at her so expectantly that Josephine tried to please her. "Monday?" she said.

The girl laughed. "Well, no, it's Saturday. But it's your birthday today."

Josephine thought about this. Her birthday. She was born on September 24, 1874, in Conca Campania, Italy, a village high up in the mountains. The villagers liked to say they lived close to God. To Josephine, that seemed to be true, even now. The village was a maze of white stone houses, cobblestone streets, fields and hills. In the center sat the church, and perched on its steeple, watching over the village and its people, was the Virgin Mary. She wore long blue robes. Her hair was a tumble of black ringlets. In her arms she held her son, the baby Jesus. And all of this was outlined in twenty-four-karat gold. That gold shimmered in the bright sunlight and glowed at night. Her halo, a large round disc above her head, was also gold. From afar, Josephine could look up and see that golden image and feel safe under its watchful eyes.

In the village, she ran barefoot. She herded the sheep for the nuns and helped the women bake the Communion wafers. She ate figs fresh from trees, and juicy grapes right off the vines. One of the things she never got used to in America was the way the fruit tasted. It didn't have the sunshine in it, the way it did in the Old Country. She never got used to wearing shoes, either. Wiggling her toes now, she realized she only had on socks. Maybe she could get this girl to take them off and then she could run barefoot through the grass.

The nurse's face was very close to Josephine's, so close that Josephine smelled the bad American coffee on her breath.

"You're one hundred years old today, Mrs. Rimaldi. And your entire family is coming to give you a party."

Josephine laughed. What foolishness was this girl giving her today?

"Do you want to wear your butterfly barrette?" the girl was saying.

Josephine struggled to tell her things: about the magic dust on butterflies' wings, and how she wanted to take off her socks and run in the grass, and that she had hidden the barrette so that she never had to wear it again.

"I can't find it," the girl was muttering.

Josephine wondered if anyone had ever told Carmine the truth about Anna Zito; if Valentina had ever wondered about her; if Tommy Petrocelli had died. She wanted to run barefoot in the grass. Was it safe to go outside? Josephine tried to ask. Or were people still dying of the Spanish Influenza? All the words strangled in her throat.

"You all right?" the nurse said, hurrying to her side. She clamped a blood-pressure cuff on Josephine, placed her own fingers on Josephine's wrist to feel the weak flutter there, like butterfly wings.

Josephine's heart slowed and she grew calmer. Her eyes met the girl's and she managed to ask, "Tommy Petrocelli? He come see?" She shook her head and tried again. "He see me today?"

Frowning at the blood-pressure machine, the nurse said absently, "Not today, Mrs. Rimaldi."

"Ah," Josephine said, unable to hide her disappointment.

"But everyone else is here," the nurse said, bringing her worried face close to Josephine's.

Something strange was going on in Josephine's chest. She'd had these feelings before. Pushing out her first baby. Falling in love with the ice man. Handing Valentina to the nun. The feeling was something like love and something like grief. But how to explain this to the silly nurse who was staring at her with such concentration.

"I'm going to take you to the sunroom, Mrs. Rimaldi," she said. "That's where everybody is waiting for you." She was talking loud, like she always did, but Josephine was having trouble hearing her. "Remember?" the girl said. "Today is your birthday."

"September 24," Josephine said.

"Yes!" the nurse said. "Good for you!"

She expertly spun the wheelchair toward the door.

Josephine's heart did twists and turns. She thought of Valentina, so small and perfect and beautiful. She remembered the feel of cold, slippery ice in her hands on a summer day.

"Here we go, Mrs. Rimaldi," the nurse said.

Josephine took a breath. The hallways tumbled past her, and she reached her hands out to try to keep her balance. She remembered a long-ago day when she tried to learn how to ride a bicycle, the off-kilter feeling as she struggled to stay upright.

"What's that, Mrs. Rimaldi?" the nurse asked. "You want to take a ride on a bicycle?"

Josephine shook her head. The stupid girl, she thought. She had not been able to learn, her fear of falling too great. *Basta*, she'd said finally, getting off the thing and leaning it against the house. She had legs, didn't she? Good, strong ones that could run across fields and climb hills.

"If there's one Italian word you've taught me, Mrs. Rimaldi," the nurse said, "it's *basta*. Enough. Right?"

The wheelchair sailed over a bump and into a room that smelled sour, like the bologna her children always begged for, that her grandchildren ate in sandwiches made with American bread and ketchup.

Slowly, the room was bathed in light. The sun came through the windows, bright and warm. Josephine tilted her face upward.

"You all right?" the nurse was asking.

Josephine gasped. She could not catch her breath. In the distance, finally, Josephine saw him. Tommy Petrocelli, carrying a big block of ice that sparkled in the sunlight. She leaned forward, again reaching a hand out.

A bell was ringing, and footsteps hurried toward it.

The stupid nurse kept calling her name, but her voice was growing fainter.

Josephine blinked, trying to bring the images floating in front of her into focus. There was Tommy, smiling at her now. Was Valentina there with him? If she could see her daughter again, then she would die a happy woman.

That was when Josephine knew: she was dying.

So this is it, Josephine thought. When we die we do not think of our children who are waiting down the hall, or of the food we've cooked to nourish them. We do not think of all the breads we've baked, or the tomatoes we've grown, or the hours we've spent at their sickbeds. We do not think of the things we hoped for. We do not think of the things we loved.

No. It is the things we did not have, the love that broke our hearts, the child we lost, that come to us finally.

As the sun sparkled and Tommy neared, Josephine's heart filled.

She smiled and thought one word.

Yes.

ACKNOWLEDGEMENTS

I AM THE LUCKIEST WRITER I know with my dream teams at W. W. Norton and Brandt and Hochman. Thanks go to them, as always: Jill Bialosky, Gail Hochman, Erin Lovett, Jody Klein, Marianne Merola, and Rebecca Schultz.

And I have a dream team at home as well, and send thanks to Mary Hector for her enormous help; my husband, Lorne Adrain, and children, Sam, Annabelle, and Ariane, who inspire and support my writing life.

Parts of *An Italian Wife* were written thanks to fellowships at Yaddo and grants from Rhode Island School of Design. And gratitude goes to the editors who published sections of the book.

I would also like to thank Rebecca Doire, Coral Bourgeois, and Catherine Sebastian.

I grew up in a large, noisy, loving Italian-American family. Sadly, I've lost too many of them. But they live on in my heart and mind: Nonna, Mama Rose, Uncle Rum, Uncle Carmine, Nuneen, Auntie Etta; my uncles Joe, Brownie, and Chuckie; my aunties Rosie, Angie, Connie, Ann, and Dora;

my cousins Cynthia and Peter; my own father Hood and brother Skip; my daughter Grace.

And for those still blessedly with me: Auntie Junie and Cousins Gina, Gloria-Jean, Tony, Becky, Chip, and all the others scattered around the country; Melissa (and Delila and Gus!); and mostly my mother, Gloria, aka Gogo, who makes me the luckiest daughter, ever.

AN ITALIAN WIFE

Ann Hood

DISCUSSION QUESTIONS

1. From her marriage to her emigration to America to raising her family, Josephine Rimaldi is not a person with a lot of choices in life. Would you consider her to be an unhappy person? Do you think she would consider herself to be unhappy? Has our definition of what happiness is, what choices a person deserves, and what makes for a meaningful life changed in the generations since Josephine's youth?

2. Describe the character of Elisabetta. Is her childhood ambitiousness a particularly "American" trait? How else can we tell that Elisabetta was raised in a different culture from her mother's?

3. Describe how the Rimaldi family's relationship to the Catholic Church evolves from generation to generation.

4. Do you blame Carmine for the hurt and pain in his relationship to Anna Zito? To what extent is his own naïveté an excuse? Describe how his experiences in World War One affect his feelings toward women. What is he responding to when he calls his sisters and nieces "puttanas"? To what extent is he a product of his time?

5. Josephine loses a daughter. Martha loses a lover. Elisabetta loses her childhood ambition. Carmine loses his grip on reality. To what extent are Josephine and her children defined by loss? What do they find to live for in the wake of their losses?

6. Compare and contrast Josephine's actual affair with Tommy Petrocelli to her daughter Connie's imaginary affair, which she only

wishes she had, with Dr. DiMarco. How are the two women's circumstances different, and how are they similar? What are both women trying to escape?

7. We meet Josephine's granddaughter Aida twice, once as a child in "Crooning with Dino" and then as a teenager in "The Boy on the Bus." How can we see her growing up and coming of age from one chapter to the next? What does she learn?

8. We see the Rimaldi family affected by three wars over the course of the novel: World War One, World War Two, and the Vietnam War. Which characters are affected directly, and which indirectly? Can we use this family and these characters as a lens through which to understand how each of these wars changed the country overall?

9. What does it mean to be an "Italian wife"? Does the meaning of that moniker change over the course of the novel and from generation to generation?

10. The novel ends in a far more sexually permissive culture than the one in which it begins. Nonetheless, are there parallels to be drawn between Josephine's introduction to sex and love with her husband Vincenzo after marriage in Italy and her granddaughter Penelope's introduction to it at boarding school?

11. When and in what circumstances did your family come to America? Do you feel that you are in touch with your heritage? Did you—or did your parents or grandparents—make an effort to assimilate, like some of Josephine's children did?

12. In the novel's final scene, Josephine and her lost daughter are finally in the same place at the same time. Josephine never knows it, although the reader does. What is unique about the reader's vantage point in *An Italian Wife*? How would the novel be different if our perspective was tied to a single character?